MARY'S REDEMPTION

MCKENNA'S DAUGHTERS
BOOK TWO

LENA NELSON DOOLEY

WILD HEART
BOOKS

ISBN-13:

Dedicated to my beautiful and fun great-granddaughters - Ava, Sophie, Everly, and Emalyn. You are dear to my heart.

I praise my Lord Jesus Christ. Every word was written for His glory.

And I can't forget Tony Chan of Chan's Mongolian Grill. He is the inspiration for Chan Tung Jia, the Tony Chan in the book.

For I will pour water upon him that is thirsty,
and floods upon the dry ground: I will pour
my spirit upon thy seed, and my blessing
upon thine offspring.

— ISAIAH 44:3

PROLOGUE

September 1867
On the Oregon Trail

enneth Murray rushed toward the wagon he shared with his wife and two tiny daughters. A stinging wind held the promise of winter, even though autumn still lingered on the horizon. Limbs of nearby trees clacked together, shaking faded leaves onto the hard-packed ground inside the circled wagons.

As he approached their campfire, his eyes homed in on his precious Melody as she came from the opposite direction. She clutched a threadbare burlap bag to her chest. The sack contained her reward for pouring out nourishment for another woman's child while she still mourned the loss of her own lost infant. Baby Rebecca's remains lay in a forlorn grave along the trail, buried more than two weeks ago. He knew how deeply Melody mourned their loss. And he hated the fact that their family needed the meager food the Oppenheimer family gave to her so she could still produce milk to nourish their child.

And each tear that streamed down her cheeks while she was fulfilling her bargain stabbed his own grieving heart.

Approaching the campfire beside their wagon, she started digging in the bag to discover what the Oppenheimer family had shared with her today. He knew Melody wouldn't eat it without sharing some with him and their little girls. Each bite stuck in his throat. If only he'd been more wise when he outfitted their wagon and more prudent at each trading post along the way. Maybe they would still have rations enough without eating part of hers. What kind of man depended on his woman to provide for the family's needs? He snorted, wanting to turn away in disgust.

Three large, shriveled potatoes and two equally wrinkled carrots were a welcome addition to the thin rabbit stew simmering over the flames. She washed the vegetables the best she could in the meager water supply and quickly cut them into bite-sized pieces. As she dropped them one at a time into the bubbling broth, a drop of fiery water popped out and fell on her already inflamed hand. She lifted the back of her chapped fingers and blew on the spot. She needed the soothing lotions she used to have before they left Missouri on this trek. With all his heart, he regretted not realizing what a necessity they would be. He probably could have stuck a few of the bottles into empty crannies in the wagon. He had been so stubborn.

"Mmmm, smells good." Kenneth wrapped his arms around her from behind, nestling his nose in her dark curls.

She jerked toward the fire, and he pulled her back to keep her from falling. He must have startled her.

He gently turned her toward him. "Are you okay? You're so pale." He brushed his callused fingers along her chapped cheek, wiping away her tears.

Losing Rebecca affected him as much as it did her, but he had a hard time expressing his pain. He shed a few tears that first day, then stoically went about his business, never mentioning their monumental loss again. He hadn't wanted to add to her feeling of loss. But had he been wrong in his decision?

"I'm just tired." Her words came out breathy. He could barely hear them.

Kenneth placed his hands on her upper arms and worked their way up to her shoulders, massaging as they went. He could feel the lack of flesh on her bones. Her muscles were sinewy, instead of soft and feminine as they were when they left Missouri. Lack of food and all the more-difficult-than-normal activities on the journey across the Rocky Mountains had drained her of the bubbling personality he loved so much. What he wouldn't give to see a smile break across her face.

"Overton has called a meeting for all the men in an hour." He dropped a kiss against her cheek.

"I know the wagon master said we need this day of rest, but I'm anxious to get to Oregon City." She glanced up at him, and he wondered what she thought about his clothing hanging like sacks on his once robust form.

Everyone had lost so much weight on the journey. He wished he had known just what a toll this journey would take on all of them. He might not have chosen to come.

"We should be there in another three days. That's what he told us while we circled the wagons." He kept one arm around her and held his other hand out toward the fire. "I agree. Reaching the end of the trail will be wonderful."

After the family had eaten every morsel in the pot, Kenneth stood. "I'll head over to see what Overton wants."

Melody nodded. She clutched her arms across her chest and gripped her upper arms tight enough that her knuckles bleached white in the cold. Kenneth wished he understood what she was going through.

As Kenneth left, he watched their daughters scrunched up next to her on the bench, Annette on one side and Carrie on the other. She put her arms around them and pulled them close. Tonight, he wished he could stay there with them.

When he started past the McKenna wagon, he heard activity within. He was familiar with the sounds inside from when he'd waited outside their wagon for Rebecca to be born. Once again, his heart hitched at the thought of the baby no longer with them.

Catherine McKenna had been riding in the back of the wagon on a pallet for over two weeks. She was the reason the group took the easier, but longer, Barlow Cutoff instead of crossing The Dalles. Maybe Catherine was finally getting ready to deliver her child.

That's all I need. Another newborn on the wagon train to remind Melody of what she lost. Kenneth knew his thoughts were selfish. This would be the McKenna's first child and he shouldn't begrudge them their blessing, but he knew the toll another infant would take on his already overburdened wife.

The doctor climbed out of the McKenna wagon and signaled for the nearest woman to approach. After a few exchanged words, Mrs. Smith hurried the opposite direction from their own wagon, and the physician climbed back inside.

What is that all about?

Soon three women came to join the doctor. One woman stayed outside and put a large kettle of water on to boil. The others slipped into the wagon.

If Catherine McKenna had her child tonight, maybe they could continue on their journey at least by noon tomorrow. Kenneth couldn't keep from smiling at that thought. He wanted to get his family to their new land as quickly as possible, so he could start providing for them the way he'd planned to all along. The main reason he'd insisted they take the trip that seemed endless. A chance for a better life in Oregon, not having to divide the family homestead into even smaller plots of land. Now they could have as much as he could take care of.

When the meeting ended, Kenneth hurried toward his family. A cold wind carried the first icy drops of rain with it. He wanted to be with Melody and hold her close to keep her warm. After he took off his outside garments, but kept on his union suit, they slid between several layers of quilts. He held her in his arms until he heard her soft snoring sounds, so familiar and so welcome. Finally, he slipped into a light slumber, thankful Melody was getting the rest she needed.

Way before dawn, Kenneth heard someone moving around outside their wagon. *Is everything all right?* Had the circled wagons lulled them into a false sense of security? *Could Indians be lurking in the shadows?* He strained his ears, trying to pick up any other sound.

"Anyone awake in the Murray wagon?" The loud whisper came from Reverend Knowles.

Kenneth slipped his arm out from under Melody and wrapped a quilt around her before peeking out around the covering at the back of the wagon. "I am."

When the preacher moved, accumulated rain dumped from the brim of his hat in the back. Kenneth hoped it wasn't seeping under the man's collar. "Sorry to bother you, but Catherine is having a difficult time. I'm asking everyone to pray for both her and Angus."

He nodded. "Of course, Reverend."

As the man walked away, Kenneth poured out his heart before God, asking him to protect Catherine and her baby. He didn't know how long he had sat there praying when something startled him.

"Noooooooo!"

The screaming wail that reverberated all around the clearing broke through Melody's slumber, jerking her wide awake, and she hit her head against the wooden tailgate. She rubbed her head where she'd hit it and glanced over at him in the soft, predawn light. "What was that?"

Kenneth slipped back beside her. "Mel, you are you okay, honey?"

"I think so," she whispered.

"I'm not sure what it was, but it didn't sound good. At least, it wasn't a wild animal. Sounded more like a man. I'd better go check on things." He started dressing. "Someone might need my help."

She moved out of his way and slid into their pallet.

When he finished buttoning his shirt and shrugged into his coat, he leaned over and pressed a gentle kiss on her lips. "Please stay in the wagon until I come back and say it's safe."

"All right."

He hurried to check out what was going on. He didn't want to leave his family very long. As soon as he finished talking to the doctor outside the McKenna wagon, his hurried footsteps took him back. He didn't hear any movement inside his wagon, so he almost didn't open the flap, but a chill wind drove him inside. He pulled back the quilt to climb into the wagon.

A slice of early morning sunlight bathed Melody's face. She opened her eyes and gave him the cozy half-smile he loved seeing when she had just awakened. Then she seemed to notice the concern on his face.

"What's wrong?" Her voice trembled between dry lips.

Kenneth raised his right hand and started massaging the back of his neck. "It wasn't good. Mrs. McKenna died giving birth to three girls."

Melody gasped. "That's horrible."

"The sound we heard was Angus when Doc gave him the word." Kenneth hunkered beside her without removing his coat. "The man is beside himself with grief."

"I'm sure he is." She bunched the edge of the quilt in both hands and clutched it to her chest. "What's he going to do?"

"You see, that's the thing. He doesn't know what to do." Kenneth huffed out a deep breath. "And those babies need to learn how to nurse. Doc wondered if...you and Charlotte Holden could help. You're the only two women on the train who can right now."

A tear slipped down her cheek. He had hated asking her. He knew she would cry, but none of this was the poor babies' fault. They needed to be cuddled and suckled, and she had the means to do both. Would it break her heart? Probably. But he knew she wouldn't refuse the request. That was just the way she was, more interested in other people's needs than her own.

"If I go over there, will you stay with the girls and get them dressed and fed when they awaken?"

He nodded and gave her a tender look. "You know I will. But can you handle being around newborn babies?"

"Yes. It won't be easy, but those babies need the kind of help I can provide." Having slept in her clothing, she quickly pulled on her shoes and climbed out of the wagon.

Kenneth watched as she walked by the wagons between theirs and the McKenna's. Charlotte Holden took Melody to the cradle set between the wagon and the campfire. Both women stared down at the three tiny occupants.

His attention was drawn toward the wagon parked beside the McKenna wagon. Former slaves, Henry and Odette Marshall were travelling with the McKennas, and they were expecting a child as well. Dr. Horton stepped down out of the back of the Marshall wagon. Perhaps Odette was in labor as well. If so, she might be able to nurse one of the triplets and relieve Melody from the task. Kenneth certainly hoped so.

~

The long day rushed into eternity. A funeral and burying. A grieving husband. A somber noontime meal. Three baby girls without a mother.

After the evening meal, Kenneth helped Melody put the

two girls to bed. Then he watched her go over to help with the new babies. After making sure their daughters were completely asleep, he headed toward the McKenna wagon as well. On the way, he whispered a prayer of thanks that their girls were alive, healthy, and would sleep until morning. They would be safe for a few minutes. Besides, the wagons were close enough, he could hear if either of them woke up crying.

He stopped a ways from the McKenna campfire. He just wanted to watch over Melody as well as their daughters.

While Angus McKenna walked across the clearing toward him, Kenneth concentrated on his wife. He wished he could take the look of pain and loss from her face. At times like this, he felt so helpless. Why couldn't he say the words Melody needed to hear? He felt the emotions, but no matter how hard he tried, he couldn't express them to others, not even his wife.

She gave the infant the same kind of tender attention she had always showered on their own children. While her hands gently cradled the child, Kenneth knew she wanted the baby to feel a mother's arms around her.

Angus stopped right in front of him, one of the tiny girls held against his shoulder. Kenneth glanced at him. The change in the man's looks surprised Kenneth. His shoulders slumped, and his haggard appearance had aged him ten years in one day. He appeared to be a broken man. All the sparks of his personality had been extinguished.

No wonder. Everyone on the wagon train had been blessed by the love shining between Angus and Catherine. Kenneth was sure that if he lost Melody, he'd look even worse than Angus.

After a moment the man cleared his throat. "I...uh, I want to talk to you...about something."

Kenneth nodded. "Go ahead."

"I'm up against a brick wall here." Angus shook his head as if to clear his thoughts. "I don't know how to take care of one baby, much less three. I want to give all my girls a chance at a good life." The shorter man glanced sideways up at Kenneth, while clutching his baby even closer. "Would you and your missus consider adopting one of them? I believe you would be very good parents that I can trust to take care of her."

Kenneth pondered the words while he rubbed his chin. He glanced toward Melody, noticing the tender expression on her face. Maybe it would be good for her to have another baby right now. "Why don't we ask my wife?"

They walked over to where Melody sat with another of the babies in her arms. She had finished feeding the child. Now she sat humming to her and patting a gentle rhythm on her back.

Angus McKenna stopped in front of her, and she glanced first at Angus and then at him. Kenneth gave her an encouraging smile.

"Mrs. Murray." Mr. McKenna cleared his throat before starting again. "I've come to ask you something...that I never dreamed...I'd ever ask anyone." His voice rasped, and he stopped, staring off into the distance.

"I've decided...it would be best to find other families to raise two of my girls." He stood straighter. "I've watched you with Mary Lenora..."

Melody gazed at the baby in her arms, and Kenneth knew her heart ached for the child.

"Mary Lenora McKenna?" She kept her attention on Angus.

The man stared across the clearing with unfocused eyes. "My wife's parents couldn't agree on a name for her. Her father wanted Mary Margaret. Her mother wanted Catherine Lenora. So they stuck all four names on her." Mr. McKenna seemed relieved to be talking about something else besides what had happened that day. "I've named this one"—he indicated the baby on his shoulder—"Catherine Lenora."

He didn't say anything about the third girl. Kenneth figured they'd find out soon enough what Angus had done with her.

He looked straight at Kenneth. "Your husband said that perhaps the two of you could take one of the girls."

Her gaze darted toward him. He gave a small nod. "But only if you want to, Melody."

"What I'm trying to say, Mrs. Murray, is..." Angus stared across the circle of wagons as he spoke. "Would you consider adopting one of my daughters and raising her as your own?" He stared at the ground as he clung to the tiny baby in his arms.

"I'll be happy with whatever you decide, Melody." Kenneth spoke gently.

"I'm just asking you to keep the name I've given her." Angus gave her a pleading look.

A slow smile spread across Melody's face. "I'd be honored to have your daughter. I love her already." She kissed the fuzz atop the sleeping baby's head.

Kenneth slipped his arm around her waist and held her and the baby close.

"Thank you. I'll send some clothes and blankets for Mary Lenora." Angus turned and trudged toward his own wagon, holding his one remaining daughter to his heart.

Kenneth held Melody and watched her as she stared down into the face of their new daughter.

"She is a blessing from God." Melody looked up at him with love shining in her eyes. "I intend to be God's blessing to this tiny girl."

He smiled. "You will be, Melody, and she will be our blessing too."

CHAPTER 1

"*P*a?" Mary Lenora Murray shouted back over her shoulder as she picked up the heavy picnic basket. "You ready to go?" *Why does he always drag his feet when we're going to church?*

Her father came through the mud room into the kitchen, letting the screen door slam shut behind him. He smelled of heat, hay, and sunshine, with the strong tang of muck from the barn mingled in. By the looks of his clothes, attending church was the farthest thing from his mind. His ratty trousers held smudges of several dark colors. She didn't even want to guess what they were. And the long sleeves of his undershirt, the only thing covering his torso, were shoved above his elbows. Grayed and dingy, the shirt would never be white again, no matter how hard she tried to get it clean.

Mary bit her tongue to keep from scolding him as she did her younger brothers and sister when they made such a racket entering the house. No doubt, he would give her some excuse about having too much work to go to church. Not a big surprise. She'd heard it all before too many times.

He set a bucket of fresh water beside the dry sink and gripped his fingers around the front straps of his suspenders. That always signaled he was about to tell her something she didn't want to hear.

"I'm not going today." This time, he didn't really make any excuses. Just this bald-faced comment.

She took a deep breath and let it out slowly, trying to calm her anger. She'd give him a sweet answer even if the words tasted bitter in her mouth. "The new pastor is coming today. We're having dinner on the grounds after the service. Remember, I told you when we got home last Sunday." She flashed what she hoped was a warm smile at him and prayed he couldn't tell it was fake.

"What happened to the last one? He didn't last very long, did he?" Pa started washing his hands with the bar of homemade soap she kept in a dish on the shelf. "Don't understand why that church can't keep a pastor. Someone musta run him off."

Mary couldn't keep from huffing out a breath this time. "I told you about that too." She clamped her lips closed before she asked the question that often bounced around her mind. *Why don't you ever listen to me?* At seventeen, she was close enough to being an adult to be treated like one, and she'd carried the load of a woman in this household for years.

"His wife died, and his father-in-law begged him to bring the grandchildren closer to where they live, so he headed back to Ohio. Living in the same community as their grandparents, he'd have a lot of help with the younger ones."

Mary had never known her own grandparents, none of them. Not her mother's parents. Not her father's parents. Not the parents of whoever gave birth to her. She didn't wonder about any of them very often, but today, her heart longed for someone who really loved her.

With bright red curly hair and fair skin that freckled more every time she stepped into the sunlight, she didn't resemble anyone in this family that had adopted her as an infant. Since they were black Irish, they all had dark hair and striking blue eyes, not like her murky green ones. And none of them had ever wanted to know what she thought about anything...except her mother.

"Well, I've gotta lot to do today." Her father reached for the towel she'd made out of feed sacks. "You and the others go ahead. I might come over that way at dinner time."

No, you won't. Mary had heard his statement often enough to know he was trying to placate her so she would leave him alone. So she would.

"Frances, George, Bobby, come on. We don't want to be late." She shifted the handle of the loaded basket to her other arm. "Frances, you grab the jug of spring water. We might get thirsty."

Her father's icy blue eyes pierced her. "Pretty warm out today. No sign of rain."

"We'll be picnicking in the field between the church and Willamette Falls. It's cooler there, especially under the trees with the breeze blowing across the water." She started toward the front door.

"Keep your eyes on the boys." His harsh command followed her. "Don't let either of them fall into the river. They could drown. Water's fast right there."

She nodded, but didn't answer or look back at him. All he cared about were those boys and getting them raised old enough to really help with the farming. He already worked them harder than any of the neighbors did their sons who were the same ages.

Six long years ago her mother and older sisters contracted

diptheria when they went to help Aunt Miriam and Uncle Leland settle in their house on a farm about five miles from theirs. On the trip to Oregon, one of them had contracted the dread disease and didn't know it until after they arrived. No one knew they were all dead until Pa went looking for Ma, Carrie, and Annette a couple of days later. He saw the quarantine sign someone nailed to a fencepost and didn't go closer until he had help. When he came home, he told Mary she would have to take over the keeping of the house. *Six long years ago.*

When did my life become such a drudgery? Had it ever been anything else? At least not since Ma died, which seemed like an eternity ago.

~

*D*aniel Winthrop whistled while he dressed for church. He looked forward with anticipation to the moment when he would lay eyes on Mary Murray. Even her name had a musical ring to it.

He'd been waiting and planning what to say when he approached her. Today he would start his subtle courting. With the situation at the Murray farm, he knew he would have his work cut out for him to convince her she could start a life of her own with him. After he achieved that, he'd ask her father for her hand.

Visions of coming home to her each night and building a family together moved through his head like the slides of photographs in the Holmes Stereopticon they had at home. He loved her already, but more than that, he wanted to get her out of that house where she was loaded down with so much work and responsibility.

Daniel had often gone with his mother when she bought fresh produce from the Murrays. So he knew what her life had been like since her mother died. Their families came to Oregon on the same wagon train so he'd known her all his life. He was only three years older than she was, and he had watched her over the last few years as she blossomed into a beautiful young woman.

Mary needed to be appreciated and cared for, and he was just the man to do it.

"Daniel, we're leaving soon." His father's voice prodded him from his dreams.

With a final peek into the tall cheval glass, he straightened his necktie before he headed out the door of his room. "I'm on my way."

He bounded down the stairs and took their picnic basket from his mother. "Something really smells good." He gave a loud sniff. "Do you need me to test and make sure it's all right?"

He welcomed her playful slap on his hand that crept toward the cover on the basket. Her laughter reminded him of the chimes he had heard in the larger church in Portland.

"Not a single bite until dinner." Like a queen, she swept out the door Father held open for her.

Their familiar ritual warmed his heart. He looked forward to creating family rituals with Mary. Once more, he whistled as he headed toward the brougham. Nothing could cloud his day.

When they pulled up to the Methodist Church, his father guided the team toward the back where a large area paved with fine gravel gave plenty of space for those who arrived in horse-drawn vehicles. While Father helped Mother down from the open carriage, Daniel took the reins and tied them to one of the hitching rails that outlined the space. He chose the rail under a spreading black cottonwood tree where the limbs were just beginning to show the leaf buds.

He scanned the lot, looking for the Murray wagon. Not there. Disappointed, he stared at the ground. *Please, God, let Mary come today.*

Clopping hoofs and a jingling harness accompanied a

wagon taking too fast of a turn into the parking area. Daniel cut his eyes toward the advancing disaster. Two of the wheels did indeed lift from the ground. Before he could get a shout out of his mouth, he heard Mary's sweet voice.

"Lean to the right, boys!"

George and Bobby, Mary's brothers, scrambled across the seat, followed by Frances. The wagon wheels settled into the gravel, and Mary pulled on the reins.

"Easy. Settle down." Even though she spoke to the horses, he heard every word.

His heart that had almost leapt from his chest also settled down when he realized she was no longer in danger. *Thank You, Lord.*

The wagon came to a standstill, and Mary put her dainty hand to her chest and released a deep breath. The green cotton fabric, sprigged with white flowers, looked good on her, setting off her red hair, pulled up into a bunch on the top of her head. Without a hat or bonnet covering it, the sun danced across the curls. He loved seeing the wisps frame her face. That's how he pictured her when he dreamed about their future.

Mary sat a moment without moving. She was probably scared out of her wits. Where was her father? He should have been driving the wagon, not her. How long had it been since the man had attended services? Daniel couldn't remember the last time. It was not a good thing for a man to neglect his spiritual nature. He'd just have to pray harder for Mr. Murray.

Daniel hurried toward them. "Hi, Mary."

She looked up, straight into his eyes, fear still flickering in the back of her gaze. "Daniel. Good morning." Her words came out riding on short breaths.

He took hold of the bridle of the horse nearest him. "I can hitch your team under the trees for you."

After releasing another deep breath, Mary nodded. "Thank

you. I'd like that." She turned toward her siblings. "Frances, you get the picnic basket, and George, you carry the jug of water. Go find us a pew, perhaps near the back of the sanctuary, and put the things under the bench. I'll be right in."

The younger children climbed out of the wagon and followed their sister's instructions. Mary watched them until they'd gone around the side of the building toward the front. Then she stood up.

Before she could try to climb over the side, Daniel hurried to help. He held out his hand to her. She stared at it, then looked at his face.

"I'll help you down." He gave her his most beguiling smile.

For the first time since she arrived, she smiled back, and pink bled up her neck into her cheeks. Her blush went straight to his heart. Oh, yes, he loved this woman.

Mary slipped her slim fingers into his hand. Even through the white cotton gloves, he felt the connection as warmth sparked up his arm like fireworks on Independence Day. She glanced down, so she could see the step. When she hesitated, he let go of her hand and both of his spanned her tiny waist. With a deft swing, he had her on the ground in seconds. He wished he had the right to pull her into an embrace. *Wouldn't that just set the tongues a-wagging?* He couldn't do that to her. Mary needed to be cherished for the treasure she was. And as far as Daniel could see, her father really didn't treat her that way.

He watched her walk toward the front of the building, enjoying the way her skirt swayed with each step, barely brushing the tops of her black patent shoes. *That is one beautiful woman.* He turned back to her team. Walking beside the horses, he led them toward the hitching rail where his family's brougham was parked, hoping it would give him the opportunity to help her back up onto the wagon seat. As he crossed the lot, several other conveyances entered, and he waved and exchanged greetings with each family.

The church was the first one established in Oregon City. At that time, it was the Methodist Mission but grew as the town did. Along the way, members of this body had a great influence on what happened in the burgeoning city. And that was still true today. His Winthrop ancestors, who settled nearby, had been instrumental in both the growth of the church and of the town. He felt a sense of pride at being a part of something that important, and he wanted to increase the town's assets, because he planned to raise his own family here. Maybe establish a dynasty of his own, watching his sons and daughters, then his grandchildren, prosper.

His woolgathering slowed the progress of tying the horses to their spot. He needed to hurry so he wouldn't miss the beginning of the service. As he opened the front door, Mrs. Slidell struck the first chord on the new Mason and Hamlin reed organ. The church had ordered the instrument from the manufacturing plant in Buffalo, New York. When it arrived only a couple of weeks before, the music added a special feeling to the worship and helped most people stay on the right tune better than the old piano did. He hummed along with the introduction to "What a Friend We Have in Jesus," his favorite hymn.

Glancing around the room, Daniel finally spied Mary and her siblings sitting on the second pew from the back on the right side of the aisle. He squared his shoulders and confidently approached the wooden bench. He asked if he could sit with them, and she scooted over to make room. Just what he wanted. He would be sitting right beside her.

Throughout the service, Daniel had a hard time keeping his mind on the proceedings. Mary sat close enough for him to touch her if he leaned a little to his right. He was so tempted to bump against her arm, but he held back. He imagined clasping her hand in his and holding it for longer than just a few seconds while helping her down from a conveyance or through a doorway. Really wrapping his large fingers around hers and intertwining their fingers. Just thinking about it caught his breath.

He whooshed it out, and she turned toward him, her eyes widening with a question. After flashing a smile at her, he glanced up at Reverend Horton. The man's delivery was smooth and his words made a lot of sense. He'd be a good pastor for them, but Daniel couldn't keep a single word of his message in his mind. Not while he could feel Mary's presence with every cell in his body.

Instead in his mind, he searched up and down the streets of Oregon City, seeking a place to turn into a home for him and his beloved. If the right house wasn't for sale, he could build her one. She could help him choose the design. That's what he'd do. Build her the home she'd always dreamed of. His heart squeezed with the knowledge of what he planned to do. He could hardly keep the idea to himself. He hoped it wouldn't take too long for him to convince her that they should marry.

He'd even hire servants to help her manage their home. Whatever her heart desired, he'd do everything he could to present her with all she wanted. He only hoped it wouldn't take too long. At twenty years old, he was ready to move on to the next phase of his life... with Mary by his side.

"Now let us bow our heads in prayer." Reverend Horton raised his hands to bless the whole congregation.

Daniel dropped his head toward his chest. How had the man finished his sermon without Daniel noticing? Next Sunday, he'd have to listen more closely. He really did want to get to know the new pastor and his family.

"Amen." After the pastor pronounced the word, several other men echoed it.

Daniel watched his father rise from the second pew near the front on the left side of the aisle and take his place beside the new preacher. He placed his arm across the man's shoulders. "Dear friends, on your behalf, I welcome our new pastor. Now let's all meet his lovely family." He waved toward a woman sitting on the front pew. "Mrs. Horton?"

The woman stood and turned toward the congregation. She was pretty, but not as young or as pretty as Mary.

"And," Father's voice boomed, "these are their children."

Four stair-step youngsters stood beside their mother. The tallest a boy, the next a girl, then another boy, and the shortest a cute little girl. As if they had rehearsed it, they bowed toward the people in unison.

Several women across the sanctuary *oooed* or *aahed* before a loud round of applause broke out. The three oldest children gave shy smiles, and the youngest tugged at her mother's skirts. When Mrs. Horton picked her up, the girl waved to the people, clearly enjoying the attention.

"I hope you all brought your blanket and picnic baskets." Father beamed at the crowd. "We're going to spread our food together. I believe there are plenty of sawhorse tables set up near the building. And you can pick a spot under the trees to settle for your meal. Just don't forget to take the time to greet our new ministerial family while you're here." Father led the Horton family down the aisle and out the front door.

Daniel turned back toward Mary. "Perhaps you and your brothers and sister could spread your blanket beside my family's."

A tiny smile graced Mary's sweet mouth. "If you're sure your mother wouldn't mind, I'd like that."

"Oh, yes. I'm sure." He stepped into the nearly empty aisle and moved back to let Mary and her family precede him, and he quickly followed behind.

His heartbeat accelerated just thinking about spending

special time with the object of his affections. Without thinking, he started whistling a happy tune.

Mary glanced back at him. "I didn't know you whistled."

"Oh, yes. I'm a man of many talents." His heart leapt at the interest he read in her gaze. Things were well on their way to working out just the way he wanted them to.

CHAPTER 2

*W*ith Daniel beside her in church, Mary didn't feel so different, so out of place. Since all the other family groups had at least one parent attending the service, her father's emotional desertion often overpowered her. With Daniel, she felt the protection of a man, even though he wasn't a part of her family.

From her earliest memories, he had been kind to her. When they were younger, she looked forward to having him accompany his mother when she came to buy vegetables from the Murray garden. They would chase each other between the rows while their mothers talked and laughed together. Even though the families took differing paths after they arrived at Oregon City, having traveled on the wagon train bonded the women as nothing else could have.

Daniel was a good man...handsome too. He worked in the family woolen goods store. Somehow, he seemed a lot older than she, even though she knew he was only twenty.

His help today made her feel feminine and special somehow. Nothing in her life up until this moment met the need she had for being appreciated. So she decided to enjoy it while she could.

She stepped from the church into the sunlight, which was much brighter than when they arrived. Such a pretty April day for the first picnic of the year. No rain. She took a deep breath, relishing the fresh clean air. Shading her eyes with one hand, she glanced down at her brothers, who were shoving each other and scuffling as usual. *Boys.* Why did little boys always do that, especially when they were out in public? Some of the women probably doubted her ability to control them.

"Since Frances is carrying the picnic basket, and George has the jug of water, Bobby, why don't you go to the wagon and get the quilt out of the back?" Her gentle words slid off them like water off a duck's back. She hadn't wanted to sound too harsh, but without raising her voice a little, she'd never gain their attention.

Before she could open her mouth, Daniel stopped beside the boys. "Hey, guys."

Like magic, the scuffling ceased, and both of them turned their faces up toward him. Now why would they listen to Daniel and not to her?

Because his voice carries more authority than mine does. She did like to hear the rich mellow baritone herself. A shiver skittered up her spine. Where did that come from? Not a single breeze carried cooler air their way. In fact, beads of sweat trickled down between her shoulder blades. She wished she could reach back there and scratch the trail they left.

"Bobby and I will go get the quilt." Daniel placed his hand lightly on the younger boy's shoulder. "While the rest of you make your way over there where my mother is laying out our blanket. Then I'll help you put the food on the table." He winked at Mary. "I want to see what you brought so I can get my share. I'm sure it will all be delicious." He and Bobby started toward the back lot.

Why had he winked at her? It made her feel a little breath-less...or was that the heat? She really couldn't tell for sure. But her stomach fluttered in a strange new way. She hoped she wasn't getting sick, because she didn't want to miss one minute of the picnic. They had so few of them.

Mary led the way through the new-mown grass toward a large maple tree spreading long branches that before too long would give a great deal of shade. As she walked, she removed her gloves and stuffed them into her handbag. No need to wear them on a picnic. She stopped beside the Winthrop blanket.

"Daniel asked if we would spread ours beside yours." Mary smiled at his mother. "That is, if it's all right with you."

Mrs. Winthrop clasped her hands together in front of her waist. "I'd be delighted to share the meal with you. We haven't visited for quite some time." The smile that lifted her cheeks lit up the area with warmth. "I should have been more attentive to your family since Melody has been gone. She was such a good friend."

Her words turned Mary's thoughts to the last time she saw her mother alive, and a lump formed in her throat, even after all this time. She tried to dislodge it, but the obstruction wouldn't move, and sudden sorrow overwhelmed her. "That's all right. We know you're busy. And thank you for allowing us to join you today." She hoped Daniel's mother didn't notice that her voice sounded funny.

"How have you been?" Mrs. Winthrop leaned closer to Mary, peering straight into her eyes. "Is everything all right at the farm?"

"Yes, ma'am."

What else could she say? Mary didn't want anyone to know how things really were going. With Pa withdrawing from anything except work and her having to take care of the house-hold, her future appeared bleak. By the time the other children were grown, she'd be a spinster. Perhaps then she could move on with her life, free from the guilt of resenting her lot in life.

"Mary!" Bobby came running, carrying the heavy bundle clutched in front of him. "Daniel let me carry it by myself, but he helped get it out of the wagon." He thrust the cover into her hands.

"His name is Mr. Winthrop." Mary wished she could always remember to teach the children proper manners. Mother had. But she was so busy with the chores that some things slipped through the cracks.

"But he told me to call him Daniel." Bobby glanced at Daniel before squinting up at her.

"Oh, he did, did he?" A chuckle crept up her throat, and try as she might, she couldn't contain it. Bobby looked so earnest.

"I thought that was Mr. Winthrop." George pointed toward Daniel's father, who walked toward them.

"He is." Mary felt another blush enter her cheeks. Maybe everyone would just think she was too hot. "That's Daniel's father, but Daniel is a man, and children should call him Mr. Winthrop too."

Bobby turned his attention toward Mrs. Winthrop. "Isn't that a problem? Having two Mr. Winthrops in the house? Do you ever get them mixed up?"

When all the adults burst into laughter, the boy was the one who looked confused. "That wasn't funny, was it?"

Mary wrapped her arms around her younger brother. "His parents don't call him Mr. Winthrop. They call him Daniel."

"I'm glad we only gots one Mr. Murray at our house." Bobby pulled away from her embrace. "Can I go play with the other boys?"

"Yes." Before she got the word out, both Bobby and George took off running as fast as they could.

"Boys." Frances huffed out a breath, as if she were too old for such goings on.

Daniel spread the quilt for her, then relieved Frances of her burden. He held out his other arm toward Mary. "I'm going to help put your food on the table. Remember?"

At some point, Daniel had removed his suit jacket. When Mary slid her hand around his elbow and rested it on his forearm, she felt his muscles through the thinner fabric of his starched white shirt with dark pinstripes. A tightening in her midsection signaled something to her, but she wasn't sure what. She couldn't get sick today. Since she lost her mother and older sisters, any kind of illness scared her. She trembled at the thought.

"Are you okay?" Daniel stood very close to her.

She glanced up. His hazel eyes held warmth she'd never seen in them before. All she could do was stare into their depths.

When she took the next step, she stumbled, but because of her hold on his arm, she didn't fall. She glanced down so she could see where she was going. The ground in this field was uneven. "I'm fine."

How could she describe what just happened to her?

"I'm glad." His husky whisper covered her with a blanket of comfort.

What was happening to her? This was just Daniel, the boy she'd known all her life. He was the same, but something was different with her. Or maybe something was also different with him too. The emotions surging through her told her she was an adult now. When had they stopped being children?

"Where do you ladies want us to put our food?" Daniel held up the basket as if showing the other women what he was talking about.

Our food? When he said that, Mary wished it really was their food, not just the Murray family's offering. The other women kept their eyes on her and Daniel, so she slipped her hand from his arm. No sense in starting any unwarranted gossip.

"There's plenty of room over here." Mrs. Slidell indicated a vacant space on a blue tablecloth.

The long tables were covered with an assortment of cotton tablecloths. The multicolored display added a festive air to the picnic. Mary set the basket on one side of the empty space and opened the top. She lifted out a platter of fried chicken covered with a tea towel. After setting it down, she removed a bowl of green beans to put beside it. Carrots glazed with butter and brown sugar soon joined the other two.

Mrs. Slidell helped remove the other two tea towels for Mary. "This looks good. Your momma really taught you well. I loved her glazed carrots." The woman started down the table a ways. "And if you have a dessert, we're putting them all down here."

Daniel pulled the last dish from the basket. "This looks like a pie to me." He gave an exaggerated sniff. "Smells like my favorite...apple pie. I love the cinnamon." He smacked his lips.

His enthusiastic response made her smile. No one had given her that kind of encouragement since her mother died. Mary lifted the nearly empty basket while he followed Mrs. Slidell to the space she indicated for the pie.

"Thank you for your help, Daniel." Mary glanced toward the place where Frances stood talking to his parents. "I need to be sure my family has enough plates and silverware to eat with."

Before she could take a step, Daniel lifted the basket from her arm and offered the other one to her. Mary quickly took it and started toward their family members. Too many people glanced toward them. She didn't want anyone to get the wrong idea about Daniel being so nice to her. She loved the attention he gave her, but nothing could come of it. Not with things the way they were at home. She could not have the kind of life other young women looked forward to, so she shouldn't let false hopes take root in her heart.

~

*A*fter they finished sharing the meal together, a couple of the men came by asking if Daniel and his father would like to play baseball. The only time the men actually played the game was at special events like this, and they really put on a show. The women watched and cheered for the men in their family.

"Not me." Daniel shook his head.

"I think I should work off some of this good food." His father patted his stomach and started rolling the sleeves of his dress shirt partway up his forearms. "Will it be the older men against the young bucks?"

With much joviality, the men hurried toward their comrades. Mother tagged along behind the men and joined the women who planned to watch.

As the others made their way across the field to where the game would be played, Daniel turned his attention back to Mary. She sat with her knees drawn up under her skirt and her arms locked around them. She looked so cute with only the tips of her black shoes peeking out. His heartbeat accelerated so much, he was sure someone close by would hear the pounding.

He got up and held out a hand to her. "Want to go for a walk down by the river?"

She glanced at him. "I've got to be sure the boys are playing in a safe place." She turned to scan the area between them and the church where various groups of all ages clustered.

"I see them over by the horses with other boys. I think they'll be safe." Daniel kept his hand extended.

She slipped her fingers into his and held her skirt down with the other hand. Another thing he liked about her. Mary maintained her modesty in every situation. She'd make an ideal wife, as well as a very beautiful one.

After she was on her feet, she searched the area until she spied her sister. "I'll go if you let me tell Frances to watch out for our brothers. Can't have them getting too near the water and falling in. Pa would never forgive me."

She made that statement with such conviction, Daniel almost believed she meant it. But surely her father would understand that an accident wouldn't be Mary's fault. But then Kenneth Murray had apparently never recovered from losing his wife and two oldest daughters.

After they found Frances and delivered the message, they headed toward the bluff above the riverbank. Daniel really wanted to hold Mary's hand all the way, but he knew it was too soon. So they walked close together, but not touching.

Finally, Mary relaxed and appeared carefree, meandering through the grass. When they approached a cluster of plants where flowers usually blossomed, she stepped carefully around them.

"I can't wait until the wildflowers bloom. My favorite is Queen Anne's lace." Mary glanced toward him. "Their name is a good description. I love lace."

As they continued on their way, Daniel pondered those words. Even though Mary wore dresses that fit well, made from fabric that looked good on her, he'd never seen a snippet of lace on any of her clothing. When they married, he'd make sure she had all the lace she wanted. Maybe her wedding dress could be made of that material too. Even her veil. Mary, surrounded by a lacy cloud, looking like an angel. His chest constricted, aching with the desire to fulfill all her dreams.

"Did you always want to work in your family store?" Mary's tone let him know she was really interested, not just passing the time.

"I guess so." He stopped, and she did too, turning to gaze up at him. "I never even thought about doing anything else. When we came out on the wagon train, my parents followed other members of our family who had settled here earlier. And when people started raising sheep, they did too. The climate is just right to produce top quality wool. Eventually, my father decided to open a store to sell the woolen products produced by the family. I naturally grew up learning all about it."

He started back toward the river, which roared past them. Mary moved to his side.

"I just love watching the water on the falls, but it's pretty loud." She turned her face up toward his. "At least the air is cooler here."

"So what do you want to do with your life, Mary?" He tried to sound casual but her answer was important to him. If she wanted to move away from Oregon City, he'd have his work cut out for him, trying to convince her to let him court her.

"Huh." Her response sounded almost like a snort. "I don't think I have any choice in the matter." Wistfulness colored her words with multiple undertones.

He cut his eyes down toward her. "Why do you say that?"

"I haven't had a choice since my mother and sisters died." She covered her lips with her fingertips, evidently trying to keep words in her mouth. But after a moment, she continued, "I shouldn't have said that. I try not to complain, and I don't want to say anything against Pa, but I can't do anything else until my sister and brothers grow up."

Although none spilled over onto her cheeks, tears glistened in her eyes. His heart broke for her. "How old were you when your mother died? About twelve?"

"I was just thinking about that this morning. I was eleven." One tear finally escaped, and she flicked it away with a fingertip.

"And how old is Frances now?"

Mary's eyes widened. "She's thirteen."

"Yes, she's thirteen, plenty old enough to take over if you wanted to do something else. That's two years older than you were when you started caring for the household." He hoped he hadn't come on too strong. "And you'll soon be eighteen. Right?"

"Yes, in September. You really have kept up with my life, haven't you?" She tried to laugh, but it sounded breathless. The sound made his heart hitch.

"Yes, I have." He cleared his throat. "And there's a good reason. I want you to think about something. I want to court you, but I won't ask your father if I can until you tell me you're ready."

"Court me?" Her voice came out on a soft squeak, but she didn't back away, and her features softened. "You want to court me, as in looking toward marriage?"

"I don't know any other kind of courting, do you?" Amusement spurred a smile to his face.

She gazed across the water and twisted her hands together. "I'd never considered such a thing."

He stood quietly, letting her get used to the idea. The fine mist from the falls floated on a breeze, cooling them even more, and swishing through the limbs of the tall trees. This verdant area was full of life, and that's what he wanted for Mary. A full life. Finally, she glanced toward his face. "If you really mean it, I think that would be nice."

Daniel wanted to jump and whoop for joy, but he maintained his decorum. Wouldn't want to display something like that in full view of the members of the congregation, even if they were all involved in other activities.

"Perhaps we should head back, so I can make sure George and Bobby aren't getting into trouble. Frances isn't always stern enough with them." Mary twirled around and started through the grove of trees.

He hurried to catch up with her. His dreams and plans were coming together. He wondered how long they'd need to court before he could actually ask her to marry him. He'd never done anything like this before, and he didn't want to talk to anyone else about it yet.

But it was actually going to happen. Soon, he hoped.

CHAPTER 3

week. Mary got out of bed and stretched as she yawned. For seven long days and agonizing nights, she hadn't heard a word from Daniel. Had last Sunday afternoon only been a dream?

The first few days after the picnic, she had basked in the warmth of his declaration. He wanted to court her. With her heart about to burst with happiness, she had agreed. Where was he? Didn't courting mean she would see him? Or at least he would make some kind of contact with her in this length of time? Even if he just sent a servant with a note. The farm was only three miles from town. He could get here quickly in his buggy.

Yesterday, Mrs. Winthrop came to buy produce from Mary's garden. Disappointment clouded her day when Daniel didn't accompany her as he often had in the past. Mrs. Winthrop hadn't given her a message from him, and Mary didn't dare ask about him. Had she just imagined him telling her he wanted to court? *Surely not.*

Were all her dreams a mere vapor in the wind, to be blown away before nourishing her parched heart? Daniel's eyes and words held the strength of truth when they were together last Sunday. Or did she read more into his intentions than he actually expressed to her? She remembered every word he'd spoken, repeating them over in her mind every day since they parted. His words were plain and to the point, not open to wrong interpretation. So maybe he changed his mind. Or his parents didn't want him to court her. That thought hit her heart like a piercing dagger. She almost doubled over with the pain.

Nothing about her should catch the attention of a man with such a bright future. Although her father made enough off the farm to keep them in food and clothing, she was no match for his social stratum.

Was it wrong to want more than the bleak future spread out before her? For those few moments, Daniel had offered a life free from the responsibility of rearing her younger siblings. Her hopes had soared like a butterfly breaking free from its chrysalis and spreading its wings in the sunlight. Now fear of rejection choked off all the hope and dreams awakened by his words.

But today was Sunday. Maybe Daniel was waiting to see her again. With a lighter heart, she arose from her bed and started her ablutions. As she splashed water on her face, she tried to decide what to wear. She had worn her favorite Sunday dress last week. Today she had to wear something else.

She looked at the garments hanging on the hooks in her bedroom and couldn't decide which of her other three nice ones to choose. Maybe the one with the cream-colored bodice and warm brown skirt. Mary liked the way the lines of the dress enhanced her figure without being immodest.

She dug through her bureau drawer to find a ribbon to match the ensemble. She could braid her hair and form it into a chignon at her nape with the ribbon winding through her curls. Wearing this more sophisticated style always made her feel elegant. If he really did change his mind, she could show him what he would be missing.

Waiting to don her dress until she had fed the younger children breakfast, she threw on a cotton wrapper she had created out of flower-printed feed sacks. She cinched the tie belt tight around her waist and headed toward the kitchen. Passing the room the boys shared, she heard soft moans. *What in the world?*

Mary opened the door and peeked inside. Bobby had thrown off his covers and moved restlessly. When she reached the bed, heat radiated from his body. She placed her hand on his forehead and jerked it back.

A high fever. Fear coursed through her. The family had been blessedly free of illness for years, ever since her mother and sisters died. Why now? Bobby rolled into a ball clutching his stomach but still didn't awaken.

Mary rushed from the room and checked the water in the bucket beside the dry sink. She picked up the dipper and poured cups into a blue-speckled dishpan. On her way back to the bedroom, she grabbed a clean face cloth and a Turkish towel.

As she reentered the bedroom, George sat up in his bed and rubbed his eyes. "Mary, whatcha doing?"

She set the small round pan on the bureau, dipped the face cloth into the tepid water, and wrung out the excess before placing it on her younger brother's forehead. Still the boy didn't awaken, but he continued to moan. Shouldn't the water have startled him?

Fear cut through her like a sword. *Please, please, God. Don't let my brother die.* She couldn't face another loss. She'd had so many in her life. Her first mother, the one who didn't want her. Gave her away like just so much trash. The mother who adopted her. Her two older sisters. Now pain joined the fear as they performed a macabre dance in her midsection.

Those long ago days were as vivid in her mind as if they

happened only last week. Mama and Mary's older sisters getting into the wagon and heading down the road. Her standing on the porch with her arms around the column holding up the roof, sad because she had been left behind. Her mother had said Mary was old enough to help Pa with the younger children for just that one day.

And they never came back.

Mary never saw them again, not even at a funeral. She fantasized for several years that they were just away on a journey, and any day they could return. Each night their absence added to her discouragement. She'd had to learn to care for a two-year-old and a three-year-old with only the help of her seven-year-old sister.

Pa had been no help. He took over a year getting to the point he could even look at the younger children. His grief was all-consuming, and he didn't seem to understand that hers was too. She had no one to share her burden of pain and loss.

Bobby slowly opened his eyes, but they looked blank. "My stomach hurts." His wail trembled through the room.

"George, go get an empty bucket." Mary gathered the warmed cloth from her younger brother's head.

After dipping it in the water again, she reapplied it. He tried to push it off.

"Shhh. I'm here, Bobby." She pulled him onto her lap.

He needed his mother, and right now, Mary was the closest thing he had. He didn't even remember their mother. If only Mary knew more about caring for a sick child. She crooned a nameless tune as she rocked him. He settled against her chest, drawing all the comfort she had to offer. She only wished she had more to give him.

What would her little brothers do if Daniel did take her away? And could she really leave them? No matter how much she wanted to be free of her responsibilities, her family needed her. Without a doubt, she loved them so much. Sometimes she almost lost sight of that fact.

Bobby nestled closer into her arms while George clanged down the hallway with the galvanized bucket. As George barged through the doorway, Bobby sat up and grabbed his stomach. George barely got to the bed before his brother leaned forward and retched into its depths.

"Ooooo, don't get that stuff on me!" George quickly dropped the bucket beside Mary and jumped back.

She grabbed it with one hand while holding Bobby with her other arm. "It's okay, Bobby." She glanced up at George. "Please get a clean face cloth and wet it in the dishpan on the bureau. Then bring it to me, along with a cup of fresh water."

He scampered out of the room demonstrating his eagerness to be away from the mess his brother made.

Oh, God, please help me. She hadn't heard Pa in the house when she got up. He was probably already working outside with no thought about what was going on with the children.

She heard George scurrying down the hall slamming into the walls in his haste and hitting the door facing as he entered. He leaned way over to hand the glass of water to Mary without getting too close. "Here."

She balanced the bucket against her leg and reached toward the glass. The second her fingers touched it, he let go. "Careful, George." She barely kept it from spilling all over the bed.

He stomped over to where the dishpan sat and dipped the face cloth into the water. When he wrung it out, some splashed onto the floor. The boys were often sloppy about things, and these two were pretty young. She didn't have the energy right now to rebuke him.

"Here, Bobby, take a swallow to clean out your mouth and spit it in the bucket."

He gave a half-hearted try, with some of the liquid splattering on her night dress. Then he leaned back against her chest and closed his eyes.

George brought the damp cloth over. "It stinks in here." He thrust it at her and backed away. "I don't want to get whatever he's got."

Before she could answer, he was out the door. "George, come back here. You haven't changed out of your pajamas." The slam of the back screen door punctuated her sentence. She heaved an exasperated sigh.

Bobby stirred in her arms. The wet cloths weren't doing anything to bring his fever down. Panic like a caged bird beat its wings inside her chest. *What am I going to do?*

∾

*K*enneth Murray had just started mucking out the stalls in the barn when his oldest son ran through the door clad only in his pajamas. And he wasn't watching where he stepped. No telling what was smeared on the bottom of his feet besides mud. He opened his mouth to yell at the boy when he noticed the expression on George's face. Something was terribly wrong.

"Pa! Come quick!" The boy slid to a stop in the middle of the barn and shot a pleading stare his way. "Bobby's sick...real bad!"

Kenneth leaned the pitchfork against the railing of the stall and rushed out with the boy running and skipping to keep up. "Where's Mary?"

"She's holding him." George didn't miss a step or fall behind.

"Where's Frances?"

"Still sleepin'."

Kenneth knew he'd been too lenient on his younger daughter while Mary carried the whole load. That needed to change, but he hadn't had the heart to interfere while Mary was doing such a good job with everything. He took the easy way out to keep from confronting any of the kids. But he hadn't planned on raising this brood by himself. Melody was supposed to be here with him.

He stopped in the doorway of the boys' bedroom and stared at Mary holding Bobby. Her arms cradled him as she crooned a wordless song with her eyes closed. For a moment, he could hardly believe his eyes. When had his daughter become a woman? An ache spread from his heart to fill his chest. And what was wrong with his son?

Kenneth walked toward them, a squeaky board announcing his presence.

Mary's eyes flew open and she stared at him. The tracks of tears marred her cheeks.

"What's wrong with him?" He hadn't meant to sound so harsh, but his parched throat made him croak the words.

"I don't know." Mary's soft voice barely reached him. "He has a high fever, and even though I've been wiping him off with cool water, it's not going down."

He was close enough now to feel the heat radiating from Bobby. "Did he throw up?"

"Yes." She nodded without jostling the boy. "After I got him to drink a little water, he fell asleep. I didn't want to put him down."

"Do we have anything to give him for a fever?" His arms ached for his son and his heart ached for the loss of his wife. If only she were still here, she'd know what to do.

"No, sir. I've done everything I can think of." She clutched the boy closer in her arms. "I'm afraid, Pa. What if he dies? Like Mother, Carrie, and Annette did."

Her words hit his heart like a sledgehammer, and he gasped in a deep breath. He didn't have the answer to her question, and he didn't dare consider that outcome. How could he manage another loss? Even in six years, he hadn't gotten over the last one.

"I'll go into town and get the doctor." He wiped his sweaty palms on his trousers.

"Can we afford the doctor?" From her stricken expression and quickly indrawn breath, he knew she wished she hadn't asked that question.

"Just let me worry about that." He headed toward the door. "If he's not at home, he'll probably be at church."

Everything always came back to church. He hadn't been going, because he wasn't real sure if he could trust God. Hadn't been since he lost Melody and the girls. But if the doctor was at church, he'd go there to get him.

"I know." He turned for one last look. "I'll be back as soon as I can."

Anxiety sparked from her eyes, and a grim expression compressed her lips. His words didn't give her comfort. She probably thought he wouldn't do the right thing.

When he started down the hall, he almost stumbled over George. "What are you doing hiding there?"

"I'm sorry, Pa. I just wanted to know how Bobby is." He cowered against the wall.

"Get Frances up. She can help Mary until I return."

He didn't look back as he rushed to saddle his horse. He didn't want to see the disappointment in his child's eyes.

A failure. That's what he was. Even his children didn't respect him. Every weekend that was evident when they went to church and left him home alone. He'd seen the way they looked at him. He knew he'd never given them a reason to respect him. But that was going to change.

He'd find that doctor and get help for Bobby. Maybe then they'd know how important they were to him.

About time I took my place as the head of this family.

CHAPTER 4

$\mathcal{D}$aniel stepped down from the trolley that connected Portland to Oregon City, his face cooled by a fine mist of rain. His trip to San Francisco had taken more than a week. He hadn't anticipated that when he left home. Even though he enjoyed being trusted enough to go on business trips for his father, he had difficulty keeping his mind on the reason for the journey. All that time away from his beloved Mary just to meet with Mr. McKenna, the head of the shipping company their family had decided to use.

Daniel wouldn't have had to stay so long in northern California if the shipping company hadn't just suffered a great loss. One that made him question the wisdom of using this company, no matter how good its reputation. A ship had been lost at sea not long before reaching San Francisco Bay. The young captain was severely injured when he saved the members of his crew, but everything else went down with the ship. What kind of businessman would entrust his large ship to someone too young to be a seasoned sailor? And did the Winthrop family really want to do business with that man? Was Mr. McKenna getting too old to make wise decisions? Did

Daniel's family want to gamble on the possibility of losing a whole shipment of woolen goods?

These were questions he planned to take up with his father and uncle when they met in the morning. If shipping by rail were more stable, they could send most of their products across the country that way, then on to Europe when appropriate.

But first he needed to talk to Mary.

Daniel headed toward his house instead of going to the store. After cleaning up from the travel, he'd seek out Garrett, their driver, and find out what Mary said when he delivered the note Daniel wrote her.

Back home, Daniel climbed the stairs and made quick work of washing up and changing clothes. Then he headed toward the kitchen. Enticing aromas drifted toward him, reminding him it had been a while since he ate. Maybe he could grab a quick bite.

Standing in the doorway, he watched Mrs. Shelton stir a pot on the stove. Finally, she noticed him.

"Mr. Daniel, when did you get home?" She put the spoon down and came toward him, wiping her hands on her apron.

"Not very long ago." He loved the twinkle in her eyes when she flashed a big smile. "Do you have anything I can eat right now? I know it's not meal time."

"Pshaw, for you, anytime." She headed toward the pantry door. "Do you want cookies, or something more substantial?"

"Substantial sounds good to me." His stomach announced his hunger with a loud roar. "I haven't had anything good to eat since I left here."

Mrs. Shelton bustled around the large room, gathering bread, then roast beef from the icebox. Now would be a good time to get the information he wanted.

"Where is everyone?" By *everyone*, he especially meant Garrett Henry.

"Your father is out at your uncle's farm in Washington Territory. And your dear mother is over at the church. The women are putting together some things to take out to the Murray family."

His heart beat double-time. The women would only do that if something was wrong. Surely nothing had happened to Mary. "What's going on out at the Murray's place? Did something bad happen?"

"Oh, that's right. You don't know." She laid down the knife and stared straight at him with not a hint of a smile. "Most of the children are sick. Dr. Childress said the measles. Only the women who have had the disease will be going out there. Your mother had me make a large pot of my chicken and dumplings for the poor dears."

"When you say most of the children, do you know which ones?" Holding his breath, he waited for her reply.

She started assembling a large sandwich for him. "I believe Mary is all right, but she's exhausted from caring for her brothers and sister. The youngest boy got it first. He was so sick on Sunday that Kenneth Murray burst into the church, disturbing the service, to get the doctor."

He whooshed out a breath. At least Mary wasn't sick... yet. But he really didn't like the sound of this. If Mr. Murray came to get the doctor, things must be very bad.

"The doctor has been out there every day since then. I heard that Mary will be fine, because she had the measles when she was young, while her dear departed mother was still alive. But that man works the girl really hard." She slapped on the top slice of bread and mashed the sandwich with a large spatula. "I'm hoping she doesn't get sick just from exhaustion. A body can only take so much, I always say." She set his plate in front of him.

"Thank you, Mrs. Shelton."

He grabbed the sandwich and headed out the door. Hopefully, Mother would let him accompany whoever was going out to the Murray's house. He wasn't going to wait a moment longer to see Mary.

Daniel arrived at the church to find Mother and Mrs. Horton overseeing Garret as he loaded a wagon with baskets of food and wooden crates. At least the rain had stopped.

"How can I help?"

"Daniel!" Mother rushed toward him. "You're finally home. How was your trip?" She raised her arms, then quickly lowered them, clasping her hands together.

He knew she wouldn't want to embarrass him in public, and he recognized her strong desire to hug him, so he threw his arms around her. "I'm glad to be home."

After the quick embrace, she stepped back and studied him. "You look tired. Didn't you rest well on the trip?"

"Not like I would in my own bed." He tried to ease her mind with his smile. "I hear the Murrays haven't been feeling well. Would you like some help? I could drive these things out to their place."

She started to shake her head, but Garrett stopped beside them. "If you don't mind my saying so, ma'am, I'd appreciate the help. I haven't had the measles myself, and I don't want to get sick. I surely don't want to bring illness home to my family."

Daniel turned to his mother. "Is that all right, Mother? After all, I've already had the measles. And I do want to help."

Mother sighed and nodded. "We'll be ready to go in a minute. We're just waiting for a few loaves of bread to cool." She waved and headed into the parsonage with Mrs. Horton.

Good man! Just what Daniel needed to hear. A real reason for him to go. He clapped Garrett on the shoulder and followed him inside to carry the last two crates to the wagon.

Thankful that no one else was in the room, Daniel stopped beside the table. "So, Garrett, what did Mary say when you delivered my note?"

The driver stopped and stared at him, chagrin cloaking his face. "Sorry, sir, I didn't have a chance to take it to her."

Daniel almost shouted, but he stopped and took a breath to calm down. "You didn't? Why not?"

"I'm really sorry." Garrett shook his head. "Your father kept me busy, and your mother went to pick up the produce, like she often does. I wasn't anywhere near the Murray place. And you said to only give the message to Mary, no one else, so I didn't ask your mother to take it."

Great! Just great. Mary probably thought he had forgotten her. Would she trust him to be a man of his word? He had to convince her he was sincere. Now he really had to accompany the women.

~

*M*ary had never been so tired. She placed her hands on her waist and stretched to try to get the kinks out. All three of her siblings were ill, and her heart felt sick. What if one or more of them died? The doctor had said that most people recover from the measles if they were careful. But she was the only person available to care for them. Pa had to work every day to keep the farm going, and he came in each night dirty and discouraged. After she fixed him a meager supper, he fell into bed while she continued to watch over the others.

Ever since the doctor came Sunday and found the horrible rash all over Bobby's body, Mary hardly had time to fix enough for them to eat. Before nightfall, George had come down with the same sickness. Then on Monday, Frances joined them. Mary kept the two boys in their room with the curtains closed to protect their eyes as the doctor suggested. Because the boys didn't feel good, they were crabby. She used wet face cloths to try to keep their fevers from rising too high, and tried to get them to take a little broth from time to time. Between making sure they stayed in bed in that stuffy room, she also did the same for Frances.

Because of the heat in the bedroom she shared with her sister, Mary had slept on the floor in the parlor. Even with several quilts cushioning her pallet, she awoke with her whole body aching. What little sleep she got was interrupted each time she had to check on her patients.

What day is it, anyway? She actually counted on her fingers to finally decide today might be Wednesday. Her brothers whined most of the morning, and she hadn't had a chance to cook anything for lunch. Pa would be in from the fields hungry as a bear, and probably just as grouchy. This illness only made him harder to get along with.

All she had time to fix were scrambled eggs and biscuits. The bacon in the smokehouse had played out several days ago. She sat down and laid her head on the table for just a minute to rest.

The next thing she knew the sounds of horses stomping and harness jingling in front of the house awakened her. She didn't want to see anyone. Not the way she felt, and especially not the way she looked. She ran her hand over the tangled hair she had just brushed back from her face that morning and tied with a limp strip of cloth at the back of her neck. Glancing down at her rumpled dress, she tried to remember the last time she'd changed clothes.

Maybe it was just someone to see Pa, and she could tell him where Pa was. She hoped Pa was close enough to notice, and she wouldn't even have to open the door.

The sound of voices, both male and female, let her know her wish didn't have a chance of happening. She stood. The movement wafted the stale scent of onions on her hands, reminding her of the poultices she'd used on her sister's and brothers' feet, trying to draw the fever out. Sometimes baking soda helped remove bad odors, but using it to try to keep them from itching hadn't removed the offensive odor from her hands.

"Mary, may we come in?" A knock accompanied the words spoken by a voice she couldn't quite place, even though she knew she had heard it before.

She opened the door only a small distance, hiding behind it. Mrs. Winthrop, Mrs. Slidell, and Mrs. Horton, the new pastor's wife, stood on the porch, each holding what looked like picnic baskets. Her stomach rumbled, and she hoped they couldn't hear it. Enticing aromas made their way around the edge of the door.

Over their shoulders, she saw a man with his back to the house picking up a large wooden crate. She wondered who he was. Then he straightened. *What is Daniel doing here?* She didn't even try to keep the frown from puckering her brow. And she wanted to drop through a hole in the floor so he couldn't see her like this.

When she turned her attention back toward the women, they were whispering among themselves. They glanced at her and the compassion in their eyes made her want to cry.

"May we come in, dear?" White curls surrounded Mrs. Slidell's face like an angelic halo. "Mrs. Horton and I want to help you. We've both had the measles. And Mrs. Winthrop needs Daniel to take her back to town after everything is unloaded."

Daniel's mother leaned closer. "We'll just have him put the crates on the front porch."

"Yes." Mrs. Horton gave her a gentle smile. "We can take them into the house ourselves."

Relief poured through Mary like cool spring water, lending a sense of refreshment. She wouldn't have to face Daniel looking like a wrung-out dishrag. She pulled the door wider, careful to stay completely out of his sight.

"But I wanted to take these inside." Daniel's raised voice sounded none too happy.

His mother's answer was softer, and she couldn't understand her words, but they had a soothing sound to them. Mary breathed a sigh of relief.

Mrs. Slidell stopped beside Mary and gently closed the door. "The first item on our agenda today is to get you cleaned up, dear one. I know you must be tired, and we're going to make sure you get some rest."

"Yes, my dear." Mrs. Horton set down the basket she carried and started removing her gloves and hat. "You haven't had time to get to know me. While Helen helps you, I'm going to get this food warmed up for you. Do you have an apron I can use?"

Mary slumped against the door for a moment before pushing away and heading toward the cupboard drawer where she had stored her mother's aprons. No one had worn them since she was gone, but the ones Mary used were so ragged, she didn't want the pastor's wife to see them.

Mrs. Slidell followed her. "Is the water in the reservoir still hot?"

Mary nodded. "The fire has died down, but the stove is still warm."

The two women helped Mary rig up a rope across one side of the parlor before they placed the bathtub behind it. With all three of them carrying water, soon there was enough in the tub to get Mary clean.

"Go ahead and get in, Mary." Mrs. Slidell handed her a large soft towel she pulled from the basket she had carried into the house. "Tell me where I can find something for you to change into."

With the two women bustling around the house taking care of things for her, Mary knew she could ignore her worries for a while. She slid down into the galvanized oblong container and started to wet the face cloth in the warm water. Now if only she could wash away all her problems as well.

CHAPTER 5

*D*aniel stared glumly at the back end of his horses as he and his mother rode back to town. He hadn't even caught a glimpse of Mary. He'd had every intention of carrying all those wooden boxes into the house. Maybe help Mary put everything away. He was desperate for a chance to have a private word with her to explain why she'd not heard from him.

Why had his mother insisted that she must get back home immediately? When they left town earlier, to hear her talk about it, she had every intention of staying to help Mary with her brothers and sister. Instead, after the organist and the pastor's wife went into the house, they quickly shut the door. Mother told him where to put each crate on the porch. Then she practically dragged him back to the buggy and rushed him until they were going down the country road at a fast clip.

"It looks as if Mr. Murray's field is ready to be planted." She waved toward the passing field where even furrows had been plowed. "That's good."

Daniel almost rolled his eyes. He could see she was trying

to distract him. Maybe Mary hadn't wanted him to see her. Of course, his mother had no idea he planned to ask Mr. Murray if he could court Mary. He hadn't wanted to say anything to his parents until he knew everything between them would work out. Better just keep that information close to his vest for now.

His mother chattered like a magpie about everything from how wonderful the people at the church were to offer so much help to the Murrays to how much she hoped his father would quickly return home. Daniel had a hard time keeping up with all the places her words took them, because his mind was fixed on Mary and what he could do about getting to talk to her as soon as possible.

"Don't you agree?" Mother emphasized these words strongly enough that he knew some noncommittal sound wouldn't appease her this time. As if to reinforce that fact, she continued, "You haven't heard a word I said."

Of course, I haven't. "I heard you." He turned the buggy onto High Street. Only a few blocks until they would reach home.

"Did you hear me say I invited Carolyn Newton to have dinner with us?" She stared up at him.

No! He gulped. He stepped right into that one. "I guess I missed that."

She laughed. "That's because I didn't say it. I just wanted to see if you really listened to what I had talked about. And you didn't."

Daniel was glad he had squelched his first reaction to her previous question. He knew Carolyn Newton had set her cap for him. Even though she was a beautiful woman and would make some man a good wife, she wasn't the one he wanted. And he wouldn't waste his time dallying with anyone he wasn't interested in. He would remain focused on his pursuit of Mary, the only woman for him.

"I'm sorry, Mother. I have a lot on my mind... just coming

back from a business trip and all." He hoped she wouldn't probe any further.

That hope was dashed when she smiled sweetly at him. "I also wondered if you'd like for me to invite Carolyn to dinner some evening."

"Not really." He kept his eyes trained on the street so she couldn't read the expression in his eyes as she usually did.

"I was really hoping you'd become interested in some young lady soon."

Her sweetly spoken words didn't fool him. She had hinted before that she was ready for grandchildren. Too bad he was an only child. No one else could produce those desired babies. And he didn't want to have them with anyone but Mary.

"I'm sure I will soon enough." Before his mother could comment on that, he noticed a commotion at the Harrison house in the next block. "What's going on over there?"

His mother glanced in the direction he had nodded. "Since Harold died, Milton and Judy have been unhappy in their home. Too many memories of their only son. The poor dears. So many people are praying for them."

He slowed the horses as they passed the house. "Looks as if they're moving."

"Yes." Mother clasped her hands tight in her lap. "Judy told me the other day. They are returning to St. Louis where they have family. She hopes living near relatives will help them get over losing Harold so young."

Daniel slapped the reins gently against the horses' rumps to get them to move faster. "But they've lived here a long time. I remember when they built that house. As boys, Harold and I played around the workmen."

"And you still miss him a lot, don't you? The two of you were nearly always together." Her voice cracked on the last word. "We all miss him."

His throat thickened with tears, but he swallowed to make them go away before they reached his eyes. "Yes, I miss him. But it's been two years. We have to move on."

She placed a hand on his arm. "That's the problem. Judy and Milton feel they can move on better by getting away from all their memories."

"I hope it works." He stared straight ahead until time to turn into the driveway. "So when should I go back to pick up Mrs. Slidell and Mrs. Horton?"

He stopped the buggy in front of the house and went around to help Mother alight.

She stood and patted her eyes with her handkerchief before answering. "Since the doctor is planning to check on the children late this afternoon, they are going to catch a ride with him." She swept up the steps to the front porch.

Disappointed, Daniel stood rooted in place, staring after her. If he didn't know better, he'd think his mother was trying to keep him and Mary apart today. Might as well rub down the horses, since he wasn't going back out there today. Why was everything conspiring against him?

While he used the curry comb, the idea of the Harrisons leaving Oregon City brought all kinds of memories back. He thought of the good times when he, Gary, and Harold were growing up. Running down the steps from Seventh Street to Fifth Street, then to Third Street to play on the banks of the Willamette River. Catching salmon swimming upstream. Hitting baseballs. Picnicking at the Chautauqua grounds. All that ended with the Gary's troubled marriage and Harold's sudden death. Daniel had never risked such close friendships again.

When the horses were back in their stalls, he dropped to sit on the bench by the tack room. Thoughts of Mary quickly took their rightful place in his mind. Just because the women were going to come back to town with the doctor didn't mean he couldn't call on the Murrays this evening.

With his head in his hands, he then said a prayer for the Harrisons. Maybe he should go over and help them today. Father wouldn't be home until late tonight, if then. He went into the house to change into older clothes and set out walking the few blocks he used to run down, eager to be with Harold.

As he approached the house, the sun broke through the clouds and cast a shaft of bright light on the front of the familiar home, bathing the white siding and green shutters in a golden glow. The light brought with it a wonderful idea. This would be the perfect house to buy for him and Mary to live in after they married. While he helped the parents of his old friend pack, he'd ask them if they had a buyer for the house.

He would have even more things to talk to Mary about when he went back out to the farm. While whistling "Love's Old Sweet Song," he rushed down the street, his mind anticipating how good his life with Mary was going to be.

$\approx$

*A*fter a long morning in the fields, Kenneth Murray headed toward the house for lunch. Drawing closer, he heard female voices, then the front door banged shut. Something was going on at his own house and he had no idea what. Didn't Mary have her hands full taking care of the other children? Why would she be entertaining guests?

His long legs quickly ate up the ground until he reached the back door. Without even stopping to wipe his shoes, he burst into the kitchen, banging the door against the wall. "What's going on here?"

Two women whirled to face him. He recognized Helen Slidell from the church. Melody had always loved hearing her play the piano. He never understood why, because the thing sounded out of tune to him. And he had no idea who the other woman was.

After a moment of staring at him, Helen clasped her hands together and came toward him. He wasn't sure what that look in her eyes meant, and he knew he didn't care to find out. He just wanted their nosiness out of his kitchen.

"Kenneth." She laid her hand on his arm, and her voice was soft and sweet. "Perhaps we could talk outside."

Without waiting for him to agree, she swept past him and stopped in the mud room. The woman had a lot of gall, coming into his home and acting as if she belonged there. He would really let her have it when they got outside. No need for the other woman to hear what he had to say. He pulled the door closed behind them.

Before he could even begin, Helen gave him a sweet smile. "I know things have been hard for you lately."

She had no idea. No one did. But he'd wait to let her have her say, then let her have it with both barrels blazing. He widened his stance and crossed his arms, staring hard at her.

Helen didn't show that she had even noticed. Her glance roved over the farm. "This is a really nice farm, and you've kept it up with all the new modern conveniences. A place to be proud of." Her gaze turned toward him.

He nodded. None of this information was pertinent to what was going on today. He'd let her dig a little deeper hole before he buried her.

"Melody would be proud of what you've done with it." Her affection for his late wife colored her tone.

When she pronounced Melody's name, his heart almost stopped beating. No one had uttered her name to him for six years.

Helen took a deep breath and plunged on. "But there's one thing she wouldn't be proud of...the way you've treated Mary."

He clenched his fists. "How dare you pass judgment on me," he growled.

She looked as if he'd slapped her face. He hadn't meant to hurt her. Just give her a taste of her own medicine.

"Oh, Kenneth, that's not what I'm trying to do. I just wanted you to realize what you have here." Her gesture encompassed the house as well as the farm. "Melody told me how God gave Mary to you as a blessing, but you've treated her as anything but a blessing. You made her take over the running of the household at a very young age. And she's done an amazing job."

"I know that." He spit out the words.

"Have you ever told her?" She stopped and sighed. "What I'm trying to get at is that with this illness, she's been taking care of the younger children all by herself. If Melody were alive and the children were sick, you would help her. That girl in there"—she waved toward the closed kitchen door—"is completely exhausted. You should have seen her when we arrived. She was a mess."

He winced. Her words found a soft spot in his stony heart.

"The people at church want to help. That's what we do. Take care of each other. And we didn't come a minute too soon for Mary. We've brought food, and Mrs. Horton and I will help take care of the other children while she gets some rest." Helen clasped her hands tight in front of her waist.

Kenneth unfolded his arms and shoved his hands into his pockets.

"I know we should have asked your permission. We assumed that since you came to the church to get the doctor, you wouldn't mind our help. Will you give your permission for us to stay?"

Her softly pleading tone slipped through the tiny crack in his armor. No wonder Melody had always liked Helen so much.

He gave a slow nod. After she went back into the kitchen, he stood and stared across his fields, mulling over all the woman had said. Her words still stung, and from that he recognized their truth. But how could he lighten Mary's load? He relied on her, needed her help with the children so he could keep the farm running. Couldn't those women see that?

He groaned as he ran a hand over his head. It was too much to handle. Just too much.

CHAPTER 6

*M*ary eased out of a deep sleep and enjoyed the quiet that surrounded her. Pulling the covers up under her chin, she relished the fresh smell of sunlight that still clung to the sheets.

What's going on? Her eyes flew open and she glanced around her father's bedroom. That brought her fully awake as she remembered what had happened earlier today. The women coming to help, insisting she bathe and rest. Her father bursting through the door. Mrs. Slidell talking to her father.

Whatever the organist said calmed him. Over a lunch of chicken and dumplings, he agreed to allow the women to stay and help Mary while she got much-needed rest. After Pa went back out to work in the fields, Mrs. Slidell cleaned up this bedroom, even putting clean sheets on the bed and braiding Mary's hair before she insisted Mary take a nap.

How long have I slept? Mary arose and pulled back the curtains. Seeing the sun sinking toward the horizon in the west, Mary knew she had slept the afternoon away. And she hadn't heard a peep from her brothers or sister.

She donned the clean clothing laid across the chair and

quickly wound the braid into a bun at the back of her neck, slipping in hairpins to keep it secure. She hadn't felt like really fixing herself up since the children fell ill. But it felt good, knowing she was rested, clean, and tidy. And an enticing smell came from the kitchen, reminding her that she was hungry.

After opening the door and starting down the hallway, she heard a knock on the front door. Mrs. Slidell answered it before Mary got close enough for them to notice her.

"Come in, Dr. Childress." The woman opened the door wider.

The doctor entered, scanning the room. "Helen, what are you doing here?" His brow furrowed. "Is Mary sick now? I thought she already had the measles."

Mary came forward. "I'm just fine. Better than I've been in days. Mrs. Horton and Mrs. Slidell came out to help me." The thought of that brought a smile to Mary's face. "I don't know what I would have done without them. They brought food from the others at church, and they stayed and did a lot of cleaning and caring for my brothers and sister."

"That's what friends are for, Mary." Mrs. Slidell slipped her arm around Mary's waist and gave her a squeeze. "You've always been a help to others." She turned toward the doctor. "Could I interest you in a piece of cherry pie?"

"That's what I smelled." Mary couldn't believe it. "Cherry is my favorite."

"Mine, too," Dr. Childress agreed.

They went into the kitchen where Mrs. Horton was cutting the dessert and placing it on saucers. "Would you like coffee with yours, Doctor? Or maybe some of this milk I just brought in from the spring house?" She set two pieces of pie on the table and went back for the other two. "And what about you, Mary and Helen?"

After everyone had what they wanted, they sat down to enjoy the treat. Mary wasn't used to having a dessert between meals. She decided to enjoy this while she could. As soon as the women left, she'd be in charge of everything again. The special break today gave her just the boost she needed to be able to face tomorrow.

After taking a bite of the confection Dr. Childress turned toward Mary. "So, Mary, how are our patients today?"

She didn't have an answer. When she hadn't heard anyone whining or making a sound, she hadn't looked in on her siblings. For a moment, she felt ashamed that she hadn't. "I'm not sure."

"Oh, they're doing really well, I believe." Mrs. Slidell patted Mary's hand. "I've been caring for them while Mary got some rest."

The doctor nodded. "I'd say she welcomed the help. Right, Mary?"

"Of course." She turned toward their old friend. "Why are they so quiet?"

"I cleaned them up, made their beds, then washed all the sheets. Mrs. Horton hung them out on the line while I made sure they all had some of the chicken and dumplings. After that, they settled down for a nap too."

Another frown creased the doctor's face. "What about their fever? And did you keep the room dark?"

His questions didn't seem to bother Mrs. Slidell. "Yes. I've cared for people with measles before. And I don't think they have a fever anymore."

Mary took another bite and leaned back, enjoying the fact that the children had been cared for better than she would have done in her state of exhaustion.

"I'll check on them as soon as I finish this delicious pie." The doctor took a drink of his coffee. "I know you helped a lot today, but Mary has been doing a very good job caring for them." He smiled at her.

The praise went straight to her heart. She hadn't gotten very much encouragement since Ma died. And the words felt golden to her, like a special treasure.

Before they finished their pie, Pa came into the kitchen. Instead of banging the door and sounding grumpy, he entered quietly. And he didn't smell as bad as he had earlier. His chambray shirt was even clean. "Pie? Is there enough for me?"

Mrs. Horton stood. "Of course there is. Actually, I baked two, so you'll have some for tomorrow as well." She bustled around and fixed him a piece. "What do you want to drink with it, Kenneth?"

Mary stared at the two of them. Her father, who hadn't gone to church in years, was on a first-name basis with the wife of the new pastor. A glimmer of hope lit in her heart that now he might start going to church with them when George, Bobby, and Frances were well again.

They all finished their pie, and the two women from town started cleaning up after insisting Mary accompany her father and the doctor to see about the patients. When the doctor completed examining the children, he said they could start getting up for a while each day, but he didn't want them to try to read yet. There was always the fear that the measles could damage their eyesight, and he didn't want that to happen.

Minutes later, Mrs. Slidell and Mrs. Horton followed the doctor to his buggy for a ride back to town. Mary and her father stood on the porch and waved goodbye until the horse-drawn carriage turned onto the country road.

"Come sit with me, Mary." Pa lowered himself into the porch swing.

Mary couldn't believe it. He hadn't used the swing since Ma died.

"I need to talk to you."

He sounded so serious... and different somehow. In a way, Mary was almost scared of what he had to say.

After she gingerly sat on the cushion beside him, he started moving the swing using one foot. He stared off into space long enough for her to become uncomfortable. He looked down at the boards of the porch floor, then glanced at her for only a moment before once more fixing his eyes on something in the distance. Finally he said, "This is hard for me."

What is hard for you? She wanted to shout the words at him, but prudence held her tongue in place.

"I'm not a man who admits weakness." Silence once more descended. He stopped the movement of the swing and clasped his hands so tight between his knees his knuckles whitened. "But today I realized I've not treated you right for years."

Stunned, she could only stare at his bowed head.

"And when all three of the other children got sick, it scared the wits out of me." His words sounded as if he were forcing each one between his lips. She opened her mouth to say something, but he interrupted. "Don't say anything until I finish. If I don't tell you this now, I might not ever be able to get it out."

Closing her mouth tight, she sat with her eyes shut, waiting.

"When Helen talked to me today, she helped me realize I had been taking advantage of you for years. I didn't mean to do that, but it was easier than facing life head-on."

Did he just apologize to me? She opened her eyes and stared at him, not recognizing the contrite man who sat beside her. He no longer had the hardness that kept her at a distance the last few years. Then snippets of memories from before Ma died filtered through her mind. Pa happy, enjoying the whole family. Pa laughing, hugging Ma. That's the man she wanted back but had given up all hope of him ever returning.

He finally looked straight at her. "It might not be easy, but I don't want to be the man I've become. I want to be a good father to you and the others.... And I don't want to rob you of the life you deserve."

This is all too much to take in. Did he really mean it? If so, what could it possibly mean to her? Long ago, she'd given up having hopes and dreams of her own. She just took care of the family the best she could, often making a real muddle of things. Only when Daniel came into her life did she allow herself to hope that life could be different.

"Mary, will you forgive me and allow me to make it up to you somehow?"

He means it. He really means every word. She only hoped he would be able to carry through with the things he promised.

His eyes pleaded with her. How could she refuse? Pa was the man who had raised her, the man who had earned the name of father. Hadn't her real parents given her away?

"Yes." She tried to sound confident, but the word escaped on a whisper. "Yes, I forgive you." This time the words were stronger, decisive.

Pa pulled her into his arms, against his broad chest. And she went willingly, resting her face on the softness of his well-worn chambray shirt.

After dropping a kiss against the top of her head, he rested his chin on her hair. "I'm going to sleep in the tack room until Frances is completely well. You can have my bed."

She pulled away and stared into his eyes with a question she hoped he read.

"I'll try to help, instead of making your work harder. I'll clean up out in the barn before I come inside, as I did today."

The smile on his face wasn't forced. Mary knew she could get to like this change in her father.

Pa got up. "I'm going to check on the others. You can stay out here as long as you want."

After he closed the door behind him, the sound of a lone horse coming down the road toward their property captured her attention. She watched the man as he slowed at the gate that led onto their farm. Before she could be sure who he was, her heartbeat quickened. Surely it wasn't Daniel returning, was it? Why would he be coming out here so late in the evening?

Mary remembered her disappointment from the last week and a half, but just watching him approach released a whole flock of hummingbirds in her mid-section. She hoped he had a good explanation about why he took so long to come see her. If he did, perhaps she could forgive him as well.

CHAPTER 7

*D*aniel arrived at the Murray farm so lost in thought he didn't notice Mary sitting on the porch swing until he had dismounted, tied the reins to the hitching post, and started toward the front steps. The lingering twilight softened her features, enhancing her breathtaking beauty. He stopped and let his eyes travel from the top of her coppery curls to the bottom of her dainty slippers. *What a beautiful woman!* He'd like to have a portrait painted of her just as she was this evening.

"Good evening, Mary." He swept off his hat and nervously tapped it against his thigh. "May I join you?"

She stopped the swing and scooted gracefully toward one end, leaving plenty of room for him beside her. Even though a tiny smile played across her lips, he'd hoped for an enthusiastic greeting after their last time together. Surely, she didn't think he had forgotten her, even if it had been a week and a half since they discussed the idea.

He dropped onto the bench seat and pushed his heel to start the swaying again. "I'm so glad to see you. I missed you while I was away." Was his tone too eager?

"Were you away?" Her question sounded almost disinterested, but the slight pucker in her brow betrayed her concern.

He placed his arm across the back of the swing being careful not to touch her. He still didn't have the right. "I'm sorry you didn't get the message I left for you."

She quickly looked into his eyes as if trying to discern the truth of his statement. "Message?"

"Yes, I asked our driver to bring the note to you. Since I told him not to give the message to anyone but you, he kept it when Mother sent another servant out here for the fresh produce."

Her eyes widened.

He reached into his pocket for the crumpled paper. "Here."

When he thrust the message toward her, she stared at it before finally reaching for the note.

She carefully unfolded the paper and peered at the writing. "It's too dark out here to read."

"So let's go inside." He stood and held out his hand. "That is if it's all right for me to talk to your father this evening."

At those words, her eyes lit up, and she clasped his hand and arose. He didn't want to let go of her soft fingers, but after a long moment, she slipped from his grip and headed toward the screen door.

Mary opened it and headed toward the kitchen where light spilled out into the hall. "Pa, we have company."

Hoping for a good reception, Daniel stayed one step behind her. He hadn't seen Kenneth Murray for months, except working in the fields, and Mary's father always appeared taciturn, even with a lot of people around. Daniel's hands began to perspire, and he wiped them on his pants and took a deep breath before following Mary into the kitchen, where Mr. Murray sat eating pie.

A brief frown furrowed Mr. Murray's brow before the wrinkles softened. "I see young Daniel Winthrop has grown up." The laugh that followed sounded rusty, as if the man hadn't used it in a long time. "Take a seat." He pointed to the chair across the table from him. "Want some cherry pie? I was just enjoying a piece."

Mary glided toward the cupboard. "I'll get it for him, Pa."

Mr. Murray leaned back against his chair. "So what brings you all the way out here from town this time of night?"

Daniel felt like he did when he'd been called on the carpet by the principal at school. He settled on the chair Mr. Murray had indicated for him, resting his hands in his lap to keep from fidgeting. "Is it too late to come calling?"

Another of those awkward laughs erupted from the man sitting across from him. "Not at all. I guess I just didn't expect you." He cut his eyes toward Mary. "Did you know he was coming?"

She turned, holding a dish of dessert. "No...I was surprised too." As she set the treat in front Daniel, she appeared as uncomfortable as he felt.

Why hadn't he thought this through more carefully? Perhaps he should have come earlier in the day, but wouldn't Mr. Murray have been working in the fields? Sometimes, it was hard to know just exactly what the best course of action should be.

Mary came back to the table with another plate holding a very small slice of the dessert. She sat between the two men and nibbled on a tiny bite.

"Mighty fine pie that new pastor's wife baked. You oughta try some." Mary's father took another forkful.

Daniel hoped it would sweeten the man's disposition, but apprehension flooded his mind. He picked up his own fork and complied. "Hmm. This is good."

He noticed Mary peeking at him from underneath her lashes before she picked up another tiny portion.

Daniel cleared his throat. "Actually, I came out here to talk to you, Mr. Murray."

The man's fork clattered to his plate, and he leaned back. "That so?"

He stared a hole through Daniel, or at least that's how it felt.

"Yes, sir." How should he approach Mary's father to get him to agree with the courting?

"So what's on your mind, young man?"

Plunging in, he blurted, "I'd like to court your daughter."

Mr. Murray turned his gaze toward Mary then back at Daniel. "I hope you're talking about Mary, not Frances. She's too young for you." This time the guffaw sounded almost normal. "Relax, Daniel, I'm not going to take your head off."

It had been years since he'd heard Mr. Murray make any jokes, although he used to all the time. Not since he lost his wife and two oldest daughters. Had something happened to the man? This had to be a good sign, didn't it?

"Yes, sir, I mean Mary." *Is it getting hot in here?* He gripped his hands together to keep from running a finger around the top of the celluloid collar he wore. *Why did I dress up so much?*

"I doubt you got all gussied up just to talk to me. Does Mary know you want to court her?"

When both men glanced at her, her eyes were downcast, and a becoming blush tinted her skin all the way from her collar to the curls surrounding her face. Daniel wanted to relieve her of her concern. He wished he could just pull Mary into his arms and comfort her as well.

Once again his throat filled with what felt like a boulder. He tried to clear it, but the lump only shifted, instead of going away completely. "I...I did mention it to her the day we picnicked at the church." He huffed out a breath. "I didn't want to talk to you until I knew if she was as interested in me as I am in her."

Silence reigned.

After an agonizingly long moment, Mr. Murray stared straight at him. "Is she?"

"I believe so, sir." Daniel felt as if his heart was going to beat right out of his chest. He turned toward her. "Aren't you, Mary?"

Finally, she raised her head. "Yes, Pa. I'd like for Daniel to...court me."

Mr. Murray dove back into his pie, taking several bites and chewing each one thoroughly while Daniel couldn't even think about putting one more bit into his mouth. Evidently, neither could Mary. If she stabbed her pie many more times without taking an actual bite, the rest of the slice would be just a pile of mush.

Mary's father finally placed his fork on the plate he'd scraped clean. "If you would've asked me before today, I would have cut you off without an answer. Probably stormed out of the house and stayed gone until you got the message and left.... But some things changed for me today."

Mr. Murray perched on the two back legs of his chair and stayed there. "I want Mary to have the life her mother and I always planned for her." He wove his fingers together and rested his hands against his stomach. "You're a good man, but both of you are really young. She's not even eighteen years old yet. I'll give my permission with one stipulation."

Stipulation? He hadn't expected that. What could the man possibly want now? Money? Some monumental task performed? Whatever it was, Daniel would perform it without fail.

"If you're willing to court her for one full year before you wed, I'll give my blessing to your marriage." The front two legs thudded to the floor, and he leaned toward Daniel. "Are you willing to do that for her?"

Daniel's gaze didn't waver from the man's stern expression. What could he do but agree? Because he wanted to court Mary more than anything else in the world. He had great plans for their life together. "I'll do whatever you require."

"Huh. You trying to be another Jacob?" This time the older

man's words contained a hint of glee. For a man who hadn't been to church in years, he evidently still knew his Bible stories.

"No, sir. I'm just a man who loves your daughter enough to wait for her, if that's what you require." He placed the force of his convictions into every word he spoke, knowing nothing could prevent him from following through on his promise.

~

*M*ary tried to swallow her sigh of relief. When Pa had said he had a stipulation, she had almost choked. She couldn't imagine what he would ask of Daniel. And she was extremely thankful it was only to wait a year. The worry she'd felt since they'd last seen each other was pushed to the back of her mind. She was special to Daniel, and nothing could come between them.

"If you'd like to sit in the parlor and visit, I will clean up our dishes."

Mary was so intent on her own thoughts, she almost missed what Pa said. Before Ma died, her parents had spent time in the kitchen talking and laughing while Ma cleaned up the dishes. More than once, Mary had seen Pa help her. But since her mother's death, he had not lifted a finger to help Mary with anything in the house.

Daniel stood and thanked him, and Mary helped carry the plates to the dry sink. Then she and Daniel went into the formal front room where she lit the lamps on the tables at each end of the settee. She didn't know whether she should choose to sit on one end of it or in one of the chairs. Finally, she settled for the longer piece of furniture.

Without hesitation, Daniel took the other end and turned sideways, so he was looking straight at her. "You are so beautiful tonight."

No one except Ma had ever said those words to her, and they sounded much more wonderful falling from Daniel's lips.

He laid his arm across the back of the couch with his fingertips close enough to her shoulder that she could feel the heat radiating from them. She hoped Daniel couldn't see how much his nearness affected her.

"Thank you." She peeked at him from the corners of her eyes. "You're very handsome too."

His fingers barely grazed her shoulder, and she forgot to breathe. Was this what falling in love felt like? This breathless anticipation? She thought she already loved him, but the ever-so-slight touch ignited a longing deep inside her.

Daniel leaned forward and propped his forearms on his knees. "I had hoped your father would have given us a shorter time to court."

"Me, too, but it's not unusually long, is it?"

"Probably not, but I have so many plans for us." He got up and paced across the room. "Do you remember Harold Harrison? He was the same age I was, two years ahead of you in school."

"The two of you were great friends, weren't you? And Gary Bowen as well?" She started to relax.

"Yes. I miss them both a lot." He stopped for a moment and just stood there as if he hadn't heard her second question.

"Don't you see Gary anymore? I know I haven't seen him in church for a long time."

Daniel shook his head and frowned. "No, he's a different person than he used to be."

"What do you mean?"

"Things aren't going well in his marriage, and he has isolated himself from friends who go to church. Almost as if he blames them for what's happening to him." He cleared his throat. "He's been making really bad decisions lately."

"I'm sorry. I didn't want to cause you grief." She went to him and put her hand on his arm. "Let's talk about something less painful."

"No." He gazed down at her with an expression in his hazel eyes so intense she could see the golden flecks in their depths. "I brought Harold's name into the conversations because his parents are moving back to Missouri, and their house is for sale. I want to buy it for us to live in."

Mary hadn't thought about where they'd live. The wedding would be so far away. But that's what happened during a courtship, wasn't it? The groom prepared a place to take his bride, like the Bible talked about. Just the thought made her feel very special.

"I went down to help them pack today. They told me I could make whatever arrangements I wanted with the banker, who is handling the sale of their house. They like me and want the best for whoever I marry." He took her hands in his and held them against his chest.

The heat warmed her through and through.

"I didn't want to tell them about you until your father agreed. Would you like us to live there?" He squeezed her fingers a bit tighter.

Mary had driven by that house many times when they went to town. It looked like a mansion to her. She'd never imagined living in anything so elegant... or large. She wasn't even sure she would know how to take care of such a house.

"I only want the best for our life together, Mary." He leaned his head close to hers, and she felt his breath ruffle her curls.

She was almost panicky. She'd never been so close to any man, except her father, and he had never made her insides turn to mush.

Daniel dropped her hands and started pacing again. The panic subsided enough so she could breathe.

"We'll have to take everything very slowly. But I have plans for lots of things we can do while we court." He stopped in front of her and cupped her face in his large hands. "You are so special to me, Mary." After dropping a kiss on her forehead, he stepped back. "I'd better head home while the moon is full enough to light my way."

She followed him out the door and watched him until he had mounted up. He turned to wave to her and rode to the end of the lane before he gave her one last wave. When he was out of sight, she stood with her arms crossed on her stomach and stared at the moon.

Mother, I wish you were here. I have so many questions.

Mary kept telling herself that everything would be okay, but in the back of her mind, a niggling doubt made itself known. Could she trust what was happening right now? Had her life really changed so much that she could be married and living in a mansion with the man she loved...in only a year?

CHAPTER 8

*D*aniel strode into the store early on the next morning. Getting right to work on straightening the stock on the shelves and making sure everything was in order before he unlocked the front door, he had a hard time pulling his thoughts away from Mary. He planned to ask Father if he could leave a little early this afternoon. If things were in order, perhaps he would be more apt to agree.

Finally, everything looked spiffy just before Father came through the back door. "The store looks nice, Daniel." Father headed toward the counter at the back where he kept the cash box.

He sounded chipper, giving Daniel hope. After turning the skeleton key in the lock, Daniel pulled the front door open, allowing early morning sunlight to flood the front half of the display room. He breathed in the fresh air, enjoying it before the buggy and wagon traffic could pollute the smell. Daniel had never liked the odor of horse droppings, even though he enjoyed the earthy aroma of Sultan after a good run.

More customers than usual entered the store in the first few hours. Both he and his father were kept busy tending to them.

"So Mrs. Fulton, would you like the blanket in the nut brown or forest green?" He pulled both colors from under the counter.

She ran her fingers lightly over the nap of the softly brushed, tightly woven woolen cover. "This is very thick. I like that. It's hard to keep our sleeping rooms heated all night."

"Yes, ma'am, they'll keep you quite toasty." Daniel had to force his voice to maintain a pleasing tone.

His father looked up from working on the books, and a slight frown warned Daniel that he wasn't pleased with what he heard. The woman had been browsing through the stacks of blankets for over an hour. He would never get a chance to talk to his father. The longer he had to wait, the more his patience frayed.

"I had always heard that Winthrop wool was top quality." A hint of a smile actually touched the woman's compressed lips. "I just hope they aren't too expensive, young man."

He spread his face into as cordial of a smile as he could. "We like to give good value for your money." A glance out of the corner of his eye showed him that his father was pleased with that answer. Good.

"So how much is one of these blankets?" Rubbing the thickness between her fingers, she leaned closer to the cover as if she were inspecting the quality of the weave.

Daniel could see his father peer over the spectacles he always wore when he worked on the books. Not a sign of a smile there now.

When Daniel quoted the price, he was surprised that she nodded.

"That sounds good." She removed her hand and reached for the reticule dangling by the strings from her left arm. "I will take eight of them. Two each of four different colors. All ours are almost threadbare. These should last us a good long time."

Now his father gave a tight smile and turned his attention back to the papers in front of him.

Daniel brought out two each in navy blue and rusty red, as well as the brown and the green, putting them in two stacks. He started pulling brown wrapping paper from the roll behind the counter, tearing it with the jagged blade. "Would you like these wrapped separately?"

"No, wrap the two of each color together." She glanced toward his father. "Should I go back and pay your father?"

He pulled the paper around the first two and cut it, starting to fold in the ends. "Go right ahead. I'm sure he'll be glad to visit with you a minute." Before she reached the back of the store, he called after her. "Would you like for me to mark the color on the outside of the paper?"

She glanced back at him. "That's a very good idea."

He noticed his father's eyebrows lift for a moment before he looked up at her. "Mrs. Fulton, how nice to see you. How are those boys of yours?" He always knew just the right thing to say to keep the customers talking.

Daniel tuned out the conversation, concentrating instead on how he would ask his father for the extra time off. He hadn't planned on telling his parents quite yet that he was courting Mary. He wanted to savor the specialness of the situation while it was still just between the two of them...and her father.

He glanced down at the jumble of products scattered along the counter. While he folded each item the best way to display the quality, he remembered Mary's curls as they were ruffled by the wind. Her hair always worked its way out of every style she wore, forming a flaming halo around her sweet face.

"With that smile on your face, you must be happy."

He hadn't even noticed that his father's conversation with Mrs. Fulton had ended. How long had the matron been gone? He glanced down the counter, looking for the four bundles he'd wrapped and tied with twine. They were nowhere in sight.

"Nice work with Mrs. Fulton." Father leaned his elbow on the other side of the counter. "She was pleased with your service."

His father's compliment gave him more hope. He cleared his throat. "There's something I've wanted to ask you."

Father straightened up. "What's that?" He folded his arms across his chest, tilted his head, and stared intently at Daniel.

"I'd like to leave work early today."

One of his father's eyebrows quirked. "And why is that exactly?"

"I'd like to..." Daniel tried to think of another reason, but couldn't. Might as well tell the truth. "...take a ride out to the Murray farm."

"Because?" Not a hint of a smile on his father's stern face.

No way was Daniel going to get off without explaining everything to him. "I asked Mr. Murray if I could court Mary."

Father's eyes widened. "I see." He shoved his hands into the front pockets of his slacks. "And what did Kenneth say?"

"He gave his permission, but we have to wait a year before we can marry." Daniel shuffled his feet and huffed out a deep breath.

"Wise man." With a pointed stare, Father frowned. "And just when were you planning to talk to your mother and me about it?"

"Sometime soon." Daniel glanced out the front window of the shop, wishing he were out there instead of here under his father's microscope. "It's all pretty new, even to me."

"Have you prayed about it, Son?" His father's stance relaxed. "The choice of a wife is an important matter, not to be taken lightly."

"Yes, sir. I've prayed, and I don't think God objects." What else could he say?

Father scuffed his shoe against the grain of the wooden floor. "I'll let you go early today, but a year's a long time. You mustn't let your courting interfere with your work. Or you won't be able to support a wife when the time comes."

What did he mean by that statement? Daniel wanted to know, but not enough to voice his question.

He would be seeing Mary this evening. He could hardly wait.

&

"*H*e's coming!" Mary heard both of her brothers screaming at the top of their lungs. Daniel had been out to the farm to see Mary every evening for over a week. Now George and Bobby, fully recovered from the measles, had talked him into spending all day Saturday at the farm. Pa was going to be gone to Portland to replace some of the farming equipment, and Daniel had offered to help the boys with the chores. She wondered if he had any idea what that entailed. He'd soon find out. At least the rain from earlier in the week had let up and the morning sun shone bright.

The screen door slammed so hard, it should have fallen off its hinges. She blew out a breath as both boys raced down the hallway, bumping into the walls in their haste. Turning toward them she placed her hands on her waist just as they tried to beat each other through the doorway.

They stopped short when they spied her.

"Do you two want Daniel to think you're ruffians?" She used her most authoritative voice.

They shook their heads in unison.

"What's a ruffin, Mary." Bobby wrinkled his nose. "Is it bad?...I'm not bad."

"No, silly. It just means you're not acting like gentlemen." She smiled as she shook her head.

"But we're not men. We're little boys. Mr. Daniel is the gentleman." Bobby sounded so earnest she had to laugh.

George pulled on her sleeve. "Can we go out to the end of the lane?"

"If he hasn't turned down the lane, how do you know he's coming?" She turned back to take the biscuits out of the oven. Pa had left so early, she didn't get up to fix him breakfast. She decided everyone could sleep a little later.

"George climbed—" Bobby's words were cut off and a muffled sound followed.

She glanced toward them in time to see George shake his head at his little brother. He had his hand clamped tight over Bobby's mouth.

"What is the meaning of this?" She quickly set the pan of biscuits on a trivet.

George pulled his hand away and put both of them behind his back. Bobby glanced over his shoulder at his brother and imitated his stance.

"If anyone wants breakfast, I'd better hear what happened really fast."

These boys were becoming a handful for Mary. She wondered how long it would be before they would completely rebel against her authority.

"George, I expect you to tell me, not make your brother have to." She tried her most stern look on him.

He hung his head. "I climbed up on the roof of the porch. You can see a long ways from there."

Before Mary could begin to scold him for disobeying her instructions not to climb on the roof again, Frances strolled in smothering a yawn. "Do I smell breakfast? I'm starved."

Mary had to bite back the words *so why weren't you in here helping me?* "You can scramble the eggs while I deal with George. I left the right amount of bacon grease in the skillet."

She pulled George out of the room and into the parlor. Before she could start scolding him, a knock sounded on the front door. She glanced up straight into Daniel's hazel eyes. His wind-blown blond waves took her breath away, and she forgot what she was going to say to George.

"Mr. Daniel, I'm so glad you're here." George pushed open the screen and threw his arms around Daniel's waist.

For a moment, Mary wished she could do that very same thing. Then she felt a blush creep into her cheeks. Maybe he would think it was from working over the stove. "You got here just in time for breakfast. Have you eaten?"

He hesitated for a moment, then shook his head. "I'd be glad to eat some more of your wonderful cooking."

Everyone enjoyed a noisy breakfast. Then Bobby took one of Daniel's hands.

"We's gotta get the eggs." Bobby pulled Daniel toward the door to the mud room.

George followed them. "I'll get the baskets."

"And just where do we get these eggs?" Daniel's laughing voice floated back toward her.

She glanced at Frances. "If we hurry, we can have the kitchen cleaned up before they get back."

"Why do I have to help? I'm tired." Frances shifted in her chair, but didn't get up. She had long ago stopped being compliant to Mary's directions.

Mary crossed her arms and gave her sister a hard stare. "I let you sleep later than usual, and you're still tired? Why?"

"Your snoring kept me awake for a long time." The droop of Frances's mouth was very unattractive.

Did I ever act like that? Mary didn't remember doing so. She was in total control of keeping the house before she reached thirteen. Her sister had things way too easy.

Mary untied the well-worn apron from around her waist and thrust it at her sister. "I cooked breakfast. You can clean up. I'm going to make the beds and straighten the bedrooms."

Frances huffed out a deep breath that followed Mary out of

the kitchen, but Mary didn't care if her sister was upset with her. She had plenty of time to get over it.

Mary stayed busy while Frances dawdled with the dishes. After airing Pa's room, she put clean sheets on the bed to welcome him home tonight. She would wash them on Monday with the rest of the laundry.

She took her time cleaning out the boys' room and straightening the parlor. Today, Frances *would* tidy up the room they shared, even though she would complain.

Their boisterous voices preceded George and Bobby into the house.

"Mary, look how many eggs we found." Bobby's shout could be heard by the neighbor about a mile away.

She went back to the kitchen. "Frances, now that the kitchen is straightened, take care of our bedroom." She didn't even pause to allow her sister to complain. "So how many are there?" She approached Bobby, who was holding the egg basket with both arms around it.

"I don't know." A smile split his face and brought a twinkle to his eyes. No telling what the soil was smudging his cheeks. "A whole bunch. More than I could count."

"I have some more eggs." George had the tail of his shirt pulled up the way Ma had often done with her apron. Eggs were cradled against him.

"Let me get a bowl for them before you drop them." She reached for a striped crockery bowl large enough to hold the surplus. *Where is Daniel?*

Mary glanced out the door, but couldn't spy him. "What have you done with Mr. Winthrop?"

Bobby hefted the basket onto the table and gently set it down. "Mr. Winthrop isn't here, but Mr. Daniel is outside."

"Mary, he helped us gather some eggs we never would have found." George stood beside the table and allowed her to transfer the ones he held into the bowl. "He's really smart."

Bobby laughed. "If he's so smart, how come he stepped in the fresh cow patty? His shoe sure does stink."

Daniel came through the doorway, wearing his socks but with no shoes on his feet. "He's right. That wasn't very smart."

Mary stared at him. She'd never been around any other man besides her father with no shoes on. Heat crept up her cheeks, and she pulled her gaze away from his thin socks.

"We've all made that mistake at some time or other." She wanted to keep him from feeling bad about what he did.

Since George's shirt was now empty, he pulled it back down. "Mary, you should have seen Mr. Daniel when the rooster took out after him. You know how he gets sometimes."

Mary glanced at Daniel. "You didn't run from him, did you?"

He shrugged. "I didn't know what else to do."

"That old bird was just trying to show that he is king of the barnyard, but he's not. We usually just shoo him away. He'll settle down." She tried to keep from laughing, but was having a hard time of it.

Now Daniel's neck turned red. Surely, he wouldn't blush. At least his eyes had a twinkle in them. She gestured toward him. "Come on, Daniel. You can help me clean up the eggs."

"I'd like to help you." The intensity of his gaze brought on more heat than a summer wind. "How do we wash them?"

A smile teased her lips. "We don't actually wash the eggs. We just wipe them clean with a wet rag."

After retrieving a couple, she plunged them into a dishpan of water, then wrung them out. When she handed one to Daniel, he tenderly clasped her fingers as well. Heat traveled up her arm, and she raised her eyes toward his face. The intensity of his gaze held her prisoner for a long moment before he released his hold on her hand, but he never looked away.

The heat of a blush climbed her cheeks, and she ducked her head. "Here's the way I do it."

While she demonstrated, she felt his attention remain on her, not on the eggs in the basket.

"I put the clean ones in this bowl."

Finally, he followed her example. Before long, all the eggs were clean, and she ventured another glance toward his handsome face. "We store them in the spring house to keep them fresh longer."

"Let me take them for you." As he reached around her, his shoulder brushed against hers, leaving a tingling trail.

He strode out the door like a man on a mission. Mary watched his long legs and the muscles stretching across his back. Everything about the man pleased her.

Everyday life being married to him would feel like this day. Sharing responsibilities, enjoying each other's company, having a family. Life with Daniel would be heavenly. A year seemed like an eternity to wait.

CHAPTER 9

*M*ary sat on the front porch, basking in the warm May sunshine. Instead of waiting on the swing that was surrounded on two sides by the large lilac bushes, she chose the rocking chair where she could see the end of the lane. Her ears strained for a hint of the sound of approaching hoofbeats.

She had been ready a few minutes before Daniel's anticipated arrival time, and now she impatiently tapped her toe on the porch floor. He was almost half an hour late. In the three weeks since he'd started calling on her, he had not been late a single time. But this waiting called forth memories of the week and a half that he disappeared without a word. Memories she didn't want to relive.

Yes, she'd read the crumpled note he had left with his servant. He had tried to send her a message. But since it didn't arrive, she'd felt abandoned, much as she did today. And she didn't like the feeling one bit. She fought against the anger that welled up inside her.

He loved her. He'd told her often enough for her to believe him. However, his non-arrival plowed up thoughts she'd believed dead and gone. Their courtship had a fairy-tale feel to it, and everyone knew fairy tales didn't come true in these modern times. Was hers about to fall apart? She could almost hear the cackle of wickedness echo at her question.

She stood and crossed her arms, then huffed out a bone-deep sigh. Was her happiness destined to always disappear like fog at midmorning?

As she turned toward the door, she finally heard someone approaching the end of the lane. Her eyes cut toward the opening between the trees in time to glimpse Daniel slowing to turn the buggy toward her house. Her stiffened spine relaxed, and she hung her head. Maybe she should keep a tighter rein on her errant thoughts. Surely, Daniel would have a logical explanation.

Since the weather was unpredictable, Mary had chosen to just pull her hair back and clasp the unruly curls with a barrette at her nape. That way, she could wear a wide-brimmed hat in case of rain. If only she could do something with her hands. Even though she put camphorated cold cream on them every night, nothing could repair the damage caused by all the work she did during the day. She wished she could afford one of the more expensive preparations. Wearing white gloves seemed pretentious to her since she had on a serviceable brown skirt and jacket that went well with the only decent hat she owned. At least Daniel hadn't seemed to mind when he clasped her hands in his so often.

"Whoa!" He pulled back on the reins and quickly hopped from the seat. "Sorry I'm late. Something came up."

He took her hand and led her to the buggy where he helped her up onto the seat beside him.

Something came up? Was that all the explanation he had for being over half an hour late? Somehow that thought didn't set well with her. She'd expected more. Should she ask him for details? Would he think she was too nosy?

He picked up the reins and clicked his tongue to start the horses. Soon the buggy was turned around and headed back down the lane toward the country road. "Are you ready for your first Friday Surprise Sale at Meier and Frank's department store in Portland?"

"Yes." She felt for the lump in the pocket of her skirt. Pa had even given her a little money she could spend. Maybe she'd find something interesting to purchase. She so seldom had money she could use any way she desired. She couldn't imagine what she'd find that would make her part with it.

Daniel leaned his head closer to her. "Have you ever ridden the trolley that connects Oregon City with Portland?"

"No. The only time I was in Portland was years ago when I was a small child. I don't remember much about the trip."

A grin spread across his face, making him even more handsome than before. He did love her and wanted to show her a special good time. How could she have doubted him? But she still wished he had given a reason for his late arrival.

They reached the trolley stop just before the car was scheduled to depart.

"Hey, Tony," Daniel called to a Chinese man waiting beside the tracks.

"Where you want buggy to go?" The man's wide smile almost hid his eyes.

"Just take it behind our store." Daniel helped Mary down while he talked. "We can walk over there when we get back from Portland. I'm not sure how long we'll be staying."

"I make sure horses brushed and fed, Mr. Daniel."

After they got on the trolley, Daniel paid their fares. He picked a seat near the front. "Do you want to sit by the aisle or the window?"

She slid across the padded bench. "I want to watch everything go by."

Mary glanced toward the people who stood in doorways

and watched as the vehicle started its journey to the adjoining town, pulled by a team of horses. She had expected the trip to take longer than it did. Within an hour, she and Daniel left the trolley and headed toward the department store. So many things going on around them called for her attention.

As the trolley pulled out to go farther into Portland, she let her gaze wander across everything. On the other side of the street, two teams of long-haired white goats appeared to be racing each other. They wore harnesses much like the ones she'd seen in pictures of dogs pulling a sled.

"What are they doing?" She couldn't help pointing, even if it wasn't the most polite thing to do.

"Training." Daniel crooked his elbow and she slipped her hand along his muscular forearm, relishing his strength.

She smiled up at him. "Training for what?"

"They're going to use them in the gold fields in Alaska." He watched the traffic, waiting for a chance for them to cross the street.

"I never heard of such a thing." Mary had to take two steps to one of his strides, soon making her breathless. "I thought they used dogs for that."

He helped her up on the curb. "It's an experiment, I think. I'm not sure it'll really work in the harsher climate that far north."

Mary had a hard time taking in everything around them, because he was moving so fast. "Daniel, could we slow down a bit?"

He stopped still on the sidewalk and stepped in front of her to face her. People walked around them, making Mary uncomfortable for being in their way.

"I'm sorry I didn't notice I was going too fast for you. You're such a tiny woman, and my legs are so long." His soft words caressed her. "Will you forgive me?"

She nodded. "Of course. How much farther to the Meier and Frank department store?"

He glanced over his shoulder. "See where all those people are going into the red brick building? That's it." He studied her face for a moment. "Are you all right?"

"Yes, let's go."

When they arrived, the store was crowded with shoppers. Mary had never seen such a large variety of goods. She took her time browsing through the lovely displays, and Daniel seemed content to follow along. At one counter, a colorful array of silk scarves enticed her. She lifted one of the lovely creations and a rough spot on her hand caught the delicate fabric. She quickly put it down so she wouldn't damage it, giving it one last gentle pat before looking up.

Straight into the eyes of a woman staring at her. A woman she'd never seen before. Tall with sleek blonde hair pulled into an elaborate bun at the nape of her neck. Exquisite jewels adorned her ears, and her gown was the latest fashion. Her intense gaze made Mary very aware of just how much her own clothing set her apart from this elegant woman. But why was she staring? She looked as if she were contemplating speaking to Mary, but then she shook her head, turned, and sauntered away.

Daniel stepped up beside Mary. "Do you like this scarf?"

She was barely aware he was talking to her. Then she turned toward him. "What?"

A concerned look flitted across his face. "Is something the matter, Mary?"

"Do you see that woman with the blonde hair, wearing the blue dress with the lace on it?"

He glanced toward the woman then back. "What about her?"

"She was staring at me... intently."

He watched the woman until she exited the store. "Why would she do that?"

"I don't know, but it made me feel uncomfortable."

With his mouth very close to her ear, he whispered, "She was probably jealous of your beauty."

Mary almost laughed out loud. A woman who looked like that wouldn't be jealous of her. "There was something intense in her gaze. Almost as if she knew me. I thought she was going to speak to me."

Daniel turned her toward him. "Forget about her. We're here so you can enjoy the store and our special day together. I'm going to buy that scarf for you."

She started to demur, but he placed his finger on her lips to stop her. "It's not too personal of a gift from a man who is courting you."

After he paid for the lovely item, he guided her to another section of the store. "It's too soon for me to buy you jewelry, but I want to see what you like."

The lovely pieces didn't have price tags so she could see how much they cost. She was hesitant to let on which ones she liked best, because they might be too expensive, but soon Daniel had her trying on several pieces of gold jewelry studded with both diamonds and colored gemstones, even pearls. She liked the pearls best, but didn't say so. What if he tried to buy her some jewelry today? How could she turn down such lovely things?

The day was filled with interesting activities, but the most important was getting to know Daniel better. He was funny, so smart, and kind. He knew the best place in Portland to eat lunch and kept her entertained through a delicious meal... yet she couldn't remember a single thing she had eaten, because he had her captivated.

When they arrived back at the trolley stop to head to

Oregon City, they both carried packages. This time, Mary let Daniel sit beside the window as they headed out.

"Did you enjoy Portland?"

"Oh, yes. I loved it. Thank you for making it so much fun."

He put his arm across the back of the seat and let his hand settle on her other shoulder. "We'll have many more times like this before we marry...and after. Our life together will be so good."

His words warmed her heart, filling her with promise. Finally, she completely believed him.

On the buggy ride home, they started singing together. Their voices harmonized beautifully, just as Mary knew their lives would.

When they reached the first field of her family's farm, Mary was puzzled to see one of the horses, with the plowing harness still on him, stretching his neck across the wooden fence to eat grass from the other side. "What is Brownie doing out here like that?"

Daniel stopped the buggy, and Mary hopped down and jumped across the water in the ditch. He followed close behind.

She grabbed hold of the reins and ran her hand down Brownie's face. "Where is Pa?"

Daniel stared out across the partially plowed field. "Mary, what's that lying on the ground?"

Mary stood on her tiptoes and scanned the area. "The plow is over there. And that looks like Pa...Pa!"

When she screamed, the lump moved slightly and a loud moan erupted from it.

"Mary, your father's hurt!" Daniel stepped on the bottom board of the fence and quickly hiked his leg over before dropping into the tall grass. "Wait here. I'll check on him."

"I can't just stand here if Pa's injured." She followed him over the fence. May not have looked ladylike, but at the moment, she didn't care.

This side of the field hadn't been plowed. She and Daniel ran, with him quickly outdistancing her. Then he stopped and turned to catch her in his arms.

"Mary, you don't want to go any closer. He's hurt bad." He started to pull her close to his chest to shield her.

She resisted him. "I have to go see about him." She pushed past Daniel, lifted her skirt high enough not to impede her progress, and ran as fast as she could, grass and weeds whacking her lower legs.

They arrived beside her father at the same time. Mary's head swam. A large cut slashed across the upper part of her father's right leg, and a pool of blood had stained the plowed ground beside him. The coppery smell overwhelmed her, making her stomach turn. She dropped in the dirt near his head.

"Pa! Please open your eyes!" Sobs garbled her words.

Daniel whipped off his belt. He hunkered beside the wounded leg. The sound of fabric being ripped grabbed her attention. When Daniel had an opening large enough, he thrust one end of the belt under her father's leg. An agonizing scream from her father tore through the air. At least, he was still alive, but Mary's heart was about to break as fear shivered down her spine.

Daniel pulled the belt tight. "I've got to cut off the flow of blood. I'll hold it as tight as I can." He held the tourniquet with both hands. "Mary, you have to go for the doctor. Can you drive the buggy?"

"Yes, but I could get there quicker by riding Brownie." She headed toward the horse that had pawed the ground nervously since the commotion started. She had ridden the horse bareback many a time when she was younger. Even taught him to jump fences that way.

"There's no saddle, and you have on a skirt." His words chased her toward the fence.

Mary hollered back at Daniel, "That doesn't matter."

She pulled the plowing harness off Brownie and dropped it to the ground, just leaving the bridle and reins so she could control the horse. Mary led the large horse to a stump at the edge of the field. Stepping up on the hunk of wood, she hiked up her full skirt and leapt onto Brownie's back. She rode him across the field far enough to give them a running start. With a shout, she urged the horse over the fence and the ditch with her leaning low over his powerful neck. She clenched her teeth so she wouldn't bite her tongue when they landed. Even so, the thud when they hit the road almost unseated her and made her head begin to throb. It had been too long since she'd ridden bareback. With her urging the horse as fast as he could go, his strides ate up the few miles into town. She knew she looked a fright with her hat bouncing on her back held only by the ties around her neck and her hair whipping in the wind. But she didn't care. Her father's life hung in the balance.

Thank goodness, Dr. Childress lived on this end of town. She slowed Brownie as they approached the place, then slid from his back and hurried up the stone pathway to the front porch of the two-story house. The doctor had his office and exam rooms on the lower floor, and he and his wife lived upstairs.

Mary prayed all the way to the porch that the doctor would be there. She thrust open the door with a bang and rushed into the front room.

Mrs. Childress got up from behind the desk and hurried toward her. "Why, Mary Murray. What's the—"

"My pa's been hurt!" Mary took a quick breath. "He needs the doctor right away." Tears streamed down her cheeks, and she swiped at them with both hands.

The doctor's wife quickly turned and went through the back doorway. She returned immediately with her husband.

He peered at Mary over his glasses. "Tell me what happened."

"We found him lying in a field, and he's got a deep cut on his leg, I think from the plow, and he's lost lots of blood." She hiccupped a sob.

Mrs. Childress put her arm around Mary's shoulders. "There, there, my dear. Clyde will help you."

"Winifred, take Mary to the kitchen and get her some water while I harness the team." He went over to the one other patient in the waiting room. "Do you mind coming back tomorrow? I'll see you first thing in the morning."

The older woman, who Mary had never seen before, stood and nodded, her brow wrinkled with concern. "You go ahead. I'll be all right until then." She started out the front door.

Mrs. Childress closed it behind the woman. "Do you need me to come with you, dear?"

The doctor stopped and turned toward Mary. "Is anyone with your father?"

"Yes. Daniel Winthrop and I found him. Daniel's with him. He used his belt to apply a tourniquet." Mary's thoughts were so jumbled, it was a wonder she could speak a complete sentence that made sense.

"Good." He took his wife's hand. "I think Daniel and I can handle it. But I'm going to take the large wagon, in case we need to bring Kenneth in town to the clinic. I'll put the stretcher in the back."

What if he's dead? Mary couldn't keep the insidious idea from invading her thoughts. *Please God, don't let Pa die. Not now that he's finally his old self.*

I can't face another loss.

CHAPTER 10

*D*aniel's arms and shoulders ached from holding the belt as tight as he could. Blood still seeped from the gash in Kenneth Murray's leg, but only a tiny amount. The man's moans had faded away, and his face looked as if it were carved from candle wax. Not a speck of color in his blanched cheeks, except the prickly black whiskers, which appeared as if they had been stuck in one at a time. Was he still breathing? Daniel leaned as close as he could without releasing any pressure on the tourniquet. He'd almost given up hope when he detected a slight rhythmic movement to the man's chest.

How much blood did the human body hold, anyway? And how much could a man lose and still live? Daniel wished he knew.

What am I going to do if he dies before Mary and the doctor get here? The invasion of that question brought a stab of pain to his heart.

Never before had Daniel been alone with anyone who was near death. His arms trembled, and he pulled the leather even tighter against the man's flesh. Another moan leaked into the air.

Mary would be devastated if she lost her father. How could Daniel face her if he let the man die? But what else could he do to help him?

"Oh, God, please let Mr. Murray live. And keep him alive until the doctor arrives. Please, Lord, heal him for Mary's sake."

Another moan punctuated his whispered prayer. His eyes flew open as he peered toward the man's face. Then Mr. Murray's eyelids quivered but didn't open completely.

"Please God, protect Mr. Murray." He spoke the words to break the oppressive silence.

"Where..." The word fluttered like a wisp on the breeze. "...am I?"

Daniel leaned a little closer to the man's head without allowing any slack in the belt. A guttural moan came from Mr. Murray's mouth.

"I'm with you, sir." Daniel's voice sounded raspy. "Mary's gone to town for the doctor."

The few words had drained any trace of energy from the older man's body, and he lapsed once again into unconsciousness. Daniel almost gave up hope. Maybe those were his final words. How could Daniel tell Mary about them? With nothing else to do besides making sure the tourniquet stayed taut, he plunged back into prayer. Time stretched into eternity with his only realities the strip of leather, the cold hard ground, and a man's life resting on his feeble efforts.

"Whoa!" Finally, a familiar masculine voice broke through his concentration, followed by the jangling of a harness.

Daniel looked up, relieved at the sight of the doctor. The muscles in his arm screamed for release, but he couldn't allow them to relax. If Mr. Murray was still alive, he didn't want to kill him before the doctor climbed over the fence.

"Daniel!" Mary's voice, though troubled, sounded like music in his ears.

He glanced toward her. She stood on the other side of the

fence, holding the doctor's bag, while the older man climbed over. Her troubled expression sank into his heart.

"Is he all right?"

That was a question Daniel didn't welcome. What could he say? He really couldn't tell if her father was still with them or not.

"I'm not sure, but I haven't stopped holding the tourniquet...or praying."

Dr. Childress took his black bag from Mary and made his way across the field to where the patient lay. Daniel watched Mary climb back up on the wagon and drive on down the road.

Everything had happened so quickly after they found her father that he didn't know how upset Mary was. Did she ever cry? Surely, she needed him to comfort her.

"Where's Mary going?" he asked Dr. Childress.

"I told her to drive the wagon to their place and bring it in through the gate." The physician dropped onto his knees in the newly turned soil. "We'll need to use it to get Kenneth out of here, and I don't want her here until I have assessed his condition."

The doctor examined the wound thoroughly, then poured a carbolic acid solution into the wound to cleanse it. He added sulfur powder before stuffing cotton wool into the gash and sealing it with gauze and cloth adhesive tape. "You can slowly remove the belt now, son. I'll watch for seepage. I believe we can get back to town with this bandage. You did a good job."

Minutes later Mary drove through the gate and carefully approached their position. Mary stared at her father, and Daniel saw her tremble.

"Is he...is he dead?" Her voice sounded as if it needed support. He put his arm around her.

The doctor folded his stethoscope and placed it in his bag. Then he stood. "No...but Mary, I'm not going to lie to you. Things don't look very good right now, but your beau here did the exact thing Kenneth needed." He clapped Daniel on his shoulder. "If he lives, this man will be the reason. Now we need to get him into the wagon. I'm taking him to the clinic in town."

Mary stiffened. She moved out of Daniel's arms and followed Dr. Childress. "Why can't we keep him here? I can take care of him."

The doctor took her hand and patted it gently. "I know you would, Mary, but he needs more than you could do at home. It's imperative he have the best of care right now. We want to bring him through this, don't we?"

Tears streamed down her cheeks as she nodded. Daniel clenched his fists and thrust them into the pockets of his slacks. He wanted to help her...comfort her...make all her troubles go away. But at this moment, he felt helpless. Some way, somehow, he would make everything better for her, but for now he could do nothing more.

~

*M*ary cringed when the doctor said he was taking her father to the clinic. No one in their family had ever been kept in the clinic for treatment. How could she take care of her sister and brothers and be with her father at the same time? And how would they pay for his care?

This would be a good test to see how well Frances could keep up with chores at the house, because Mary *was* going to stay by her father's side. She refused to lose him while she was at home and he was in town. If he died, she wanted to be there with him. She wanted to see him, to say her goodbyes to him. Not like when Ma, Carrie, and Annette died so far away.

She took a deep breath and turned to watch the men. They carried the canvas stretcher by the wooden poles and laid it on the ground.

"Mary." The doctor glanced up at her. "Would you please go

to the wagon and use all but one of the quilts to make a pad to lay your father on?"

At last, something constructive she could do to help. Mary folded several blankets a couple of times lengthwise and stacked them down the middle. On the way to town, her father would be jostled enough without him having to bounce against the hard bed.

By the time she finished, the men approached carefully carrying the stretcher with her father on it. Daniel led the way.

"Mary." As he spoke, the doctor kept his eyes on her father. "Please lower the tailgate."

She complied and jumped to the ground.

"Daniel, place your end of the stretcher on the wagon, then climb in and slowly lift it again."

Daniel eased the stretcher onto the tailgate. After he was in the wagon, he picked up the poles and carefully raised them high enough to set the stretcher down on the quilts without disturbing them. The doctor made sure his end was level with the other one. Daniel backed up and spread his legs toward the sides of the wagon with each step. Slowly, they lowered Pa onto the blankets. Mary released the breath she hadn't even noticed she'd been holding.

Daniel jumped down and pulled her into an embrace. Mary rested her head against his chest, drawing comfort from him.

She clutched the lapels of Daniel's jacket. "I want to go into town with the doctor."

Before he could answer, the older man shook his head. "I want Daniel to drive the wagon. I'll ride in the back with your father. If you want to come, you'll have to drive Daniel's buggy."

As tears streamed down her cheeks, Daniel hopped up onto the wagon seat. How would she ever get through all this?

He picked up the reins and turned toward her. "Climb up here with me. We can give you a ride to where the buggy is."

When they approached the farmhouse, Frances, George, and Bobby stood waiting for them. Mary didn't want them too upset, but at least with them seeing the shape Pa was in, they would understand her need to leave again.

Daniel stopped the wagon beside where they waited.

Frances ran to the wagon and screamed. Pa groaned and turned his head toward her without opening his eyes.

Dr. Childress pulled the extra quilt over Pa. "We're taking him to the clinic, Frances."

"I want to go with you," Frances cried.

Mary hated having to disappoint her sister. "You can't. You have to stay with the boys... and take care of them."

Although tears streamed down Frances's face, she nodded. "But you'll come home soon, won't you, Mary?"

The question tugged at Mary's heart. How could she answer? She had no idea how long she would be gone, because she wasn't going to leave her father's side until he was on his way to recovery.

"I'll come as soon as I can." She clutched her jacket closer around her. She didn't even want to contemplate what might be ahead...for all of them.

As they pulled out of the lane, she glanced back at her forlorn siblings. *Lord, please take care of them while I'm gone.*

Daniel stopped when they reached his horse and buggy and climbed from the wagon seat. When she stood, his strong hands spanned her waist and he lifted her down, pulling her into a last embrace before he climbed back onto the bench.

Mary had been looking forward to him holding her in his arms some day. Never in a million years would she have thought their first real embrace would arise out of tragedy instead of passion. Her life had turned completely topsy-turvy.

She watched the wagon head toward town before she climbed into the buggy. The packages on the floor brought back memories of the wonderful time she and Daniel had spent in Portland. Those images were quickly replaced by all they had experienced later in the day. As she drove the buggy down to the lane to turn it around, she wondered if they would ever return to the happiness they had experienced today.

CHAPTER 11

wo hours! Mary had been sitting alone in the waiting room outside the door to the clinic where Dr. Childress and Daniel carried her father as soon as they arrived in town. Daniel had returned to sit beside her a few minutes before the doctor asked for his help. Even though Mrs. Childress soon brought her a pot of tea and some sandwiches, Mary hadn't been able to force a bite past the large lump in her throat. The tea had been welcome, but the remnants had long since grown cold. Just like Mary's heart.

She leaned her head against the back of the upholstered chair and closed her eyes, willing away the horrific sight of her father between the plowed furrows, looking like a dead man. Perhaps she should pray again, but she'd already done that several times and nothing had changed so far.

What am I going to do if Pa dies? Tears seeped from under her eyelids and started their trek down her cheeks. She was too tired to wipe them away.

The front door to the doctor's office opened, but Mary didn't lift her eyelids. Probably someone needing help. She hoped Mrs. Childress was close by. Mary didn't feel like talking to anyone right now.

The swish of skirts accompanied the sound of multiple footsteps approaching her. She glanced up just as Mrs. Horton and Mrs. Slidell stopped beside her. Straightening, Mary tried to smile, but felt sure her expression was more of a grimace.

"Are you all right, dear?" Mrs. Slidell perched on the chair closest to Mary's. "What happened?" The pastor's wife stood behind the organist.

"My father has been injured."

The two women tsked in unison, and Mrs. Slidell gave Mary's hand a couple of soft pats.

"I'm not sure what happened exactly. The doctor has been working on him a long time." Mary gulped back a sob that threatened to explode.

The door of the clinic opened and Mrs. Childress bustled through. "Ladies, how good of you to come."

Mrs. Horton turned. "We came as soon as we heard about the accident. We'd like to help any way we can."

Can you make time turn back so Daniel and I arrive at the farm before Pa is injured? Mary squelched that thought, sure the women would think she was crazy if she voiced it.... Maybe she was.

"Is someone at the farm with the other children?" Mrs. Slidell asked.

Mary shook her head. "Frances is thirteen years old. She can look after the boys." Mrs. Horton moved closer. "We know that, dear, but I'm sure they're scared and just as worried about their father as you are. We could take food and help comfort them until you can come home."

The idea of someone besides herself taking responsibility for Frances and the boys sounded like a gift from God. "That...would be...nice." She swallowed the threatening sobs between the words.

Mrs. Slidell stood up. "We knew you would feel that way. Several of the women are busy cooking things to take out there. You don't have to worry about a thing." With a few more words of comfort, she and Mrs. Horton bustled away.

Mary wished she could relax. Yes, the other children would be taken care of, but what about all the outside chores that Pa did by himself? And what about the plowing? Without the preparation of the field, their garden couldn't be planted. And they couldn't get by without selling most of the produce they grew. At least, that's what she had been able to glean from watching and listening to Pa. He never really told her any details about their financial situation, but he had talked to other men in her presence.

The enormity of all they would have to face, even if her father recovered quickly, almost drowned her. And if he didn't...she couldn't even let her thoughts dwell on that eventuality.

Suddenly the front door opened. Surprise overcame her when Daniel came in, followed by the Chinese man who had taken care of the horses when they left the buggy at the trolley station that morning.

Mary stood and stared at Daniel. "I thought you were in there helping the doctor with Pa."

Daniel nodded. "I was, but I went out the back door to get Tony."

Her gaze moved past him to the Chinese man. The young man bowed his head. "Chan Tung Jia at your service, ma'am. Mr. Daniel call me Tony Chan." A large smile brought a hint of pride to the man's eyes. "Easier for him to say."

"Tony is going to the farm to take care of the outside chores," Daniel explained. "He's a hard worker."

At Daniel's words, the man nodded vigorously. "I plow too. Take good care of things."

This was almost too much for Mary to take in. So many

people willing to help. Her knees felt weak, and she dropped back into the chair. Now she didn't have to face all of this alone.

"Thank you. I want to stay with my father, but I've been worried about my sister and brothers and the farm."

Daniel hunkered beside her. "I knew you wanted to stay with your father. I'll be here with you as long as you need me."

Comforting words. She would need him forever. Tears gathered in her eyes before breaching her lower lids and pouring down her cheeks. This time, she pulled her handkerchief from her handbag and swiped them away.

Two more hours passed and the sun had set before Dr. Childress sat down with Mary to talk about her father's condition. Daniel had stayed by her side through the long wait. Even though they really didn't talk much, just having him there strengthened her. Gave her hope.

"Mary, you are a young woman now, so I won't gloss things over. You need to know what lies ahead for your father...and for your family."

She didn't like the ominous sound of those words. Without an answer, she stared into his face, noticing how his brow puckered and he gazed at her intently, with seriousness written in every plane of his face.

"We have no way of knowing how long Kenneth was injured before you and Daniel arrived." He took off his eyeglasses and pinched the bridge of his nose a moment before replacing them. "He lost a lot of blood. Because it drained into the soil, we don't know how much. That is a very serious problem." He wiped a hand across his chin, the short whiskers rasping as he moved over them. "I cleaned out the wound with carbolic acid solution before stitching it together. Then I treated it with Columbia Healing Powder under the bandage. I'm a firm believer in using antiseptic practices. And we'll need to change the bandages and check the wound often."

He leaned his head back against the winged chair and took

a deep breath. Mary noticed that total exhaustion seemed to weigh him down.

"We need to add a large dose of prayer. Your father has a long way to go to regain his strength, and there's always the worry about infection." Huffing out a deep breath, he arose. "If gangrene sets in, I'll have to amputate his leg, and I know Kenneth wouldn't want that. We have to watch him closely. I'm keeping him here as long as it takes to get him over the worst of it."

He held up a hand when Mary started to disagree. "I know you want to take him home, but I can't let you. He must stay here until I can see he's out of danger. You do want him to get well, don't you?"

She jumped out of her chair. "Of course, I do."

Daniel put his arm around her shoulders. "Calm down, Mary."

Then the starch went out of her, and she dropped back into the waiting chair. "I want him to get well, but I'm not sure we can afford for him to stay here."

"Let's not worry about that now." Dr. Childress leaned forward and clasped his hands between his knees. "All those matters will work out. The important thing is to get Kenneth well. Right?"

She couldn't do anything but nod. Half afraid he wouldn't agree, she asked, "May I see him now?"

The doctor arose. "I don't see why not. I have given him laudanum for the pain. He'll be sleeping a lot, but sometimes he comes out of it. It might do him good to have you there with him. You are very important to him." He led the way through the clinic door with Mary and Daniel following behind.

When she first saw Pa, she had to take a deep breath. He looked so weak, almost as if he had shrunken somehow. And his bandaged leg was propped up on a couple of pillows. The dressings made it look huge.

"I've raised the wound higher than his heart, so it won't throb so much. Hopefully, it will help relieve some of the pain." Dr. Childress must have noticed her staring at her father's leg. "Daniel, would you bring the chair Mary has been sitting in and place it close to the bed?"

Without saying a word, Daniel followed his directions.

Mary hadn't realized just how shaky she was until she dropped into the chair. She leaned forward and touched her father's limp hand, rubbing her fingers over the rough calluses on his palm. Each one revealed how hard he had worked to support their family. He hadn't shared his grief over losing Ma and the older girls, which had built a wall of resentment between them. But all the time he was dealing with his losses, he still poured himself into making a living for the rest the family. She wished she had realized and honored him as she should have, instead of resenting some of the things he did.

Not knowing whether he could hear her or not, she leaned close to his ear. "Pa, please get well. We need you.... I love you."

"Can we get you anything, Mary?"

She hadn't realized that Mrs. Childress had slipped into the room until she heard the soft question. Raising her head, she could think of only one thing. "Would someone bring me a Bible? I want to read Scriptures to him."

"Of course." The woman exited the room, returning quickly with the book.

After Dr. Childress and his wife left, Daniel took Mary's hand. "I will be praying for you, and I'll come by first thing in the morning."

"What time is it, anyway?" Mary had no idea, even though night had long since dropped its dark cloak on the world outside the windows.

With his other hand, Daniel pulled the fob on his pocket watch, extracting it from its small compartment in his slacks.

He leaned a little closer to the lamp in order to read its face. "It's half past nine."

Mary wondered if her siblings had gone to bed or if they were trying to wait for her return. She hoped they weren't giving grief to whoever went from the church to help them.

He slipped the timepiece back into its place. "Before I go home, I'll ride out to the farm and let the others know that your father came through his surgery."

Tears once again rolled down her cheeks. She felt drained, and she couldn't hold them back. Daniel erased each one with the pad of his thumb. His gentle touch comforted her.

"I wish I could take away your pain. I love you, Mary. One day...soon, I hope...everything will be all right." He leaned forward and placed a soft kiss on her forehead. "Good night."

She sat frozen as she watched him slip out the door. If only she had the energy to really do something else to help, but it took everything she had in her to sit beside Pa and start to read the Psalms over him. The words droned on into the night.

Her voice had turned hoarse before he ever moved. First, she felt a slight squeeze from his fingers. She stopped reading and studied him. *Did his eyelids move?* She wasn't sure.

She turned the page with her other hand, but before she got one word out, the squeeze came again. This time with a little more strength. And when she looked up the eyelids did indeed flutter. Finally, they opened completely, but his eyes looked glazed, like a hazy mirror.

"Mary?" He spoke her name like a gentle breeze that blows by and immediately disappears.

She closed the Bible in her lap and leaned toward him. "Yes, Pa."

"It...is...you."

"I couldn't leave you here alone." She dropped a kiss on his blanched, leathery cheek. At least, it felt cool to her touch. She knew that if he was too warm, it could signal an infection.

He started to turn his head, but stopped as if pain shot through it. "Where...am...I?"

"You're in the clinic. Dr. Childress performed surgery on your leg."

She watched his face, almost afraid he would quickly lapse into sleep again, leaving her more alone than before.

"What...happened?" Each word worked its way out of his mouth.

"You were injured. Daniel and I found you in the field where you'd been plowing. We don't know what happened, or when it happened."

Clarity leaked into his eyes like drops of rain on dry soil. "Lightning."

That didn't make any sense. It hadn't rained in Portland or even Oregon City, because everything was dry when they returned.

For a long moment, everything was still... too silent. Then he stared at her again.

"Big rock in way... I tried to move it." He took a deep, raspy breath. "Dark clouds. Lightning struck tree...spooked Brownie."

Well, that explained why everything was out of place in the field. Mary had so many questions to ask her father, but his grip released and his eyes closed.

Please, God. Help Pa to heal. We really need him.

She clasped his hand as tight as she could without hurting him. Maybe if she held on to him, he wouldn't slip away...the way Ma had.

CHAPTER 12

*D*aniel stared out the front window of Winthrop's Wool Emporium. Although there were plenty of people out and about today, none came into their store. He had lost count of the number of customers going into Clyde Huntley Drug and Books store, two doors down. If he could have his way about it, he would just lock up and turn over the closed sign. All he really wanted to do was go to the clinic and see Mary. She needed him more than this store did.

In the two weeks since her father's accident, Mary had spent almost all her time in the clinic sitting beside his bed. She only allowed Daniel to take her to the farm every couple of days to bathe and change clothes. Then she insisted on returning to her vigil.

Mr. Murray had lost so much blood by the time they found him that his recovery was moving at a snail's pace. Sometimes, he was awake enough to carry on a conversation, but most often he was not. The man looked as if one of those head-hunters Daniel had read about had taken his whole body and shrunk it. His muscles were wasting away from disuse. Daniel no longer held out much hope for the man's recovery.

When Daniel mentioned that fact to the doctor, he said that Kenneth needed to start eating more solid food. And they should get him up to sit in a chair at least once a day. But that hadn't happened yet. Perhaps when he finally shut the store, he and Mary could help him to a chair.

Noticing a neighbor boy walking by rolling a hoop, Daniel rushed to open the door. "Hey, wait up, Philip."

The boy grabbed the hoop in one hand and pushed the hair out of his eyes with his other. "What d' you want, Mr. Winthrop?" He scuffed his toe on a crack in the boardwalk.

"I'll give you a nickel to take a note to my house."

Philip's eyes lit up like those new electric lights in Portland. "Sure thing!"

He stepped back and opened the door wider. "Come on in. I need to write it."

While the boy walked all around the store eyeing the merchandise, Daniel went behind the counter and grabbed a piece of paper, an envelope, and a stubby pencil. Philip whistled a nameless tune that Daniel tried to block out of his mind while he composed the message.

After sealing the envelope, he thrust it toward the boy. "See if Mrs. Shelton wants to send back an answer. If she does, I'll give you another nickel to bring it quickly."

The boy grabbed the envelope and stuffed it in his pocket. "You bet, I will!"

He hurried out the door and down the boardwalk. Daniel smiled. He figured that Mrs. Shelton's chicken and dumplings could heal nearly anyone.

Two hours later, his father hurriedly entered from the back of the building. "How has business been today?"

Daniel really didn't want to answer him. "Not a single customer."

Father set the box he carried on the counter and looked all

around as if he were checking everything. "The store looks good. I see you kept yourself busy, anyway."

Indeed, Daniel had swept the floors, dusted the displays and shelves, straightened the merchandise, checked the inventory, and counted the money in the till. "Yes, sir." Daniel couldn't keep a smile from creeping onto his face. "But I finished quite a long time ago."

His father clapped him on the shoulder. "I'm proud of you, son. I know I don't tell you as often as I should."

Daniel wasn't expecting that reaction. But he liked it. "If you're here to stay, I'll head out to check on Mary and her father."

"You go right ahead. I need to put these things away." Father turned toward the box.

Whistling "Clementine," Daniel headed toward home. After stopping there to pick up the pot of food, he drove his buggy to the doctor's house. The enticing aroma of Mrs. Shelton's chicken and dumplings made his stomach rumble.

He tied up his horse behind the clinic and entered through the back door. Mrs. Childress was folding sheets in the workroom.

"What are you carrying, Daniel?" She took a deep breath. "It smells like one of my favorites."

"I remembered that it's a favorite of Mr. Murray as well." Daniel set the covered pan on the other end of the table. "I thought maybe we could entice him to eat more than he has been."

"That's a good idea." She set the final sheet on the stack and went over to a cupboard to retrieve a couple of bowls and spoons. She dipped some of the food into a bowl. "You can take it into his room. I'll bring another serving for Mary too. She hasn't left his side for more than a couple of minutes today."

Balancing the bowl in one hand, Daniel quietly opened the

door to the room Mr. Murray occupied. Mary had her head bowed, and she clasped one of her father's hands in both of hers. *Probably praying.* He knew she had been doing a lot of that. He moved across the room toward a shelf near the bed. With his second footstep, the floorboard squeaked.

Mary's head shot up and her eyes turned toward him. "Daniel, I'm so glad you're here."

"How is your father?" He set the bowl down. The man didn't look a bit better than he had yesterday.

"Seems to be the same." She huffed out an exasperated breath and stood. "What do you have there?"

"Some of Mrs. Shelton's chicken and dumplings."

A low moan emanated from the bed. They both turned to look at Mr. Murray. His eyes were open. "Chicken...and dumplings?"

"Yes, sir." Daniel dropped into the chair beside the bed. "I thought you might like some. Maybe we could get you up sitting in the chair, so it will be easier for you to eat."

When Mary glanced at him, worry lit her eyes. "I'm not sure that's a good idea."

"Of course, it is."

Mrs. Childress entered with another bowl of food for Mary. "My dear husband would like nothing better than getting Kenneth into a chair. That would show real progress in his recovery." She set the second bowl on the shelf and leaned closer to the patient. "How about it? Will you let us help you up?"

Mr. Murray gave a slight nod. Hope lit a flame in his eyes.

"All righty then." Mrs. Childress took charge. She picked up one of the bowls and handed it to Mary. "Mary, dear, why don't you take this into the kitchen and eat a bit to give you some strength. Daniel and I will get your father into the chair."

Daniel could tell Mary wanted to object. He moved closer to her. "We'll get you back in here when's he's settled."

He turned her toward the door. She gazed back over her shoulder before leaving the room.

Mrs. Childress had Daniel move the deeply upholstered, wingback chair close to the bed. They eased Mary's father up, and with their arms around his back and supporting his legs, slid him over to the waiting chair. Then the doctor's wife grabbed a quilt and covered the man up to his waist.

"Are you all right, Kenneth?" Mrs. Childress hovered around like a mother hen.

"Yes...thank you." He leaned his head against the back of the chair and closed his eyes for a moment before he opened them and stared up at Daniel. "Now...where are those...chicken and dumplings?"

After pulling a straight chair next to the patient, Mrs. Childress retrieved the bowl and sat down. She quickly lifted a spoonful of the delicious soup and fed it to the man.

His lips closed around the loaded spoon and a smile lit his eyes, bringing new color to his face. She withdrew the utensil, and he slowly chewed.

He swallowed and sighed. "So...good."

Mrs. Childress gave him another taste. "This is wonderful. We'll have you strengthened in no time at all."

Daniel went after Mary. He opened the door and found her leaning against the wall in the hallway, enjoying her own food.

"Is he in the chair?"

"Yes, and Mrs. Childress is feeding him." Daniel was glad he had good news.

Mary's face revealed her high hope for her father's recovery. She had never given up on him, even though at times Daniel had doubted the man would even live. He wanted to take Mary in his arms and hold her close to his heart...forever.

"He's letting her feed him?" Incredulity threaded between Mary's words.

"I think he's finally hungry."

Mary placed her hand on his arm, branding him through his shirt sleeve. "We owe all this to your thoughtfulness, Daniel. I don't think I would have made it these last two weeks without you."

"Anything for you, Mary." He meant every word. Maybe today he could finally share his plans with her and her father.

❧

*M*ary followed Daniel into her father's room. Seeing him sitting up in a chair and eating almost brought her to tears. For the first time since the accident, instead of flapping around in her muddy thoughts, her hope took wing.

Since both of the chairs were being used, she sat on the side of his bed. "Isn't this food delicious?" She put another spoonful in her mouth, and this time she really tasted it. "Since you like it so much, I'm going to have to ask Mrs. Shelton for her recipe."

Pa turned his head toward her and gave her a tentative smile. Was he tiring out? Did they need to get him onto the bed? She finished eating and set her empty bowl back on the shelf then went to stand beside his chair. She wanted to hug him, but she didn't know if it would hurt him.

"Here, Mary." Mrs. Childress held her father's bowl out for her. "You can help him finish this, and I'll change the sheets on his bed. That should make him more comfortable."

Mary sat in the chair she vacated and offered Pa another spoonful. "You're really looking better."

She noticed tears pooling in his eyes, but she didn't say anything about them. She didn't want to embarrass him. A man had his pride.

"Good...food." He turned his attention toward Daniel. "Thank you."

Daniel hunkered beside her father's chair. "I know how much her dumplings make me feel better when I'm not well. Happy to do it for you, sir."

"You're a good man...Daniel Winthrop." His voice trembled on the last word. "Glad Mary...has you."

"I'm the one who is blessed to have Mary." Daniel glanced up at her and gave her a wink.

She couldn't help smiling at him. That wink sent a shiver through her. How had she ever caught the eye of such a wonderful man?

"When I'm better...we'll talk again...about your waiting time." He gave Daniel a teary smile. "Make it shorter."

Mary gave him another bite before dropping the spoon into the empty bowl. A shorter waiting time. *Does he mean we can get married sooner?* She hoped so. Nothing would make her happier.

"Your bed's all ready, Kenneth." Mrs. Childress headed toward the door. "I'll get Clyde, and we'll get you cleaned up as well." When she reached the door, her husband stood in the opening. "Look who's here." She glanced toward Mary and Daniel. "You can go out into the waiting room. We've closed the clinic for the day. You won't be disturbed."

Mary rose to her feet and kissed Pa on the cheek, a cheek with more color in it than he'd had since the accident. "We'll be back soon."

He nodded.

Daniel followed Mary out the door and closed it behind him. He put his arm across her shoulders. "We have a lot to talk about."

"Yes, we do." They went into the waiting room and she dropped into one of the chairs.

Daniel pulled another one facing her, so they would be closer. "I have so many plans for us."

"Plans?" This sounded intriguing to Mary. "What kind of plans?"

"If your father cuts down our waiting time, we could get married soon. The Harrison house now belongs to me. There are a few things I want to have done to it before we move in, but we can set up our household there." He stared at his hands. "I can hardly wait until we'll be together as husband and wife. You can have servants, so you won't have to do so much work."

Mary was stunned. *Was he completely oblivious to reality?* Even though her father had finally turned a corner in his recovery, he had a long way to go. She wouldn't want to be in Oregon City in some mansion far too large for two people while her father needed her.

"Daniel, it could take months, or even years, before Pa will be completely well."

"Then we could marry, and he and your sister and brothers can move in with us. Maybe they could sell the farm—"

Mary quickly stood. "Pa won't want to sell the farm. He wants it to be an inheritance for the boys." She paced across the woolen rug.

Daniel stood too. "They won't need an inheritance. I'll have enough money to give your family a good life."

She whirled toward him. "The farmhouse is the only home the children have known. We can't take them from their home. They've lost so much already." She couldn't stand still, so she once more moved across the room. "Besides that, Pa won't want to leave the farm and move into town."

"But what if he can't ever do all the work that's needed to run the farm?" Was that the sound of desperation in Daniel's voice?

"With me there with him, we'll work it out somehow." She crossed her arms and clenched her fists. "Tony Chan has been doing a good job."

Daniel raked his fingers through the waves in his dark

blond hair. "I know. *I'm* paying him to do the work. We could keep him on the farm to help your father."

"You don't understand, Daniel. Frances, George, and Bobby will need me during this time. I'm the only mother they have." She stopped and whirled to stand in front of him. "We could live on the farm with them. My family is very important to me."

"That's not what I have planned for us. I want to give you a better life." His words were so insistent, as if only his ideas had merit.

"Maybe your idea of a better life and my idea of a better life are totally different." She thrust her fisted hands onto her hips and glared at him.

He stared at her with a look akin to horror on his face. "I can't believe you're saying this. I can give you everything." His eyes bored into her, almost burning a trail.

"Maybe I don't want everything you can give me." She knew her voice had gradually risen to a shout during the conversation. But she didn't care. He wasn't listening to her. He only wanted his own way without taking her thoughts into consideration. Was that how a marriage was supposed to work?

Her words hit him hard, because he flinched as if they were stones she had thrown at him. Maybe she didn't really mean them the way they sounded, but how could he not understand how important her family was to her? How could he even consider her abandoning them when they needed her so much?

Without another word, he turned and slammed out the front door.

Tears streamed down her cheeks. *What just happened?* Everything had been going so well for her and Daniel. Now she didn't know where their relationship stood. She didn't even know if they still *had* a relationship.

The front door opened. Daniel reentered. "My buggy is in the back." He bit out the words like bullets.

He stomped through the room and down the hallway. She felt each of the heavy footsteps on her wounded heart. Why had she let all her anger and frustration boil over onto Daniel? She regretted every angry word she'd hurled at him. Surely, he would come back, and they could apologize to each other. Couldn't they?

CHAPTER 13

*D*aniel couldn't believe he'd been such an idiot. To storm out the front door of the doctor's house when he had parked the buggy at the back. Going back inside to get to his buggy took much of the power from his exit. At the ripe old age of twenty, he wanted everyone to know he was a man. He was thankful no one else witnessed this embarrassing event, and he hoped Dr. and Mrs. Childress hadn't heard the argument.

He couldn't imagine what had gotten into Mary. Never before had he seen this side of her personality. He thought she loved him for who he was... and for his wisdom. Couldn't she see that everything he had planned for them was in her best interest as well as his own? How wrong he had been. Each time her voice raised another notch, it fueled his anger. Why did she do that to him?

Dr. Childress came through the back door behind him. "Could I have a word with you, Daniel."

Forcing an insincere smile to his face, he turned. "I'm sorry about—"

"I didn't want to intrude, but there are a few things I can't tell Mary about her father. I felt that you should know, since you're courting her." Frown lines emphasized the man's concern.

Daniel stuck his hands in the pockets of his slacks. "Yes?"

"I'm pleased that Kenneth roused so well today, but he's not out of the woods yet...and he may never be." He stared intently into Daniel's eyes. "I cannot take away Mary's hope, but someone needs to know that there's a strong possibility her father may never be able to work the farm again. These things need to be considered when making long-term decisions."

Daniel nodded. "Thank you, Doctor. I appreciate your candor with me."

After a moment, the other man pivoted and reentered the house.

At least the doctor respected him as a man. Otherwise, he wouldn't have entrusted this information to him. This just reinforced the turmoil raised by their disagreement. Perhaps he wouldn't have any choice in the matter, and marrying Mary would mean living and working at the farm. Could he face that? He felt a growl deep inside, but he silenced it with his will. Everything was so out of his control.

He untied his reins and climbed into the driver's seat. He really didn't want to go home while he was in this frame of mind. And he didn't want to answer any questions his parents might have about his foul mood. He turned the buggy away from town and drove into the country.

Even being in the buggy, instead of riding his horse, raised his ire. If he were riding Sultan, his Arabian stallion, he'd run him full-out.

The only reason he chose this conveyance was so he could drive Mary home in comfort. He had planned to spend time with Tony Chan, checking on how the work at the farm was progressing. He would iron out any problems the man might have while Mary visited with her siblings, bathed, and dressed. Then he would return her to her father's side.

Thinking back he realized that their misunderstanding probably started when Mary didn't agree with him about getting her father out of bed. After all, he was trying to follow the doctor's orders to move Mr. Murray's recovery along. He'd been taken aback when she hadn't agreed. Then from that moment, everything took a downward spiral.

Mary had been disrespectful...and she shot down his plans and dreams about their life together. She wasn't willing to marry him and live in town while they helped her family with the farm, and she wouldn't consider not taking care of them herself. Any other woman would have jumped at the chance he offered her.

He wanted to build a life with Mary, but it didn't include starting that life in a country farmhouse with an ailing old man and three children around. Besides, a man and his wife needed privacy in their home at the beginning of their marriage, didn't they?

What could he do about it? He wanted her to understand that he would be the head of their family from the very beginning of their marriage. But he didn't know how he could approach the subject with her. Not in her present state of mind. Or his.

As he drove along other thoughts kept coming to mind. His childhood friend Gary Bowen had a similar problem after he and Debra married. Having to take care of her family after a disaster had almost destroyed their marriage. Just thinking about how Gary had changed made Daniel's stomach muscles clench. He did not want to face something like that. He didn't think he would make the choices Daniel had, but he didn't want to have to face the possibility.

Instead of stopping at the Murray farm, he drove on down the country road, finally turning the buggy around at a deserted farmhouse and heading back to town. The evening breeze cooled his anger as it brought a chill to the evening. By the time he reached his house, he had his temper under control.

"Is that you, Daniel?" Father came out of his study and met him at the foot of the curving staircase in the foyer. "I need to talk to you."

Even though his father sounded serious, Daniel couldn't detect any anger in his tone. He didn't want to experience any more anger this evening.

"Is something amiss?" Daniel followed him back into the wood-paneled office. Father sat in the leather chair on the other side of his large cherry-wood desk. "Something has come up, and I want to ask your opinion."

He dropped into a wingback chair across the desk from his father. "Fire away."

His father picked up a yellow piece of paper from his desk. "This telegram came a short time ago. It's from your uncle Clarence. He fell and broke his leg. He will need help for a while." Father laid the paper back down. "I know you have the Chinese boy helping out at the Murray farm. Do you know anyone else who's a good worker we could send up north to help Clarence? Maybe a young man who will be able to work on the sheep farm? It's time for shearing, and it takes someone who is strong and has stamina."

Father was right. Tony Chan would have been a good choice. He worked hard and was willing to take on almost any kind of task. But Daniel didn't want to take him away from the Murray farm.

Maybe this would be a good opportunity for Daniel to get away. He had a lot to think about.

He cleared his throat and looked his father straight in the eyes. "How about if I go help Uncle Clarence? I was there during the shearing once when I was younger."

His father steepled his fingers under his chin. "Are you sure you want to do that? What about Mary and her family?"

"I really want to help *my* family." No need to let his father know that he was running away from his problems here. "You could keep Tony working out there. Make sure he gets paid. That will help the Murrays. And the women at the church are pitching in with cooking and the housework."

Father gave him a steely-eyed stare, and Daniel almost broke under his scrutiny. But he was too old to have to go to his parent with his problems. He'd work this out his own way.

After a long, agonizing moment, his father nodded. "If you're sure. I know Clarence would appreciate the help. Can you be ready to leave tomorrow morning? If so, I'll send the telegram."

For a moment, his heart felt as if it was in a vise. Somehow, his decision hadn't brought the peace he'd expected. But he couldn't face another argument with Mary right now. Although he had planned to go back and take her home this evening, he knew nothing had been resolved, and she would want to rehash everything. Didn't women always talk things to death?

With him gone, she would have time to simmer down and be more agreeable to his plans. If he could come up with a solution for their dilemma in the meantime.

$\sim$

*M*ary couldn't believe what a shrew she was before Daniel stormed out of the house. And she didn't say a word when he came back through slinking like a dog with its tail between its legs. She should have said something.

She didn't remember a time when she had been so exhausted. Even though Pa's slight recovery perked her up, it didn't take away any of the burden she carried for him... for

Frances, for the boys...for the farm. Sometimes, she felt as if the weight of the world rested on her shoulders.

This evening, Daniel was supposed to take her home for a while. At least today, she'd have good news for her siblings. Rejoicing with them for the small victory in their father's recovery should lift her spirits, at least a little.

She went back into her father's room. "How is he, Mrs. Childress?"

The woman tucked the covers under Pa's chin. "He'll probably sleep for quite a while now. Getting him into the chair and feeding him was a real breakthrough, but it tired him out completely."

"I'll just sit here until Daniel returns to take me home. Maybe Pa will sleep all the time I'm gone." Mary pulled the wingback chair closer to the bed and dropped into the seat.

"Would you like another serving of the chicken and dumplings Daniel brought? There's plenty." Mrs. Childress had her hand on the doorknob.

Mary's stomach gave a big rumble, and she rubbed it with both hands. "I guess that's your answer. I didn't realize I was still hungry, but I haven't eaten much in several days either."

"I'll be right back, dearie." She exited the room.

Mary leaned her head against the cushioned chair, trying to relax. But the awful conversation she and Daniel had kept repeating in her mind. If he loved her, wouldn't he want what was best for her family? Maybe he didn't understand the need for members of a family to take care of each other. He was an only child, and his family had always had plenty of financial resources. The life she had led must be foreign to him.

When he came back, they would need to have a calm discussion. She wanted him to listen to her, but she would also listen more closely to what he was saying. Perhaps they could find common ground for understanding each other.

Mrs. Childress returned with a tray. "I brought you a pot of tea too. It should perk you right up."

Mary stood and cleaned off a place on the bedside table. "Thank you. I know I'll enjoy it."

After the doctor's wife left, Mary tasted the chicken and dumplings. *Delicious.* She had made the dish many times, but hers never tasted as good as Mrs. Shelton's. She finished eating, then poured a cup of the steamy beverage. She added a little sugar and milk, then leaned back in the chair and sipped, letting the warmth infuse her. At home, she didn't often take the time to steep a pot of tea. But she really enjoyed this.

Taking time to relax didn't erase the hurtful memory of her last conversation with Daniel.

Where is he, anyway?

Mary had expected him to return by now. It had to be past eight o'clock. She picked up one of the ginger cookies from the plate beside the teapot and nibbled on it. She was anxious for his return for more than one reason.

Even though she chose to stay by her father's side until he recovered, she missed seeing her sister and brothers. She knew they worried when she wasn't there. This time when she got home, she had good news to share with them. Although Pa had only made a little progress, she would stress how much better he was eating and how some color had returned to his cheeks. Everyone needed hope.

Mrs. Childress returned to pick up the tray. "I thought you were going home this evening for awhile."

"I am." Mary put the empty cup back on the saucer. "As soon as Daniel returns."

"It's getting a little late, isn't it?" Concern outlined the woman's features. "Perhaps he's not coming."

"I'm sure he's just gotten delayed by something important." Mary clasped her hands so the doctor's wife wouldn't notice them trembling. "He'll be here soon. He's a man of his word."

"All right." Mrs. Childress headed toward the doorway. "I won't bother you again."

Mary crumpled into the chair, limp as a wet dishrag. *Where is he?*

She had hidden her feelings while the doctor's wife was in the room, but now her doubts returned full force. Did her anger drive him away? What would she do if it had? Dropping her face into her hands, she let the tears flow. But still she refused to believe that Daniel wasn't coming back.

As evening slipped into the wee hours of the night, her belief faltered. *How could he do this to me?* She didn't want to go to sleep, but she couldn't fight off its tentacles.

She awakened when the morning sun peeked over the windowsill with a strong ray bathing her face with both heat and light. Sitting scrunched down in the chair, she felt like a knotted clothes line left to dry in the sun. Every muscle screamed to be released, and her neck ached.

After unfolding from her uncomfortable position, Mary finally stood and walked on shaky legs to stare out the window at the new morning. *He. Didn't. Come.* The enormity of his absence almost knocked her to her knees.

He had to be here soon. Anything else was unimaginable.

CHAPTER 14

"Good morning, dearie." Mrs. Childress's cheerful voice announced her entrance into Pa's room.

Please, please, please, don't ask me any questions. Mary didn't want to face the ones in her own mind, much less those from other people. If she had to talk about Daniel not coming to take her home, she knew she'd burst into tears. And she didn't want Pa to know what had happened. He needed to concentrate on getting well, not worry about her and Daniel.

"Did you sleep well?" The doctor's wife set a tray on the table near the bed.

Mary forced a smile to her face before she looked at the woman. "Yes, after I finally fell asleep."

"And just look at your father. He's awake too." Mrs. Childress clasped her hands and smiled down at her patient.

Mary whipped her attention toward him. His eyes *were* open, and he looked more alert than he had yesterday. She rushed to the bed and dropped into the chair beside him.

"Good morning, Pa." She brushed her lips across his forehead, noticing the coolness of his skin. Not a hint of an infection. Dr. Childress would be as pleased as she was.

"I love you, Mary." Her father's gaze remained on her eyes.

The words sounded foreign coming from him. Yet they fed a hunger deep inside her. She could almost taste the sweetness they conveyed.

"Of course, you do." Mary pushed his dark hair back from his face. He needed a haircut. She wondered how long it would be before he could go home. When he did, she would need to cut his hair right away. "And I love you too."

Relief lifted the ends of his mouth into a smile. Did he still think she hadn't forgiven him for the way he'd withdrawn from them after Ma was gone? How could she settle his mind about that?

"Well, now." Mrs. Childress came close to the bed as well. "I do believe the two of you are ready for breakfast. Kenneth, would you like to sit in the chair again?"

"Yes. Must get strong enough to go home." He tried to shift by himself then fell back against the pillow, releasing a deep breath that sounded like an angry sigh.

"Be careful." The doctor's wife slid her arm under his shoulders and helped him sit up in bed. "You still need a bit of help, but your strength will come back quicker when you start eating more."

Sharing breakfast with her father took away some of the sting of Daniel's abandonment. During lulls in their conversation, fragments of the argument they had yesterday rebuked her. She needed some way to put things right between them. But how could she do that if he didn't even come see her?

While she ate her oatmeal, she also helped her father with his. Mrs. Childress bustled about straightening the room.

"When Clyde returns, we'll get your father cleaned up and back in bed." She fluffed the pillow and gave the crisp white sheet another tug.

A gentle knock on the door drew Mary's gaze toward the opening.

Mrs. Horton stood there, peeking inside. "Is this a good time?"

"Come on in. Pa's getting better now." Mary wondered what the pastor's wife wanted. Maybe she was just making a sick call on her father.

"I'm going out to your place this morning to help with the house. I thought you might like to ride along."

"That's such a wonderful idea." Mrs. Childress practically gushed. "Clyde has gone out to the Simmons farm. He'll be there for a few hours. It's Mary Lee's time, but she usually doesn't take very long. He can stop and pick you up on his way back into town."

"But he won't know that I need him to stop." Mary couldn't keep exasperation from her tone.

Mrs. Horton came over beside her. "I saw the doctor before he left, and he was the one who suggested I give you a ride. He told me he would bring you back, so I could stay and help your sister the rest of the day."

This sounded as if they conspired to set it up, but Mary didn't care. She did want a chance to clean up, but what if Daniel came by the clinic this morning? Well, he wouldn't find her waiting for him like some lap dog. He should have been here last night as he said he would.

"I'd like that...a lot." Mary turned back to her father. "Do you mind if I go?"

He lifted his hand to clasp hers. "You go ahead. I have a good nurse." He nodded toward Mrs. Childress. "Tell the kids I love them."

In two shakes of a lamb's tail, Mary found herself riding in the Horton's buggy. After a few polite but meaningless comments, they lapsed into silence. She was thankful the pastor's wife wasn't a chatterer. Since Mary didn't get much sleep last night, all she wanted to do was rest, except she couldn't keep Daniel from invading her thoughts. Some of her memories were happy, but that awful argument kept pushing itself to the forefront. She fought to hold back her tears.

"I know you're tired." Mrs. Horton kept a firm grip on the reins. "After you bathe and spend a little time with your sister and brothers, you can take a nap. I know how exhausting it is to sit with an ailing parent."

Mary didn't know much about the woman's history, but from the sincerity in that last statement, she felt that perhaps Mrs. Horton had spent time sitting with one of her own parents. Feeling good to be with someone who could understand what she was going through, Mary relaxed.

"I appreciate how you and the other women at the church are helping us." A lump formed in her throat, cutting off the other words she wanted to say.

"That's what the good Lord told us to do." Mrs. Horton flicked the reins. "Help each other. I'm sure you do your share for others. I've heard wonderful things about you, Mary."

The words fell on her parched spirit like a welcome spring rain. It had been so long since anyone had complimented her...besides Daniel. And now she wondered if any of the things he'd said had truly been the way he felt about her. Why did her thoughts always come back to that exasperating man? *Because I love him.* Whether he loved her or not.

When they reached the edge of the farm, eagerness to see her siblings made Mary's heartbeat accelerate. Her being home for awhile today would be good for all of them. The other three wouldn't want her to leave, or they would probably beg to go to the clinic to see their father. Neither option was possible right now. Their energy and neediness would tire Pa.

As they approached the lane, Mary spied Bobby walking from the barn back toward the house, carrying a pail. Milk sloshed over the side, and Mary wondered if her youngest brother had been milking the cow. She didn't remember his knowing how. He always took care of the chickens instead.

"Be careful. You spill some." Standing in the open doorway to the barn, Tony Chan called after him. Perhaps the young Chinese man had done the milking.

Mrs. Horton stopped the buggy beside the gate to the yard that surrounded the farmhouse.

Tony hurried toward them. "I take care of horse and buggy." He reached toward the harness, talking to the animal as he ran his hand down the side of the horse's head. "I brush him and put him in stall."

"Thank you, Tony." The pastor's wife tied the reins to the rail on the front of the buggy, then climbed down, followed by Mary.

"Mary!" George burst through the door, slamming it against the front wall with a bang. "Hey, Francie! Mary's home." After bounding down the steps, he slowed to a quick walk and opened the gate. "Are you going to stay?"

Mary smiled at her brother's enthusiasm. "I'll be here for a while, but then I must go back to stay with Pa." She ruffled his hair, and he leaned his head away from her. Was he growing up so much that he no longer wanted anyone to bother his hair?

As soon as Mrs. Horton and Mary were through the gate, he closed it and ran toward Bobby, who stood like a statue in the middle of the lane, still holding the milk bucket. "I'll carry this for you." He took it from his little brother and headed toward the back door.

Frances met them in the hallway, wiping her hands on the apron that swathed her. "I'm glad you're finally home, Mary. I worried when you didn't come yesterday."

Mary swallowed before answering, hoping to dislodge the tension in her throat. "Something unexpected came up." She hoped no one noticed that her voice wobbled a bit. And she hoped no one would ask what came up. She wouldn't have an acceptable answer.

She pushed her way past her sister and hurried to the room

they shared. As usual, Frances had left her clothing scattered around—some on the floor, the chair, and even piled haphazardly on Mary's bed. She felt like grabbing the garments in her way and throwing them to the floor beside the others. Anger swelled within her, but she knew it wasn't really aimed at her sister. The object of this emotion hadn't even bothered to seek her out late yesterday or today. She growled deep in her throat and dropped onto the empty end of her bed.

"Mary?" Mrs. Horton's kind voice called from beyond the door.

She had shut it hoping to keep anyone else from seeing her break down. Wiping her eyes, she took a deep breath before opening the door. "Yes."

"I am getting the tub ready in the bedroom downstairs so you can have a bath."

"All right."

When Mary came down to the bedroom, she found that Frances had already filled the galvanized tub with water from the well. Mrs. Horton came in carrying hot water from the reservoir in the stove. She poured it in, stirred the water, then tested it to make sure it was the perfect temperature. Then she stood and removed a cake of Cashmere Bouquet soap from her pocket, still in its paper wrapper. "I thought you might enjoy using this." She handed it to Mary.

Tears streamed down her face. "Thank you."

Impulsively, she hugged Mrs. Horton. The other woman's arms closed around Mary, cradling her. All she could think about was how much her arms felt like Ma's had when she held Mary as a child. How she missed those times.

After the older woman left, Mary plunged into the water and soaked away some of her weariness. She even washed her hair, though it would take a while to dry. When she emerged clean and smelling so nice, she felt renewed.

She dressed and went into the kitchen where Frances and

Mrs. Horton were cooking a pot of stew. The enticing aroma of cornbread brought a growl from Mary's stomach.

Mrs. Horton turned around. "Mary, you look lovely with your hair down like that. I love the curls." She reached up and caressed a few. "And the color is wonderful, like a flaming sunset."

Tony Chan came through the back door with a load in his arms. "I brought more wood for stove."

When he finished, Mary followed him out the back door. "How are things going, Tony?"

"Good." He nodded. "I help boys with chores, then work in field like Mr. Daniel tell me."

"Right." She knew she would hate herself for asking, but she couldn't hold back the next question. "Did you see Daniel this morning?"

Tony frowned. "Yes, Mr. Daniel go away to help uncle on farm."

Why would Daniel go somewhere without telling her? "Did he say how long he'll be gone?"

"No." Tony glanced at her face, then away. "He did not."

Stunned, she stared at him as he walked away from her. That's what Daniel did too, walk away from her. She couldn't stop the tears streaming down her cheeks as she clenched her fists in anger.

CHAPTER 15

*M*ary dragged herself up onto the front porch and dropped into the swing, Tony Chan's words ringing in her head. Surely, their quarrel wasn't enough to send Daniel away indefinitely. *But what if that's why he left?* She felt as if a giant hand had grabbed her heart and squeezed, draining the life out of it, one drop of blood at a time. *Rejected...abandoned...unworthy.* Familiar words she didn't want to face fought for the dominance she couldn't allow.

How could he do this to her? Did he have any idea how she felt? Probably not, or he wouldn't have shouted those words at her, words that sliced through her, leaving her decimated. He didn't come back to the clinic when he said he would. Now he was gone for who knew how long.

Would she have to face the problems in her family without his strength supporting her? Panic rose up inside her like a river flooding out of its banks. She needed a man she could depend on, not someone who would turn and run at the first sign of trouble. Everyone had hard days, and yesterday was a major one for her. Didn't Daniel realize she was under a lot of strain? What kind of man left the woman he professed to love in such circumstances? Not the man she needed in her life.

For now, she'd concentrate on taking care of her family. They were all that mattered.

Too bad her heart didn't understand this truth the way her head did.

Wishing she'd remembered to stuff a hanky inside her cuff, she used her sleeve to wipe the moisture from her cheeks and eyes. Crying would get her nowhere. Taking a deep breath, she arose and turned her face toward the sunlight, hoping the warmth would bathe away the chill that had invaded her bones.

"I don't know how I'll get it all done, but I have no one to depend on except myself." Saying the words out loud didn't bring the strength she'd hoped for, but she wouldn't let go of her determination.

If she could only keep her chin from wobbling.

"Whoa!" The voice of Dr. Childress penetrated her thoughts even though the sound of his horse and buggy approaching had not.

Mary hoped her face wasn't all blotchy and red. But if it was, maybe the kind doctor would think her tears were for her father. She hoped against hope that he hadn't overheard her argument with Daniel.

"Are you ready to go back to the clinic?" Dr. Childress laid the reins over the horses and headed up the porch steps.

She cleared her throat. "Yes, sir. Just let me go hug my sister and brothers before I leave."

"I'll go in and see if Mrs. Horton needs me to send anyone or anything out from town." The doctor hurried to open the screen door for her.

George charged through the doorway from the kitchen and stopped short right in front of them. "Oh no, Dr. Childress is here," he called back over his shoulder, then stared straight at the man. "Is Pa all right?"

"I believe your sister saw him after I did." The doctor glanced at Mary expectantly.

She forced a smile. "He was sitting up in a chair when I left. We had just finished sharing breakfast."

"Does that mean he's better?" George wasn't going to let the subject drop.

Dr. Childress intervened. "That does mean he's better, but he's not ready to come home yet. Maybe soon."

Mary knew that Pa wasn't anywhere near ready to come home, but she kept her thoughts to herself.

"So are you here to take Mary back?" George clutched his arms over his chest just the way Pa often did. In the last month, he looked as if he had gotten much more mature, especially for a boy barely ten years old.

"That's right." She put her arm around his shoulders and went into the kitchen with him. There she announced to her other two siblings, "Dr. Childress will be taking me back to town now."

Both Francie and Bobby came close enough for her to hug. She clutched them to her chest and had a hard time letting go.

When the good-byes were finished, she went out and climbed into the buggy while Dr. Childress finished jotting down a list for Mrs. Horton. Mary wasn't ready to leave her siblings, and she wasn't ready to once again see her father languish in the bed at the clinic. Why had her life taken this turn when everything had been looking rosy? Didn't God know that she couldn't take much more?... Or did He even care?

The buggy dipped to the side with a loud squeak when Dr. Childress climbed aboard. "Ready, Mary?"

"Yes, sir." She hoped he couldn't hear the note of panic in her tone.

"Everything's going to be all right." He clicked his tongue to the horses and drove the buggy in a tight circle to turn back up the lane. "It really is."

When she didn't comment on his observation, he glanced at her. She caught the movement out of the corner of her eye, but she didn't give any indication that she had. She didn't feel like talking to anyone right now, even a kind man like Dr. Childress.

After they reached the road, he set the horse at a fast clip, and they soon arrived in town without exchanging another word.

Mary wondered what she would find when she went back in to see Pa. Would he still be sitting up? She hoped he hadn't gotten too tired, that all the movement hadn't set him back in his recovery.

"You've been very quiet." Dr. Childress stopped the buggy near the back door to the clinic. "Do we need to talk about things? I know you are facing really tough times."

The kindness in his tone touched her heart, but she didn't want to put any of her troubles into actual words. Speaking them would make everything even worse. Keeping her eyes trained on her hands clasped in her lap, she shook her head.

"All right. But Mary, I'm here if you change your mind."

Before he could climb down from the buggy and turn to help her, Mary jumped to the ground and hurried through the back door. The sound of laughing voices drew her like a magnet. When she approached her father's room, they grew louder.

She stepped through the open doorway and had a hard time believing her eyes. Pa sat forward in the chair with Mrs. Childress hovering near. Neither of them noticed her because of their shared merriment.

"What's so funny?" She had to raise her voice to cut through the other sounds.

Pa turned toward her with a twinkle in his eyes. "Did you enjoy your time at home? How are the kids?"

Could this possibly be the man who only a couple of days ago couldn't even sit up in bed without help? What in the world had happened?

The doctor's wife smiled at her. "We're so glad you're back."

Loud enough that everyone in the room could hear them, hunger pangs growled in Mary's stomach.

"Oh dear, do you need something to eat?" Mrs. Childress came toward her. "I'll go fix you a sandwich. Mrs. Newton brought a nice ham and some fresh-baked bread just a little while ago." She gave Mary a quick hug before exiting.

Mary stared after the woman, then turned back toward her father, who was waiting expectantly. "The kids are worried about you. They really want to come to town to see you."

A twinge of pain flitted across his face. "I don't want them to see me here." He changed the subject. "You look refreshed."

"Yes, I enjoyed a bath and a nap at home." Mary frowned when she remembered what else happened while she was there.

"What's brought that troubled expression to your face, Mary?" He stared intently at her.

She turned toward the open window. "Nothing, really." At least nothing she wanted to share with her father...yet. She was having a hard enough time understanding what had happened, and she wasn't ready to delve into the situation with him. The story might upset him and slow his recovery.

"What was going on when we got here?" Maybe her question would get his attention off her and her problems.

He cleared his throat. "I don't want to stay here one minute longer than I have to, so I'm trying to gain strength. I've had one of those sandwiches and some applesauce. And I'm going to eat every bite they bring me for supper."

Holding the arms of the chair, he pushed himself farther back, then relaxed. "While I ate, Winifred and I shared tales of our childhoods. Some of them were very funny. I do believe the

Scripture that says laughter is good medicine. I feel much better now...stronger."

Mary couldn't remember him talking about Scriptures. Maybe he did when Ma was alive, but not since.

"What's this I hear about my patient being so much better?" Dr. Childress accompanied his wife as she brought Mary's food.

Mrs. Childress settled Mary in a chair and joined her husband as he examined her father.

Pa spoke up. "Doc, I want to go home."

Mary recognized that tone. It was the one he used when he didn't want any backtalk or sass from them. His this-is-final tone.

"I know you do, but we don't want to rush it. I'm not sure you're strong enough." The doctor opened his bag and took out his stethoscope. After listening to Pa's chest and back, he put his instrument away. "You are better, but it's too soon, Kenneth."

Pa got that stubborn look on his face Mary had seen often enough. "I don't agree. If you'll get me some crutches, I can go right away."

"I don't recommend it." The deep frown that covered the doctor's face concerned Mary. And she agreed with him. What in the world made her father think he was ready to go? He hadn't even taken a step without someone helping him. How could she manage him and the whole household?

The doctor rubbed his forehead as if he were thinking hard. "We almost lost you, Kenneth, and you nearly lost your leg. The wound was all the way to the bone. It was hard for me to close up. If you should fall and break it open again, there probably wouldn't be anything I could do to help you."

"Mary." Pa looked straight at her when she started to take another bite. "Is that Chan boy still helping at the farm?"

She laid the half-eaten sandwich down on the plate. "Yes, Pa. He works really hard, getting a lot done every day."

Her father stared at the doctor. "He can help take care of me when it's too much for Mary. I want to go home."

Dr. Childress crossed his arms over his chest and continued to frown. "Not a good idea."

Pa gritted his teeth and gave an angry glare at the doctor. "Are you holding me a prisoner here?" The words sounded harsh and unforgiving.

Mary couldn't believe he said that after all the ways Dr. Childress had helped him. She expected the man to get angry at Pa's question.

"Now, Kenneth, you know I can't force you to stay." His voice held more authority than Mary had ever heard in it. "I'm just saying I don't think it's best for you to go yet. You've had a rough time of it. You need to build more strength before you leave."

Pa grasped the arms of the chair again and pulled himself forward to perch on the front of the cushion. "I'm saying that I want to go home tomorrow. Can you make that happen?"

The doctor rubbed his chin as if he were thinking about it. Mary hoped he wouldn't agree. How would she be able to take care of Pa and the other children? If Pa went home probably the women at the church would stop helping them, and she couldn't face the added work alone.

Everything was piling up on her shoulders, more than before. She was still hungry, but she didn't think she could force another bite down her throat.

"All right." Dr. Childress didn't look happy. "I can't keep you here against your wishes. We'll have crutches tomorrow. And I'll see if I can rustle up one of those invalid chairs with wheels on it."

Tomorrow?

How was Mary ever going to face tomorrow?

CHAPTER 16

*T*rying to ignore the squalling baby inside the passenger compartment, Daniel stared out the window of the train. He had never run away from anything in his life, but this felt like running away. He'd gotten used to things coming easy to him. Right now nothing looked easy. And he was afraid the answers he sought would be hard to accept. Had he been too hasty when he decided to leave town? With the way all his plans were falling apart, he didn't want to think about what was going to happen next.

But on the whole trip, that's all he did...think. About Mary. About how he wanted to give her so much...make her life easier. About how much help her family needed now. About the house he'd impetuously purchased. He'd even ordered a catalogue from a company in Seattle. After making inquiries about the best furniture for sale on the western coast of the United States, someone told him about Stanton Fine Furniture. Old Mr. Stanton had made a fortune in the logging business. When he sold that, he started manufacturing sturdy, but beautifully wrought, furniture. Just the kind Daniel wanted in the home he expected to share with Mary. If there ever was a new home for them to share as husband and wife.

How could she jettison his plans as if they were just so much garbage? Didn't she know that a woman should respect the man she planned to marry? Her words yesterday didn't carry one iota of respect for him as a man...or as a future husband. His reflection in the smoky glass frowned back at him. He stared at the anger in his own eyes and clenched his teeth until his jaw ached.

Did he love Mary? Of course, he did. Why else would he ask her father if they could court? A man wouldn't go through all that without having a goal in mind. And his goal was marriage, with him as head of the household consisting of just Mary and him... until they started having children of their own.

He hadn't planned to take on the burden of her siblings and ailing father, but he'd been willing to compromise by bringing them into the home he would prepare for the two of them. His whole future hung in the balance. Daniel had a lot to mull over while he was at his uncle's sheep ranch in southern Washington Territory. He had to make important decisions that would affect all of them—including Mary, her siblings, and her father.

Could he just throw away his job at the store and dreams of living in town and move out to the Murray farm with her? *Why should I have to do that?* With Mary, he felt as if his hands were tied—it was either her way or no way at all. Could he live with that? He shook his head. Could he live without her? That was the final question. The thought of losing her dismayed him even more.

The mournful sound of the train whistle pierced the foggy air as the clacking of the wheels began to slow. This stop was where he would leave the train.

A half hour later, Daniel had stored his luggage at the station and retrieved his horse from the train. Then he mounted Sultan for the long ride to Uncle Clarence's sheep ranch, glad to be in the wide open spaces where his head could clear. Hopefully, so would his thoughts. He didn't want to tire Sultan too much, but the horse urged a good run after being penned in for so long on a moving train. After giving him his head for a while, Daniel reined him in to a gentle lope.

He spent the next thirty minutes allowing the breeze from across the rolling fields to cool him and take his mind off his troubles. Sheep huddled in flocks or dotted in twos or threes across the green grass looking much like the lumpy clouds moving across the sky. He tried to lose himself in the natural beauty, but niggling at the back of his mind were the angry words he and Mary exchanged before he left. Accompanying the words was the feeling that he had somehow let her down, even if she had also shot down all his plans. What could he do to restore the good relationship they had enjoyed?

A more pressing question was, did he really want to? Or should he just cut his losses and move on? When that last thought entered his head, pain slashed across his heart. What was he going to do?

"Hey, Daniel!" His ten-year-old cousin's words awakened him to his surroundings. He had arrived at the gate to the Winthrop Sheep Ranch.

He pulled on the reins. "Whoa, Sultan." Turning his horse's head, he went through the opening where Jerry held the gate for him.

"What are you doing here?" Jerry's blue eyes twinkled from behind the mass of freckles draped across his nose. "Nobody told me you were coming. Did you ride your horse all the way?"

Daniel couldn't keep from laughing at that. "It's much too far for that."

The tow-haired boy ducked his head. "Thought so, but where'd you get him? He's a beauty."

Daniel dismounted and walked beside the boy as they

headed toward the house and outbuildings. "I brought him with me on the train."

A frown wrinkled Jerry's brows. "I ain't never rode a train, but your horse has? How'd you get him to sit still that long, and didn't he make a mess?"

The laugh that burst forth from Daniel felt good. "They had a stall for him in the baggage car. I rode in the passenger car."

"Someday, I'm gonna ride a train." The boy dragged the toe of his shoe in the gravel paving the drive. "When I'm old as you."

His cousin lifted his spirits and took his mind off his problems for a little while.

Jerry eyed the animal that towered over him. "What's his name?"

"Sultan." Daniel stopped and studied the boy's earnest expression. "Want to ride him?"

"Can I?" Disbelief and longing colored the youngster's tone. "Really?"

"He's too tall for you to mount without help." Daniel looped the reins around his upper arm and clasped his hands to make a foothold for the boy.

Jerry placed one foot in his hands and jumped. Daniel kept his momentum going until he was in the saddle that was much too large for him. After shortening the stirrups, Daniel once again grasped the reins.

"I'm going to lead him. You hang on."

They made their way up the lane. Not much activity around the house, which surprised him. "Where is everyone?"

"Pa's laid up with a broken leg." Jerry kept a death grip on the pommel. "The sheep are penned, ready to be sheared tomorrow. You here to help?"

Daniel stared at the buildings created mostly from native stone. The scene was peaceful, not at all like the hustle and bustle of Portland, or even Oregon City. That's what he needed right now. Some peace in his life.

"That's why I came. When Father found out about Uncle Clarence's accident, he knew you would need help. So I caught the train." That's all Daniel was going to tell his curious cousin or anyone else around here.

His problems were his own, and he'd figure out what to do about them. In the meantime, good, hard, manual labor should take his mind off his worries.

~

*O*ver the next two weeks, time flew as Daniel threw himself into the work of shearing sheep. He fell into bed each night with aches in parts of his body he'd never used before. Hard work hardened his muscles and was good for his soul. Much of the tension he brought with him had released, and strength flowed through him like his life's blood.

Uncle Clarence had used a wheeled chair when Daniel arrived, but he'd moved on to crutches soon enough. He had welcomed Daniel's help with the shearing, showing him how to direct the crew, and he seemed delighted when Daniel worked as hard as the other men.

His time at the ranch gave Daniel a better understanding of this end of the family business. It took thousands of the animals to produce all the fleeces needed to manufacture the woolen fabric and blankets they sold in the store and shipped all over the country. He was thankful his thoughts were concentrated on the business during the daytime. And he enjoyed family time around the table at suppertime.

But when no one was with him in the long night hours, he could not keep his mind from dredging up memories of Mary and the reason he'd left home so hastily. All she'd meant to him. Their quarrel. The information Dr. Childress gave him about Mr. Murray's chance of a full recovery. But most of all, Mary's sweet face surrounded by all those red curls.

This morning, he stared into the mirror above the washstand while he shaved. Even his face looked different. Not just the tan he'd earned through hard work or his longer hair, but he noticed subtle changes such as tiny lines fanning out from his eyes. He was too young to be wrinkled. But nevertheless, there they were.

With a final swipe of his jaws with the thick Turkish towel, he removed every trace of the shaving soap. He thrust his arms through the sleeves of his clean shirt and quickly buttoned it before stuffing the tail inside the waistband of his trousers. Daniel wanted to look his best when he approached his uncle about what else he could do to help on the ranch. He planned to do that as soon as breakfast was over.

When he arrived in the kitchen, the whole family was already seated at the table. Uncle Clarence teased him, "Did you oversleep, Daniel?"

He felt every eye trained on him. "I was restless during the night."

After pulling out his usual chair, he took his seat.

"You mean I'm not working you hard enough to help you sleep?" A chuckle followed his uncle's observation. "We'll have to remedy that."

Knowing he wasn't deriding him, Daniel laughed too. "I'm here to help you as long as you need me."

His uncle nodded. "I know. When we finish eating, we'll have a chat in my office."

Conversation ebbed and flowed around the table while Daniel dove into the food on the plate his aunt set in front of him. Good country cooking. Crisp bacon, a mound of scrambled eggs, and fluffy biscuits drizzled with melted butter and honey. He wondered how he had kept from gaining weight, but his trousers were slightly looser than when he arrived.

Within half an hour, Daniel followed his uncle down the hallway. While Uncle Clarence maneuvered into the chair behind his desk, Daniel dropped into the seat facing him. "What's on the agenda for today?" He leaned forward with his forearms on his thighs. "I mean, now that we're finished with the shearing."

Uncle Clarence settled into the padded chair and clasped his hands on the desk. "That's not why I want to talk to you."

Daniel wasn't sure he liked the sound of this. Had he done something he shouldn't have? If so, he had no idea what it was, even as he ran through the events of the last two weeks. He couldn't keep the puzzlement from his face.

"Now don't start worrying about it." His uncle studied his face as if reading a book. "I think you have something you need to talk to me about. I just wanted you to know that I'm here for you. Sometimes we old guys have learned things through our mistakes that could help you youngsters."

Daniel didn't know what to do. Should he tell his uncle about his dilemma? Uncle Clarence didn't know any of the people involved, and maybe he could help Daniel see things more clearly.

"I could tell you were running from something when you came up here so precipitously."

The man had hit the nail with a sledgehammer. And here Daniel had thought his uncle had accepted his presence at face value.

"Would you allow me to pray with you?" His uncle's voice contained kindness, not censure.

"Fine with me." Daniel tried to give the impression that he didn't care either way, but somehow he understood that Uncle Clarence saw through his façade.

When his uncle bowed his head and closed his eyes, Daniel also lowered his chin, but he peeked under his brows at the man sitting across the desk. Although his uncle had a plaster cast on his leg and could only get around using crutches or the wheeled chair, strength surrounded him. Not a physical strength. More like spiritual as the words poured from his lips. His prayer brought the presence of God right inside that room.

Daniel closed his eyes and really listened to the words. He almost felt as if he were on the outside looking in on a very private conversation. The type he never had experienced before. The words didn't really matter, just the Presence.

When Uncle Clarence said *Amen*, Daniel gradually opened his eyes and looked straight into those of his uncle. Finally, he realized that his cheeks were wet with tears he hadn't even felt. He pulled his handkerchief from his back pocket and swiped them away. Uncle Clarence leaned back in his chair but still didn't say a word.

Daniel had to speak to fill the silence. "If I were to talk to you, it would just be between the two of us, wouldn't it?"

"Yes." His uncle's nod was emphatic. "I don't have loose lips."

For the first time in his life, Daniel finally understood that saying. "I need someone who can help me see the way through a situation."

Uncle Clarence just sat...waiting for him to continue.

He stood and paced across the office to stare out the windows at the paddock full of shorn sheep. They frolicked as if they had been relieved of the burden of the heavy wool. He wished it would be as easy to lift the burden from his heart.

"I thought I had found the woman I would marry."

Daniel waited for his uncle to comment on that statement, but not a word came. He pivoted toward the man. "She's beautiful...and sweet...and everything I want in a wife. I think you'd like her."

"So why does she have you tied up in knots?" His uncle picked up a pencil and started tapping it on the blotter on top of his desk. "If she's so ideal."

Daniel stuffed his hands into the front pocket of his trousers. "There are lots of complications."

"Such as?" Uncle Clarence quirked his brow. "Maybe you should just start at the beginning and tell me all of it."

Daniel dropped back into the chair and haltingly started talking about Mary. How long he'd known her. How hard she'd always had to work. How he wanted to make her life easier than what it had been. How he'd bought the house and wanted to hire servants so she wouldn't have to work so much.

"Does she know this?"

"Not all of it. I didn't tell her about the house at first, but I even asked her father if we could court. He said we had to wait a year before we marry. She's not quite eighteen, but she will soon be."

"Didn't she agree?" Uncle Clarence sounded confused.

"Oh, um...everything was going along just fine until her father had a terrible accident. We found him when we came back from spending the day in Portland." He stopped, in his mind reliving Mr. Murray lying in the dirt with a pool of blood around him. The horror it brought into Mary's life...and his. "Life became difficult after that."

He enumerated each of the ensuing events, ending with their fierce quarrel and the information the doctor had given him that day before he went home and found out that Uncle Clarence needed his help as well.

"Sounds as if she was under a lot of strain."

"Of course she was." His defensive words exploded between them.

"I still don't see the problem. Everyone has a bad day, which is probably what that was for her. Then you didn't go back and make things right. Instead, you ran away."

Coming from someone else's mouth, the words painted an ugly picture. Daniel didn't feel as justified as he had when it all took place. Not wanting to say anything else, he nodded.

"The way I see it, there are several things going on, and maybe we should deal with each of them separately." His uncle steepled his fingertips as he leaned his elbows on the desk. "First, you wanted to be her savior."

Daniel opened his mouth to object.

Uncle Clarence held up his hand. "Don't say anything until I get finished with what I'm trying to say. *You* wanted to be the one who made everything better for her. But she already has a Savior. You can't take His place, no matter how hard you try."

Unfortunately, his words made sense. Daniel had been trying to make everything better for her. "But I thought she wanted the same future I did."

"Why did you decide that? Did you even ask her?"

"I asked her if I could court her." He didn't like the tone that emerged from his own lips. As if he needed to justify what he did.

"Not the same thing." Uncle Clarence shook his head. "From what you said about your quarrel, you ran roughshod over her feelings without really listening to her."

"I listened. I just didn't agree with her." Daniel stopped, realizing how harsh that sounded. He decided to take another tack. "I thought the man is supposed to be the head of the household. That's what the Bible tells us, doesn't it?"

"Taken out of context, it does." His uncle picked up the pencil again and started doodling without looking at the pad of paper in front of him. "But we can't pick and choose what parts of the Bible to believe. You have to take it as a whole to get the correct interpretation."

Confused, Daniel stared out the window without noticing anything. "I'm not sure what you mean."

"Other Scriptures give us a different slant on the same idea. Jesus said He came to serve, not to rule, and He told us to do the same thing. Serve others. Whoever would be first shall be last and all that. A good marriage isn't made by a man forcing his ideas on a woman. He has to try to understand her and serve her to show his true love for her." The pencil dropped from Uncle Clarence's hand, and he leaned back in his chair. "Maybe he makes the final decision, but never without asking her opinion and really considering what she says. I always ask your aunt. Then I go before the Lord and spread it all out between us, asking Him to give me wisdom. You treat a woman with this kind of respect, and you'll have a firm foundation for your marriage. Without understanding, you won't ever have a good one."

His uncle was preaching him a sermon but every word pierced Daniel's heart. He dropped back into the chair and clasped his hands. "But what if I can't handle it? Taking care of her father...raising the children...keeping the farm going. It's just too much. And there's another thing that keeps running through my mind.

"Gary Bowen grew up with me. He got married when he was eighteen. Soon after the wedding, a fire destroyed his in-law's farmhouse and burned her father badly. Evidently, her mother had a hard time recovering from all the losses. So Gary and Debra had her parents move into the house with them, and Debra took care of her father while he recovered.

"But his recovery took a long time, and he never returned to full strength. He hated all the scars and wouldn't go around other people. Gary felt as if he had lost his wife... and the life they planned together."

He stood and once again rubbed his brow. "Within a few months, everything fell apart in their lives. They were always quarreling. Gary started drinking and lost his job in the mill. Things have gone from bad to worse."

Turning again, he studied the pattern in the carpet. "I don't want anything like that to happen to Mary and me."

Uncle Clarence shifted and his leather chair squeaked.

"Daniel, you're dealing with fear, and we know where fear comes from, don't we?"

He scratched his head. "Yes, I memorized that verse. 'For God hath not given us a spirit of fear; but of power, and of love, and of a sound mind.'"

"So where is this fear coming from?" A smile accompanied Uncle Clarence's question, taking away the sting.

"If it's not from the Lord, it has to be from our enemy, Satan." Daniel's word carried the authority of the Bible with them.

Uncle Clarence stood and reached for his crutches. "You control what happens in your own life. If you choose to live for Christ, you'll have the strength to deal with anything that comes your way. Think about it." He headed toward the door. "You've worked really hard for two weeks. If you want to take it easy today, I'll understand."

Daniel followed him into the hallway. "Don't you need my help anymore?"

"Since the shearing is finished, we'll do just fine if you want to go home." He clumped down the hall a ways, stopped, and turned back. "Not that I'm telling you to go. You're welcome here as long as you want to stay." Then he continued the way he was headed, leaving Daniel alone.

Daniel went to his room. He bowed his head and started talking to the Lord the same way Uncle Clarence had done in the office. When he finished, he picked up his well-worn Bible and flipped it open to where he had been reading. One section jumped out at him.

But so shall it not be among you: but whosoever will be great among you, shall be your minister: And whosoever of you will be the chiefest, shall be servant of all. For even the Son of man came not to be ministered unto, but to minister, and to give his life a ransom for many.

These verses from Mark 10 seemed like an answer from God to him. He was going home, and if Mary couldn't forgive him, he'd become her servant to prove that he was a changed man.

Still, a part of him wondered if he could do it all. Care for a farm, look after children, and help nurse a man who was desperately ill. Did he really love Mary that much?

Only time would tell.

CHAPTER 17

*A*lmost three weeks since Daniel left, and Mary felt as if it were an eternity. Every problem in her life had expanded to enormous proportions. Of course, Pa wouldn't listen to anything she told him. In addition to taking care of the house, laundry, cooking, and watching out for her siblings, she had to try to take care of him. And that wasn't an easy thing to do.

He was back to being a bear of a man, emerging from hibernation, roaring on his way to find something to devour. He was determined not to use the invalid chair the doctor brought for him. So it sat in the living room like a statue made of rattan and metal with wheels. A couple of times, she had to rescue it from her brothers, who thought it was a new toy to ride. She didn't think her family could afford to replace the thing if they broke it. Of course, she didn't really know the details of their finances, since Pa kept all that information to himself. She was good enough to do all the work but not to know something so important.

The time of day she enjoyed the most was early morning when no one else stirred. After twisting her hair into a lumpy bun, anchoring it tightly to the back of her head with hairpins, and covering it with a cotton scarf tied behind her neck, she headed toward the porch swing to watch the colorful sunrise. Those few minutes would bring the only peace she'd see all day.

Today her respite was short-lived. The irregular thumping pattern announced Pa's approach long before he opened the screen door.

"What're you doing out here, Mary?" Already his voice displayed his bad mood, and his scowl could curdle milk.

"Trying to enjoy the early morning before I have to go to work." She hopped up in case he lost his balance when he stepped over the high threshold.

He squinted so tight his bushy eyebrows met over the bridge of his nose. They formed that old familiar wooly caterpillar that used to make her laugh. Not today.

"Are you ready for breakfast?" She grabbed the door, so the spring wouldn't slam it shut against him and his crutches. "I'll go start it."

He maneuvered toward the edge of the porch above the steps. "No hurry. I'll just be out in the barn, milking the cow."

"Tony Chan will do that when he gets..." Her voice evaporated from the heat of his glare.

"That Chinaman won't need to come out here once I'm able to take care of the farm by myself." He cleared his throat but sounded as if he were choking.

Mary knew her father wouldn't be able to do all the work on the farm for a long time... if ever. And he wouldn't welcome her commenting on that fact. The beginnings of a headache started pulsing behind her eyes. Today was going to be another trial to bear.

After watching his painful journey across the yard and down the lane to the barn door, she reentered the house. Maybe she could take out her frustration whipping up a batch of biscuits. She'd have to remind herself not to handle the dough long enough to keep the finished product from being light and fluffy. She could apply the rest of her annoyance to the scrambled eggs. Extra beating only helped their texture. She blew a breath to move an errant curl from her eyes and set to work.

When she kept busy, she could keep herself from thinking or feeling anything. But today she couldn't keep her thoughts from wandering back to Daniel Winthrop, the man who captured her heart, then trampled it in the dust.

They had shared good times—very good times—before everything fell apart that last day at the clinic. Even though she didn't want to dwell on the hurtful words, remembering the wonderful excitement of their courtship made today feel even more dark and dreary.

That man had been a charmer, worming his way under her defenses. She hadn't wanted to fall in love with him. *Had that been love?* Her heart had been sure it was.

He brought out delicious emotions she'd never imagined before. Why hadn't he left her alone from the beginning since he left her in the lurch at the end?

Memories of his blond, wavy hair blowing in the wind while they rode the trolley to Portland and back invaded her mind. And those hazel eyes that danced with anticipation with every new thing he shared with her. The lovely silk scarf he bought her which still held a hint of his spicy masculine scent. She'd put it in the very bottom of her dresser drawer, so she wouldn't see it or smell it. Someday, hopefully, she would be able to use the luxury item without thinking about him.

A pungent, slightly acrid scent imposed itself over the memory. *The bacon!* She grabbed a fork and quickly flipped the thick slices onto a plate, then bunched up a towel so she could grasp the hot handle of the cast iron skillet. Quickly she set it on an iron trivet beside the sink. That man just kept on making trouble for her, whether he was here or not. Tears streamed down her face. *Why can't I forget him?*

She covered the bacon with a tea towel before pouring most of the bacon grease in the partially filled can. After setting the skillet back on the stove, she poured the liquified eggs in. The accompanying sizzle raised a plume of steam. Since every remnant of spring had fled and summer had arrived, the heat hovering over the stove almost took her breath away.

The fragrance of the meal awakened her siblings. She could hear the boys quarreling as they dressed, and Frances wandered into the kitchen.

"Please put the silverware on the table." Mary kept stirring the eggs with a wooden spoon instead of looking to see if her sister complied. "As soon as I pour these into a bowl, I need to remove the biscuits from the oven. When you're finished, go to the spring house for the butter."

The sigh from Frances filled the room. "Why don't you send George?"

"Because he's not in here yet."

Why can't everyone cooperate? Mary's life would be much easier if they would.

"I thought Pa would be in here. He's not in his room." Frances dropped a fork on the floor, then picked it up and placed it on the table.

"You need to get another fork." She echoed her mother's instructions from memory. "We'll wash that one before we use it again." Mary put the skillet in the sink and opened the oven door. Heat poured out making her sweat like a horse, no matter what the old adage said. "Pa went out to milk the cow, but he should be finished by now. Of course, he can't carry the bucket of milk and walk on crutches, so someone needs to help him. I'll send George for that."

Although she'd always hated to have Ma or Pa holler at her

from another room, Mary found herself doing that very thing to her brother. He came running.

"Whatcha want?" His surly question set her teeth on edge.

She had to clamp them together to keep from unloading all her anger on him. "Please go to the barn and help Pa carry the bucket of milk to the spring house."

"Sure thing." His frown turned into a smile, and he slammed out the back door. He loved being out of the house.

"Boys." Frances sounded disgusted. "They make so much noise. Why can't he just walk out like everyone else does?"

When had her sister started minding the noise around the house? Maybe she was starting to grow up a little. Mary held her tongue instead of saying what she wanted to about Frances needing to change some things in herself.

"Mary!" George's screeching holler sliced through the morning like a sword. "Come quick! Pa's hurt again!"

Her stomach dropped like a boulder into the millpond, and the fear nearly drowned her. She rushed out the back door, heading toward the barn, wiping her hands on her apron as she went.

Then anger took over. *Why won't Pa listen to me?* She'd told him not to go and try to do the milking. Just because she was his daughter didn't mean she had no sense. Evidently he had lost all of his.

She stopped and called back to her sister, "Francie, take the biscuits out, then come help me."

When she turned around, George stood before her, eyes wide and alarm leaching the color from his face. Pa must be hurt worse than she expected. "Go in the house and keep Bobby occupied until we bring him inside."

He ducked his head and hurried by her without any objection. He must really be worried about Pa.

Mary glanced toward the other end of the lane, hoping to spy Tony Chan turning in. Of course, she would have heard the approaching hoofbeats. She broke into a run and the pounding of her feet kept rhythm with the throb of her escalating headache. *Why is all this happening at once?*

Frances caught up with her. "Do you think he'll be all right?" Fear laced her words.

"I hope so." Arriving at the barn door, Mary stopped and took a deep breath, blowing it out slowly to try to slow the beating of her heart.

Even though Pa had lost weight since his injury, he was still a large man. She and Frances would have a hard time getting him to the house if he was too injured this time to help them. After a whispered cry to God, she straightened her shoulders and entered the darkness. A shaft of sunlight from the doorway lit only a small portion of the cavernous barn. The cow and horses shifted in their stalls, and the scent of straw mixed with manure overpowered the fresh morning air.

She paused allowing her eyes to get used to the dimness. "Pa?" She didn't hear him moving or making a sound. "We have to find him." She waved to her right. "You go that way. I'll look over here. Call me if you see him."

When she rounded the end of the last stall, she almost tripped over him. She pulled back and stared. She couldn't detect any movement, and the way he was lying, she couldn't tell if he was breathing. Blood pooled around the injured leg, just as it had in the field that day. This time Pa lay amid filth and animal waste, not good clean dirt.

"Here he is." She barely squeaked out.

He still didn't move. She didn't want Frances to see Pa like this. She turned back toward her. "Go see if Tony Chan is coming down the road. If he is, let him know I need him right now."

Frances just stood there a moment trying to see beyond Mary.

She moved closer to the stall and blocked her sister's view. "Quickly!"

Finally, her sister came out of her trance and ran out the door.

Mary turned and wished she had brought a lantern. Since no one went out to the barn in the night without one, they kept them all in the mud room. Should she go back and get one?

Instead she dropped to her knees and reached out and touched him. Her fingers connected with his warm skin, and she could feel the slight movement of his breathing. *He's alive. Thank you, God.* She ran her fingers lightly over him, starting at his head. When they encountered a large lump, she knew he had hit his head when he fell. Should she turn him over...or what?

The sound of voices approaching the barn brought relief. She rose and crossed to meet Tony Chan. "Do you think we can get him to the house, or do we need Frances to help?"

The young man walked around her and knelt beside her father, examining him and moving him a little. Pa emitted a low moan.

Relief rose inside Mary like a tidal wave.

"Need scarf." He held out his hand.

Scarf? Mary could go inside and get one.

"Scarf off head." He waved his hand for emphasis.

She'd forgotten she had one on her hair. She snatched it off and dropped it in his hand. He quickly rolled it into a strip from opposite corners then slipped it under Pa's thigh. He tied it really tight, and no more blood seeped through her father's pants leg.

"Have sister go to town. Get doctor." He glanced at Francie standing in the doorway. "Take my horse. Ride fast."

Frances stared a moment before whirling around and obeying his orders.

"What he doing out here?" Concern wrinkled Mr. Chan's brow.

Exasperated, Mary shook her head. "I told him not to try to milk the cow. That you'd do it when you got here. But he wouldn't listen."

"Old men so stubborn." With the vehemence in his tone, Mary understood Mr. Chan wasn't talking only about Pa. He must have someone just as bullheaded in his family.

"Can we get him to the house by ourselves?" Mary's voice shook. She knelt beside her father's head. Tears fell to her chin, and she swiped them against her shoulder.

"Think so." The man stood and looked around. "I bring wagon close."

With all the clattering and thumping intermingled with the sounds of disturbed animals, Mary wondered why her father didn't awaken. He must be hurt as bad as he was before. Maybe even worse. *What am I going to do?*

Right now, she needed Daniel as much as she had the last time Pa was injured. A sob caught in her throat. *God, what have I done to deserve all this trouble?*

No voice from heaven answered, not that she'd expected it to. Even God had turned His back on her. Once again words whispered through her soul, taunting her. *Worthless. Unlovable. Abandoned.* Her shoulders shook with the force of restrained weeping.

"Missy, don't cry." A gentle touch from the Chinese man did nothing to soothe her. "I get board." He hurried outside toward the lumber piled haphazardly by the other end of the barn.

When he returned with a long, wide board, he also carried a coil of rope. Together they eased her father onto the plank. Pa moaned a lot but didn't open his eyes. Soon their helper had the rope wound around her father and tied so he wouldn't fall off the plank.

Tony Chan made sure the brake was set on the wagon then

he let down the tailgate. "Put foot against end of board, like this." He demonstrated what he meant. "I pick up this end."

He must be stronger than he appeared, because he made it look easy. While Mary steadied the wood to keep it from sliding toward her, Mr. Chan leaned his end of the plank against the edge of the wagon bed. He moved down to where Pa's knees were resting on the board. Slipping his arm under it, he lifted the lower end and pushed it completely into the wagon.

"You want me to harness Brownie?" Mary needed to do something else to help.

He thrust his right thumb against his chest. "I pull wagon."

Pa was heavy. The wagon was heavier. How did the rather small man think he could just pull it up the lane to the house?

His sinewy arms must be all muscle, because he picked up the tongue of the wagon and started pulling it as if it didn't weigh more than a feather pillow. One good thing Daniel did for her family was bring Tony Chan into their lives. Mary wouldn't have been able to face this without his help.

Despair draped her shoulders, weighting them down. Her headache intensified almost beyond endurance.

CHAPTER 18

$\mathcal{M}$ary hiked her skirt up so she wouldn't trip on the hem and ran ahead of the lumbering wagon. She flew through the back door, letting it slam behind her. Her brothers huddled together beside the kitchen table, eyes wide. Not only were they probably worried about how badly Pa was injured, but her careless disregard of her own rules about letting the door slam probably scared them more.

"What's going on, Mary?" Though he tried to display a brave face, George's voice shook. "Is Pa...alive?"

She hurried and grabbed one brother in each arm and held them close to her heart. "Of course, he is."

Bobby turned his eyes toward hers, and she noticed the shimmer of tears that hadn't fallen. "Where'd Francie go?" His voice wobbled more than his brother's.

"She's going to get the doctor to help Pa." She dropped a kiss on top of each of their mussed heads, and they didn't pull away as they usually did. They really must be frightened.

She needed to get them away from the back part of the house. They didn't need to see Pa up close in the shape he was in. Taking a deep breath, she released them and grabbed two plates. She heaped breakfast on each and stabbed the mounds of food with forks.

"Today, you're going to have a picnic breakfast." She forced as much excitement as she could muster into her words, but they fell flat on the floor. "George, you help Bobby, and both of you go out on the front porch. Whatever you do, do not come inside the house until I say it's all right." She leaned down until her face was even with his. "Do. You. Understand?" She waited until both of their heads bobbed in assent.

With a stiff smile that made her jaws and neck ache, she accompanied them to the front screen door. When they were seated on the swing, she headed back toward the kitchen, releasing the tension on her face, fighting to keep her own tears from falling. For a moment, she stopped in the hallway and leaned her back against the faded wallpaper. If she hadn't, she might have fallen. When she had better control of her emotions, she hurried toward the back door. She arrived just as Tony Chan finished backing the wagon up to the stoop outside the mud room.

She breathed in as deeply as she could, trying to calm her own fears. Her heart hurt so badly that every breath was agony. *God, couldn't You have stopped this?* Her angry prayer didn't relieve her one iota. The words from her mind didn't even make it past the ceiling of the sweltering room. She felt them bouncing around her, mocking her wavering faith.

"We need to get Pa into his bedroom. How are the two of us going to do that?" She hoped the young Chinese man had an answer that would work.

"We slide board off wagon." The man made fast, choppy gestures to illustrate what he was talking about. "We pick up board. Carry into house."

Everything inside her quivered. She didn't have enough strength to carry her father on a board two feet, let alone through the mud room, the kitchen, the hallway, and into the bedroom. She probably couldn't carry a feather pillow tied to a board that far. *Will Pa die because I am so weak?*

Tony Chan looked at her...really looked at her. "Maybe not work." Evidently, he recognized the precariousness of her strength.

He walked around three sides of the wagon with his hands clasped behind his back. He stared at her again then walked the other way.

The sound of a fast horse on the road gradually increased as it neared the end of the lane.

"Maybe help come." His face stretched into a smile.

"It's too soon for Frances to reach the doctor's clinic and return." Mary didn't want to dampen the man's enthusiasm, but what else could she say?

The horse slowed on the other side of the windbreak trees. She focused her attention on the end of the lane. Maybe someone else was coming here. Someone strong, who could assist Tony Chan. She held her breath and prayed once again. *God, please send us help.*

Just as the last word died away in her mind, Daniel rode into view. If it would have been any other man, she could envision him as a knight in shining armor, but now a fortress wall stood between them, protecting her heart. Even so, she needed help right now. And he was the only one here able to give aid to Tony Chan.

Never taking his eyes from her, he rode up to the tongue of the wagon and leapt to the ground. "How can I help?"

She couldn't stand the hopefulness on his face. No matter, he could help, but she wouldn't encourage him about anything else. "How did you know we needed assistance?" She bit out the words.

His face fell, and he turned to tie Sultan's reins to the spoke of a front wagon wheel. "I was on my way here, and I met Frances halfway to town. She stopped only long enough to tell me there was a terrible emergency with your father, so I sent her on to complete her mission. I got here as soon as I could. Where are your brothers?"

"I said for them to stay on the front porch until I told them they could come in." Mary glanced at her father, who hadn't made a sound for quite awhile. "I didn't want them to see him like this. It's bad enough that George was the one who found him."

Tony Chan stepped toward his friend and employer. "Mr. Murray fall in barn. Hurt he's leg bad. We bring to house. Can't get inside."

Daniel stared at her father for only a moment. "We'll get him inside." He turned to Mary. "Make sure his bed is ready and scoot the kitchen table out of our way."

Without taking exception to his bossiness, Mary hurried to do his bidding. Pa's bed was a mess. She pulled off the quilt Ma had made and piled it on the chest of drawers to protect it from the mess Pa had fallen into in the barn. She straightened the sheets, re-tucking them. On her way back toward the men, she stopped to scoot the heavy table in the kitchen against the wall.

"I'll hold the doors open for you." Concentrating on the emergency at hand, she pulled the one to the mud room as far back as it would go.

Daniel and Tony Chan made quick work of doing just what Tony had previously described to her. With Daniel holding the end closest to her and Tony carrying the other, they smoothly marched through the house, keeping the board level between them. She knew that had to be hard, since Tony was hardly taller than she was, and Daniel towered over him.

When they arrived at the side of Pa's bed, Daniel glanced at her. "What do we do now?"

She frowned and shrugged. "I don't know. Anything we do could hurt him more."

The little Chinese man once again took charge. "Put board on bed."

Mary was glad she hadn't made the bed with clean sheets, because the board was filthy from being on the floor of the barn.

The two men removed the rope holding Pa to the wide piece of lumber. His agonized moans while they were doing this made Mary's heart ache even more. She wished Pa would open his eyes. At least, she knew he was still alive.

"Slide Mr. Murray off board." Tony motioned how it should be done.

"Please don't hurt him any more than you have to." Mary wrung her hands as she watched.

Daniel gently shifted the upper end of Pa's body over onto the bed. Pa groaned and his eyelids fluttered but didn't stay open. Then he moved Pa's legs. Another, louder groan accompanied that movement. Tony Chan slid the board off the bed, leaving a nasty smear of muck behind, and headed outside with it.

Mary dropped into the chair beside her father's bed. "At least Tony stopped the bleeding. He looks pretty bad, doesn't he?"

When Daniel didn't answer, she glanced up at him, catching a look of worry on his face. "We really don't know as long as we can't see the wound. Should I cut the trousers off his leg?"

"Yes. I'll get you a pair of scissors and some water to clean the wound." Mary turned to go out of the room.

The front screen slammed, and voices came down the hallway toward them. Francie and the doctor had finally arrived.

Mary stopped at the door and waited for them. "Dr. Childress, I'm so glad you're here."

Francie latched onto her and wept into her shoulder. Her

younger sister depended on Mary, just as the two boys had earlier. An even stronger sense of responsibility overcame her. They needed her more now than they had when Pa was first injured.

Mary led her sister from the room and stopped a ways down the hallway. "It's going to be all right."

Frances raised her head and stared at Mary's face. "How can you know that?"

Mary nodded. "You're right. I don't know for sure, but with the doctor here, he'll tell us how to help Pa. We'll pray that everything will be all right." Even as those words tumbled out, she remembered her last prayer that probably still resided in the mud room.

~

*D*aniel followed Mary and Frances from the room. He watched as Mary comforted her sister and ached to be the one to comfort Mary the same way. He could almost feel her leaning against his chest. He would cocoon her in his arms and let her cry until all her fears and frustration had leaked from her body, maybe even drop a kiss on top of her red curls. But judging from the reception he'd received when he arrived, the time when he could do that might never come again.

With her father once again in trouble, she had no one else. When she first saw him ride up on Sultan, he thought he saw a glimmer of relief in her expression before it hardened. Could she move beyond the harsh words they spoke when they quarreled? When he left Washington Territory, he hoped she had already forgiven him, and they could return to courting immediately. The hope that had surged through him like the rapids on the Willamette River dried up to desert sand. But he would not give up on their relationship.

When the girls headed on down the hallway toward the

front screen door, he started to follow. Dr. Childress stuck his head into the hall and gave him a hard stare. "Daniel, I need your help." Then he glanced toward the girls. "And Mary, please bring me warm water, soap, and plenty of towels."

"Yes, sir." Mary motioned Frances toward the porch and headed back to the kitchen.

Without hesitation, Daniel returned to the bedroom where his maybe-never future father-in-law lay almost unresponsive. *Lord, please don't let him die. Mary needs him to recover.*

"We must get his trousers off, but every time I try, he moans in agony." Pain filled the doctor's eyes. "We're going to have to cut them off."

Dr. Childress dug through his black bag and pulled out a large pair of scissors.

"You cut the material. I'm going to try to keep Kenneth calm and settled while you do." He handed Daniel the shears. "Pull the material away from his leg and be very careful."

Mary returned with the things the doctor requested. She set them on the table beside the bed.

"Thank you, Mary." The doctor dipped a cloth in the water and wiped Mr. Murray's face. "You go on back with the other children. We'll call you when we're finished."

She stared at Dr. Childress as if she wanted to resist, then she swiftly turned and left.

Daniel thought he had steady nerves, but his hand shook before he started. He stared at the filthy trousers, not really wanting to touch them. He pulled the fabric away from Mr. Murray's leg and slid the lower blade under it. The first two cuts were easy, but then progress became difficult. Dried blood stuck the material to the man's leg and made the fabric harder to cut. No matter how gently he tried to pull the trousers loose, the denim wouldn't let go. Daniel slid the blade of the scissors out and glanced up at the doctor.

"All right." Dr. Childress laid Mr. Murray's hand down and

came to stand beside Daniel. "Let me see what I can do. You go hold his hand and try to keep him calm."

"But he hasn't even awakened since I've been here."

"When I work this loose, it could hurt him, and that will awaken him." The doctor took the scissors from him.

God, help me. Those were the only words he could think to pray.

Sure enough, when Dr. Childress began to work the material loose from Mr. Murray's leg, Mary's father started to groan. Then his eyes fluttered several times before staying open. He stared up at Daniel as if he were the one hurting him.

Daniel clasped the man's hand and started talking to him in a low, even voice. Without him thinking about them, the words slipped between his lips. "I know that's not comfortable, but the doctor has to get the fabric away from your wound... He's trying not to hurt you... Just grip my hand as hard as you need to. Don't worry about hurting me. I can take it."

A spasm tightened their grasp, but the weakness of Mr. Murray's grip alarmed Daniel. This man really might not make it through the day. If he didn't, Mary would be devastated. If Daniel could take his wounds upon himself, he would. To save the man. To wipe the fear off the faces of her sister and brothers. To keep Mary from encountering more grief.

"There. I'm far enough to uncover the damage." Dr. Childress laid the bloody scissors on a cloth atop the lamp table beside the bed.

He ripped the fabric of the trousers farther open, and Daniel almost gasped. At the site of the previous injury, the skin once again gaped. A tourniquet had been applied over the trousers leg above the wound. No blood flowed from it, but seepage had been going on for quite a while. Bile rose in Daniel's throat. This wound was even worse than the other one out in the field.

As the doctor worked on Mr. Murray, Daniel turned toward

the man's head, watching for signs of pain. When Mary's father opened his eyes, they intensified the pain visible in every line of his face.

"You're going to be all right." He squeezed the callused hand. "Dr. Childress is cleaning the wound."

He dropped into the chair beside the bed. "Can you speak?" The man ran his tongue over his dry lips. "Thirsty." The word rasped out, soft as a whisper.

"I know." Daniel tried for a soothing tone. "When he's finished, I'll get you whatever I can."

Mr. Murray's eyelids drooped.

"What were you doing in the barn?" Daniel glanced down at the muck smeared on the bed linens. "You were in the barn. Right?"

A slight nod accompanied a deep moan.

Daniel looked back toward where the doctor worked. He really couldn't see what was going on with the leg. "You weren't supposed to be in the barn, were you?"

Mr. Murray's gaze moved away from Daniel to stare at some point on the ceiling across the room.

"Hasn't Tony Chan been doing all the farm work for you?"

"I wanted to...myself." Those few words drained what remaining energy the man had, and his hand went limp, but his eyes stayed open.

"Kenneth." Dr. Childress interrupted their conversation. "I told you that you shouldn't come home yet."

Daniel wondered whatever possessed the man to go against the doctor's orders. "So how long has he been home, Doctor?"

Dr. Childress continued to work on the leg. "The day after you left town. Mary's been trying to take care of him for almost three weeks. But he's not been a very cooperative patient."

Chagrin fell like a mask over Mr. Murray's face, and he turned away from Daniel.

The doctor didn't mind speaking plainly to Mary's father.

Daniel wouldn't have imagined saying something like that to him.

Did my leaving cause any of this? Daniel didn't want to voice his question, because he really didn't want to hear the answer. This mess could be another major roadblock to his and Mary's relationship.

I was such an idiot to go off half-cocked like that. He hoped the damage he'd inflicted wasn't permanent in Mr. Murray's life...or his own.

CHAPTER 19

$\mathcal{D}$aniel stayed beside Mr. Murray with a firm hold on the man's limp hand. Occasionally, the man's fingers twitched as he tried to return the grip. Prayers bounced around inside Daniel's head, as if the words had a mind of their own. This was the first time Daniel had experienced the Holy Spirit uttering prayers for him with groanings he couldn't understand. Peace flooded his spirit, because he knew those were the best kind of prayers for the present circumstances.

The doctor muttered something under his breath. Daniel wished he knew what the man said.

"What's that... Doc?" Evidently, Mr. Murray wanted to know as well.

Dr. Childress washed his hands in the warm water and dried them with a clean towel. He came to stand beside the head of the bed. "It's not good news, Kenneth."

The injured man swallowed, his Adam's apple bobbing several times. "Tell me... I can take it."

The doctor stared out the window without focusing on anything beyond. Finally, he wiped his hand across his mouth and looked down at his patient. "There's no easy way to say this."

Daniel held his breath.

Mr. Murray closed his eyes for a moment. When he opened them, they revealed a watery sheen. "Don't just leave me...hanging."

The doctor clasped his hands behind his back. "Since this latest fall reopened the older wound, and because you were in the barn with all the muck, if we're going to save your life..."

Daniel stared straight at Dr. Childress, wondering what measures he'd employ.

"The last time I was here last week, you were doing better. That's the only reason I agreed to wait longer between visits. But things have changed since then. Didn't you realize this was becoming infected, Kenneth? Why didn't you tell Mary?" He stared at Mr. Murray as if requiring his answer.

When none came, he continued. "I really hate to say this, but to keep the infection from spreading, you're going to lose that leg." Dr. Childress winced as he spoke with a there-I've-said-it finality.

The shock on Mr. Murray's face reflected what Daniel felt. *Lose his leg?* That was a devastating step. Not the kind of thing any man wanted to hear. Daniel's stomach muscles clenched at the thought. In his weakened state, Mr. Murray might not recover from this calamity. Tears filled Daniel's eyes, and he blinked them back. He vowed to do everything he could to help this family that faced so much devastation.

The doctor shook his head as he studied the wound. "We need to get you back to the clinic as quickly as possible."

"I'm not..." Mary's father leaned his head up as if he wanted to rise, but it quickly dropped back on his pillow. "I'm not going to the clinic."

"Things are much more sanitary there." The doctor

sounded stern, all business. "I've almost stopped doing surgery anywhere else."

"But in extreme cases...you could." Each word stole more of Mr. Murray's waning strength. "Right, Doc?"

"It would be most unwise." The clipped words from the medical man hung in the air like a specter.

Daniel recognized the battle of wills where neither man wanted to give an inch. Something had to happen to make it better. He turned toward the doctor. "Are you sure Mr. Murray is strong enough to travel to town? Wouldn't the rough road be hard on him jostling in the back of the wagon?"

Dr. Childress rubbed his forehead with the fingers of one hand. He stared down at his patient. Then he whooshed out a deep breath. His gaze turned toward Daniel. "You may be right. We'll need some things. Please go ask Mary to come back in here, but caution her to keep the rest of the children where they are. We shouldn't upset them needlessly."

Daniel headed toward the door. Tony Chan met him just inside the room. "You need my help?"

"Yes. Stay right there," Dr. Childress answered before Daniel could.

As he hurried down the hallway, he tried to think of a way to approach the children. Make it easy for them to understand. They'd all be worried about their father. He didn't want to add to their burden.

The screech of the screen door opening announced his presence. Four pairs of eyes filled with expectation immediately turned toward him.

"Mary, the doctor needs to talk to you."

With a quick nod and a "Thank you," she headed through the door and out of sight.

He gazed at the other three huddled together on the porch swing. "I know how much you're worrying about what's going on in there. And you want to go be with your father." He cleared his throat to give himself time to plan what to say next. "You'll get to see him, but not yet." He glanced toward Frances. "You'll need to watch over your brothers until it's all right for all of you to come in. Maybe take them down to the creek to see if they can catch something for supper."

George stared at him with his chest puffed out as if he were trying to appear older. "I ain't going anywhere till I know Pa's all right."

Daniel knew why he said that. It's exactly what he'd do in the same circumstance. The boy had spunk.

He gave the boy as wide of a smile as he could muster and patted him on the shoulder. Right now, he couldn't say much. He was worried about their father. If the man didn't pull through, these three would be as devastated as Mary, and they'd had enough hard times in their lives. He wished he could somehow protect them from the future they faced.

"I'll sit here with you till your sister returns." With those words he lapsed into silence, hoping his presence was at least of some comfort to the grieving children.

~

*M*ary perched on the chair beside her father's bed with her back ramrod straight. "Pa, why won't you go to the clinic?" Her tone carried a wagon load of exasperation.

Dr. Childress moved beside her. "As Daniel pointed out, the trip into town might be too much for him right now. He doesn't have much strength. We need to use your kitchen for the surgery."

"My kitchen?" Mary could hardly believe what the doctor said.

Earlier she had been worried about getting muck on the

floor. Now the kitchen needed to be clean enough for surgery. Could she pull it off? She wasn't sure she had enough strength to go through all this. She felt her stamina leaking out of her like water through a sieve. She gripped her hands together until her knuckles turned white.

"I know what you're thinking, Mary." Dr. Childress laid his hand on her shoulder. "Before we opened the clinic, I did all my surgery in people's homes. I'll tell you what to do to get ready, but then when you're finished, you'll need to go back with the other children. Daniel and Mr. Chan can assist me."

She slowly rose and started toward the door, her steps slow and deliberate.

"Do you have any whiskey?"

The doctor's question surprised her. She whirled around. "No!"

"Yes." Her father's weak reply followed hers.

Her attention shot to his face. Why did he say that?

Pa turned his head away. "In the tack room."

He had been drinking, and she didn't know it. She stiffened her spine. What he'd done in the past didn't change the present. Right now all that mattered was taking care of Pa. Everything else could wait.

Pa motioned Tony Chan to come close. "Top shelf...behind the liniment."

The doctor nodded. "We will use it during surgery to help deaden his pain."

When Tony Chan left for the barn, Mary headed for the kitchen. She could hear murmurs from Pa's bedroom, but she didn't understand the words being said. Her thoughts were otherwise engaged. When did her father drink? She had never seen him drink, nor had she ever smelled it on his breath. Maybe because he had kept himself aloof from them since Ma died. Was anything else going to happen to shake her very foundation?

Tears streamed down her face, and she swiped at her cheeks with her open palms. Did all the men in her life have to disappoint her? First her real father, then Pa, and then Daniel. She didn't know if she'd ever trust a man again.

A very unladylike sound came from her throat. What she'd really like to do was scream. At the top of her lungs. Wouldn't that upset the vegetable wagon? She could imagine the reaction from all the men here as well as from her siblings. But this was her cross to bear, and bear it she would. No matter what.

Daniel came through the door from the mud room. "Are you all right?" His tone told her that he knew about the surgery.

"I'm fine." Her words weren't true, but she couldn't tell Daniel what she really felt.

Right now, Mary didn't have enough strength to face what was about to happen to Pa and deal with this thing with Daniel. She glanced up at his face. Tender concern covered his features. Tears sprang to her eyes.

"Mary." He took a step closer to her. "What can I do to help?"

She turned away, using a brisk tone to hide her feelings. "We need to give the kitchen a thorough scrubbing since the doctor is going to do the surgery here. Help the children haul in water from the well, and I'll stoke the fire to heat it."

As he left to do her bidding, she rubbed her forehead. For some reason, just having him here did make her feel better, even if it were an added complication. She didn't know why he arrived just when she needed help, but she wouldn't question it right now. At least she wasn't alone in this situation.

≈

The long day stretched into night with Mary concentrating on each task she was given and trying to block out everything else. Now that the horrors of the day were behind her, she sat on the porch swing and stared at the stars, trying to wrap her mind around what had just happened.

Even in the quietness, snatches of the day kept intruding on her peace. The sounds of her father screaming. The smells of whiskey and burning flesh. The groans that continued long after the awful task was completed.

At least Tony Chan had taken Francie, George, and Bobby into town when he went to pick up the things Dr. Childress needed to perform the surgery. They were to stay with Mrs. Horton in the parsonage overnight and longer if needed. At least one of Mary's worries was taken care of. Now for the rest of them.

If Pa recovered...*when* Pa recovered, how would he deal with the loss of his leg? He would have to use the crutches or wheeled chair for the rest of his life. No doubt he would experience as much melancholia or even more than he had when Ma died.

Mary covered her face with both hands. What would she do if that happened? *God, I need a lot of help.*

Yes, people at the church had done more for them recently than she'd ever seen before. But they had their own families and businesses. They didn't have time to spend out here working the farm as well.

Tony Chan wouldn't always be here either. She knew Daniel had paid him to come, but would he stop now that she and Daniel were no longer courting? Did she even want him to continue, even though they needed someone's help?

As for finances, Mary had no idea if they had any money...or a bank account. She couldn't find out until Pa got better, and their supplies might run out before then.

The shrill squeak of the screen door opening sliced through the silence, bringing her head up.

"Mary."

An eternity ago, that masculine voice sent delicious chills

all over her. Not tonight. What did Daniel want now? She stared across the porch at his silhouette bathed in the silvery moonlight, his features barely discernable.

"Yes." What more could she say? *Go away. Please leave me alone. I can't handle you right now.*

"I know this is probably not the best time for it, but I need to talk to you." He leaned his shoulder against the column supporting the roof of the porch, then crossed both his arms and his ankles, looking relaxed.

Tall. Virile. Handsome. But not for her. She scooted and placed her feet on the wooden floor, setting the swing into motion.

After as long a moment of silence as she could comfortably stretch it out, Mary frowned. "About what?"

Even in the shadows, she saw him wince at her words. Why would he do that? She hadn't hurt him. He had hurt her...deserted her without any notice. Broke his promise to return and take her home that night.

He stood away from the column and thrust his hands into the front pockets of his trousers.

"I came back to apologize to you."

"Huh! It's a little late for that, isn't it?"

His eyes glowed in the moonlight, as if filled with fire or fervor. She didn't know which.

"It's never too late to admit a mistake." His voice softened on the last word. "At least, I hope it isn't."

"And just what mistake was that." She could think of several.

"I was a fool, Mary. You trusted me with your unconditional love, but mine had conditions." He stopped and stared at her.

She hadn't expected him to say anything like that. She supposed he would try to justify what he said to her... what he'd done.

"I know you have no reason to believe me."

She could agree with that thought, but she didn't reveal her reaction to him.

"I've changed since I went away. Realized how wrong I was. I really want you to forgive me." He glanced up toward the nearly full moon.

The light revealed all his features. He looked sincere, but she knew she couldn't take his word for it that there had been a change in him. It would take a long time to convince her, if at all. His leaving hadn't been the first way he'd disappointed her. She could enumerate the others if she wanted to, but she was too tired to even try to recall all of them.

"I know I was stubborn and didn't listen to what you were telling me." Looking down, he scuffed his shoe across a knot hole in the floor of the porch. "I didn't know how to handle our disagreement, so that's why I jumped at the chance to leave. My uncle broke his leg and needed help with the sheep shearing. But he helped me see that running away was taking a coward's way out."

He stared at her with darkness once again veiling his features. She didn't know what he wanted her to say, so she remained silent.

"I know I must prove it to you. I came back to serve you. Help you every way you need until you can see into my heart."

"What about helping your father work at the store?" She wasn't convinced.

"We've talked, and he knows why I'm here."

Words. Words. Words. Anyone could say pretty words. That didn't make them true. If he was going to regain her trust, he had his work cut out for him. The last few weeks had shown her how dramatically different their lives were. Daniel was an only child, pampered by his parents, coddled at a storekeeper's job, free to come and go as he pleased. What did he know of the demands of a farm and family? Her time of taking care of her family could extend for years. Was he really ready to take that on?

Too tired to express her doubts, she rose from the swing. "All right. If you could sit with Pa the next few hours, I'll try to get some sleep."

With that, she went into the house quickly, the squeak of the screen door blocking out his reply.

CHAPTER 20

For the first week, Mary and Daniel took turns sitting up with her father. Being able to go to sleep knowing her father was in good hands kept Mary from going insane. During the day, Daniel helped around the farm doing chores. When her father was past the worst of the danger, Daniel went home at night to sleep then arrived first thing in the morning with Tony Chan.

Even now, Mary heard Daniel and Tony ride their horses down the lane to the barn, their discussion animated, but too far away for her to understand the words they exchanged. Standing in the kitchen, she pulled the faded gingham curtains aside and peeked out, hoping they wouldn't notice her. Daniel sat tall in the saddle with a commanding presence, just the kind of presence she had enjoyed those weeks when they were courting. Now she just felt disgust. Disgust at him, and disgust at herself for letting him invade her thoughts so often.

With a snort, she lowered the curtain and shook her head. She had too much to do to dally here by the window, staring at a man she didn't want... couldn't have. Lifting the coffeepot from the stove with a wadded tea towel, she poured a cup for

Pa. She added two spoons of sugar and a swirl of fresh cream. Dr. Childress told her the added sugar and cream would help her father.

She took the mug and headed toward his bedroom, careful not to spill any of the scalding liquid. She tapped on the door. "Pa, are you awake?"

"Yes."

Did his voice sound stronger today? Mary thought so.

When she opened the door, he was trying to scoot up in the bed, but the grimace on his face revealed that his pain might keep him from succeeding. She set the cup down. "Let me put some pillows behind you."

She headed toward the linen closet where they stored a few extra pillows. When she turned from the closet with the pillows, she ran into Daniel, who had come up behind her unheard. His warm arms closed around her as he kept them both from tumbling onto the floor.

Thank goodness, I'm holding these pillows. If she hadn't been, the embrace would have been far too intimate. Wrapped in his arms, she stared up into his eyes that in the dimness of the hallway took on a smoky brown color. Their intense gaze connected and she had a hard time pulling free from it.

He hasn't proved himself yet, she reminded herself as she wrenched away from him. He dropped his arms with disappointment.

She ducked her head. "Sorry. I didn't realize you were behind me."

"I came to check on your father. To see if he needed my help." His words followed her as she darted around him and down the hall toward her father's open doorway.

When she stepped into the room, she hoped her father wouldn't notice the fluster flaming her cheeks. She didn't need him asking her questions she wasn't ready to answer.

Daniel followed her through the doorway. "Mr. Murray,

you're looking better today." He dropped into the chair beside the bed. "You have a lot more color."

Pa scowled at him. "I am getting tired of this bed."

Sure she also had more color than normal in her own cheeks, Mary went to the other side of the bed and gently pushed the pillows under his head. "He wants to sit up in bed, but we need to help him."

Pa started to object.

"Everyone needs help sometime." Daniel cut him off as he slid his arm under her father's shoulders and pulled him up a ways from the mattress. "Mary, put the pillows against the headboard."

There he goes being bossy again. Even with that thought, she complied.

Daniel gently tugged her father by hooking his hands under his arms. "Watch his leg. Make sure nothing bumps it."

She knew what to do. This was *her* father, and she had cared for him plenty well while Daniel was off traipsing across the country. She gritted her teeth corralling those words before they exploded from her mouth. Sometimes that man really vexed her.

As soon as Pa was sitting up against the pillows, Mary hastened out of the room. Having to get breakfast for her family was a good enough excuse to keep her from spending one more minute with Daniel Winthrop.

"I didn't have time for breakfast before I left home." His words stopped her short right outside the door. "Any chance I could beg some from you?"

She turned and stared at the tableau of Daniel and her father. Both men smiled at her.

Pa gave Daniel's hand a pat. "You don't have to beg." Her father glanced toward where Mary stood in the hallway. "Isn't that right, Mary?"

No matter how much she wanted to disagree, she couldn't.

Not with her father's gaze burning a hole through her. And he wasn't well enough for her to get him upset. She nodded. "Of course."

After spitting out that answer, she retreated into the kitchen. Daniel followed, his powerful steps inches behind hers. After grabbing himself a cup of coffee, he retreated to Pa's room.

She tried to be quiet as she started breakfast, but the skillet banged as she put it on the stove and put in the bacon she'd already sliced. With two more people added to the table this morning, the servings of the smoked meat would be skimpy. No more hung in the smokehouse.

The bowl she got down from the shelf clattered against the table when it slipped out of her hand. As she dumped in the ingredients for biscuits, somehow the white powder ended up on the floor as well as in the bowl and on the table. What a mess she would have to clean up.

She wasn't even sure she put in all the ingredients in the correct amounts. The proximity of Daniel and the way his arms felt wrapped around her chased every other thought from her head.

All the while she mixed the dough, she muttered under her breath. Halfway through cutting out the biscuits, she had to stop and take the bacon from the skillet because it was almost too brown.

When she finished cutting the dough, the tin biscuit cutter slipped through her fingers and banged against the edge of the table on its way to the floor, adding yet another dent on its side. No wonder her biscuits were so lopsided. After perching on a chair, she squeezed her eyes tight, trying to hold back tears of frustration.

"Mary, what's going on in here?" Frances yawned as she came through the door. "You could have just told me it was time to get up instead of making all that racket. I'm sure Pa is probably awake too."

"Oh, yes, he is." Mary got up to grab a dish rag so she could wipe the mess off the table. "Daniel is in there with him. They're drinking coffee and waiting for me to finish breakfast."

She threw the dishrag in the sink and started breaking eggs into another bowl. After she had done a dozen and a half, she started whisking them with a fork.

"So what's going on between you and Daniel?" Frances started setting the table without having to be told. "He wasn't around for a while. Now he's back, but the two of you don't seem very friendly to each other. At least, you're not very welcoming to him."

Mary knew that eventually one of the younger children would start asking questions, but she had hoped it would take longer than this. "Sometimes relationships take different turns. Ours did."

Her sister stared at her. "What does that mean?" She stood with her fists on her hips, just the way Mary used to when she was scolding one of her siblings.

What could she say? "Some things don't work out like we think they will."

She turned away and stirred the eggs into the skillet, fluffing them. "Why don't you go tell the boys if they aren't dressed and in the kitchen in ten minutes, they'll miss breakfast? Then go ask Tony Chan to join us. He is really working hard to keep everything going the way Pa did."

Within a quarter of an hour, everyone was in the kitchen sitting at the table. Except Pa, of course. And Mary still rushed around getting the food ready. "I'll take Pa his food and stay with him."

Frances stood up from her chair. "Let me. I want to help take care of him more often."

What has come over Francie? Whatever it was, Mary

welcomed the change. She fixed a tray for her sister, with two plates of food and a glass of milk for Frances. Her sister disappeared into Pa's room, and Mary breathed a sigh of relief and took Frances's place at the table.

Daniel gave her a gentle smile. "Do you mind if I say a blessing over the food?"

She wasn't sure why that startled her, but it did. Why would he want to do that? His treatment of her before he abandoned her didn't exhibit Christian love. But she had no reason to deny his request, so she shook her head before bowing it, her eyes sending a message to the boys to do the same.

"Dear Father in heaven, we thank Thee for Thy merciful hand in our lives. We pray for Mr. Murray's recovery and comfort to our hearts. Protect this man who means so much to each of us. We trust You to know what is best in our lives and look to You for our provisions. Bless this food to the nourishment of our bodies and bless the hands that prepared it. Amen."

When he raised his head, their eyes met. Mary was startled by the intensity of his gaze. She quickly looked away.

Although she knew he prayed, Mary had never heard him utter a prayer before. His words had rolled over her, carrying a wealth of spiritual truth and simplicity. Why did he have to do that now? These words didn't go well with those he spewed when he raised his voice to her in their quarrel. How could such different ones come from the same man's heart? These new words comforted and lifted her up, and that wasn't something she wanted *him* to do. She had to keep him a safe distance —far from her own heart so he couldn't worm his way back into her good graces.

George and Bobby loved having Daniel and Tony Chan eat with them. Usually, it was only for lunch, but today was different.

"So Mr. Daniel." Bobby stuffed a biscuit and jam into his

mouth. "Whatcha want me to do today?" The words came out a little garbled.

"Bobby, don't talk with your mouth full." Mary gave him a gentle smile. "Remember, it's not polite." The boys didn't get bored anymore since Daniel assigned them chores to finish each day. And Mary didn't have to worry about keeping them out of trouble. She had to admit that Daniel was good for her brothers.

Her little brother frowned. "Why do we need to be p'lite?"

Daniel replied for her. "Our world would be a terrible place if people weren't polite." Daniel stressed the correct pronunciation of the word. "And we don't want things to be terrible, do we?"

"No!" Both boys answered in unison as if they had practiced to get it right.

George cocked his head and stared at Daniel. "So, Mr. Daniel, are you always polite?"

Daniel laughed out loud. "Unfortunately, I'm not." He turned his attention toward Mary. "Sometimes, I do things that are completely stupid and out of line, and they hurt other people." The blaze in his eyes almost scorched her. "I've done that a few times, and I'm doing everything I can to repair the damage."

She tore her gaze from his as heat traveled up her neck into her face. Suddenly, she had trouble catching her breath. She pushed back from the table and quickly arose. "I'll butter more of the biscuits. Does anyone want anything else?" She dared not look back at Daniel.

"Mr. Daniel, you didn't tell us what chores you want us to do this morning." When she glanced at Bobby, her youngest brother was pulling on the man's sleeve.

Daniel turned all his attention to the boy. "I want you to feed the chickens and gather the eggs for your sister. I'm going to teach George to milk the cows."

Mary whipped back toward the table so fast she had to use her other hand to keep the biscuits from sliding from the plate. "Isn't he a little young for that?"

George's eager expression wilted.

Daniel studied him a minute. "How old are you now, George? Aren't you nine?"

The boy puffed out his chest. "Almost ten."

"I believe that's plenty old to learn to milk a cow." Daniel's words gave George's smile added width. "Don't you agree, Mary?"

From the look he shot her way, he might back down if she didn't agree. But how could she disappoint her brother? So many things had changed in their lives. If this was all it took to brighten his day, she'd go along with it.

She took a deep breath and let it out slowly. "I'm sure Mr. Daniel will show you the safest way to handle the milking. Won't you?"

He agreed and continued talking to her brothers.

Mary turned away from them, lost in thought. So far, Daniel had proven himself capable not only of hard work, but also of handling her brothers. But the question still remained of whether she could trust him with her heart.

CHAPTER 21

*W*orry wouldn't let go of Daniel's thoughts. Although Mr. Murray's outer wounds had begun to mend over the last two weeks, his inner wounds were not so quick to mend. The crippled man spent much of the day sleeping or staring out the window, and he resisted all attempts to amuse him or involve him in the life of the farm, seeming to take refuge in his status as invalid. Daniel was glad that Dr. Childress was due to check on him today. Daniel planned to have a private word with the doc while he was here. He hoped the signs he'd seen weren't anything serious. This was one time he'd love to be wrong.

While he hoed the large garden plot, Daniel kept glancing at the road, hoping to see the doctor's buggy or perhaps Tony returning from town. He had sent Tony to sell vegetables and milk at the grocery store. By doing this, Mary had built up a line of credit that she could use when she needed anything. She had given Tony a list of supplies to pick up as well.

The sound of the farm wagon coming down the road at a faster clip than Daniel expected caught his attention. He made his way through the field of fresh vegetables, being careful not to trample any of the produce. When he reached the fence, he climbed up to sit on the top railing to wait for Tony. Daniel heard the wagon slow down before it rounded the curve. He waved at his friend.

"Mr. Daniel, I looking for you." Tony pulled on the reins, tied them to the brake, then jumped to the ground and hurried toward him. "Terrible...terrible." His head wagged from side to side.

Daniel hopped off the fence and met the man in the roadway. "What's terrible?"

"Many people hurt, some maybe dead." He spoke so fast, Daniel had a hard time following his accent, which became stronger the more upset the man was.

He took the short man by his shoulders and looked him in the face. "Tony, slow down."

The Chinese man stopped, then took a deep breath.

Daniel let loose of his shoulders. "Now tell me slower. What happened?"

"Oh, Mr. Daniel. Really bad fire. Hotel near river... many people stay there... some not found yet."

Daniel frowned with concern. He should go to town and help fight the fire, but he couldn't just leave while Mary's father was weakening. He'd never forgive himself if something tragic happened and she had to face it alone.

"Is the volunteer fire department working the fire?"

"Yes. Many men work at fire." Tony trembled from head to toe.

"And a bucket brigade?"

Once again, the Chinese man's head bobbed up and down. "Many people make two lines."

What a relief. Daniel knew how fast those wooden building could go up in flames.

"Many friends work there. My friends. Not found yet. No

one knows where they go." His voice trembled more with every word he uttered.

"Do you want to go back to town and help?"

Tony nodded his head so fast, Daniel was afraid he would get dizzy. Then he shook his head. "No can go. Must work for you. You pay me."

Daniel put his arm across Tony's shoulder and turned him back toward the wagon. "It's fine with me if you go back to help. I won't dock your pay." He walked with him until he was safely ensconced on the wagon seat. Then Daniel joined him and picked up the reins. "So I guess that means the doctor will be too busy to come out here today."

Tony nodded. "Too busy many days. Many, many hurt people."

Daniel didn't welcome that news, but it couldn't be helped. With a smaller town like Oregon City, one doctor was usually enough to care for everyone. But that wouldn't be the case with a catastrophe of this proportion.

Nevertheless he hoped Dr. Childress might make it out here today... or tomorrow at the latest.

Daniel turned the wagon into the lane and stopped by the fence around the yard. "Did you get everything Mary ordered?"

"Yes." The other man jumped down and headed toward the back of the wagon.

Daniel met him by the tailgate. "I can unload all of this if you want to ride your horse back to town."

"I go." Tony clasped his hands together and gave a small bow to Daniel, then hurried to the barn to retrieve his horse.

Daniel hefted a fifty-pound bag of flour onto his shoulder and headed through the front gate then around the house toward the back door. Mary was in the kitchen kneading bread dough.

She glanced up as he dropped the bag on the kitchen table. "Good. Tony's back from town." She stretched the dough and folded it over on itself before pushing the heels of both hands in the sticky mound. "I used the last of the flour for this batch of bread. With two growing boys and now both you and Tony taking meals here, we use a lot of bread."

When he didn't reply, she stopped and stared at him. "Is everything all right? I saw Tony Chan hurrying toward the barn, and he seemed extremely agitated. That's not like him at all."

She quirked her eyebrow in a way that had endeared her to him long ago. He had been missing that particular habit, since she had been so serious and aloof from him lately.

He leaned both hands on the back of one of the kitchen chairs. "You're right. He's really upset. While he was in town, one of the hotels near the river caught fire. Too bad there isn't any rain today. That would be a big help for those fighting the fire."

"Which hotel?" She turned from pummeling the dough, concern puckering her brows.

"You know, I forgot to ask." Daniel shook his head. "He was so upset, he went on and on about other buildings being in danger, people being burned, some people dead, and even others missing. I just didn't get to that question."

She turned back to her task and divided the dough into three equal lumps. "Did you send him back to town?"

"I let him go. That's a big difference." Daniel enjoyed watching her movements as she formed each piece into a soft oval shape and placed it in a loaf pan. When she turned with her back to him, he could take his time watching without her thinking he was ogling her. "I told him I could finish the work today."

He wished he had the right to move close behind her and drop a kiss on the nape of her neck. With her hair pulled up on the top of her head, he would have easy access to the exposed skin. He shook his head and tore his gaze from her. Good thing he did, because she turned around right then.

She came over, wiping her hands on her apron as she came. She stopped across the table from him and grabbed the back of the chair, hanging on tight enough for her knuckles to blanch. Something was bothering her.

"I want to ask you something."

His heart leaped. After two weeks of little more than small talk, was she going to initiate something more intimate?

"What do you think about Pa?" She clamped her lips together as if trying to corral other words.

He dropped his gaze so he wouldn't reveal his disappointment that they were merely discussing her father. "In what way?" He didn't want to add to her distress if she hadn't noticed what he had.

She leaned toward him. "His wound seems to be healing." Her voice was softer as if she didn't want her father to hear. "But he's withdrawn. I have a hard time getting him to eat, and he doesn't want to spend time with the boys. He's sleeping more, like he's getting weaker. Have you noticed?"

He would not lie to her. He raised his eyes to hers. "Yes. It's been bothering me too."

"He won't let me change his bandages. You know he only lets you." Her voice hitched on the last word. "Does the leg look different...worse or something?"

"I'm not sure. It doesn't look like it's healing as well as it did at first, and it does have a strong smell." He wanted to cradle her in his arms and comfort her, but knew she wouldn't welcome that connection. "I had hoped Dr. Childress would come today. If he doesn't come tomorrow, I'll go to Portland and try to get someone from the hospital there."

Hope bloomed in her eyes. "Do you think a doctor would come?"

Daniel clenched his fists. "I'll do my best to make it

happen." If he had to, he'd pay the doctor extra for making the journey.

He glanced over at Mary. Tears filled her eyes, but they didn't fall. Nervously, she turned away, going to dampen a tea towel to spread across the pans of dough.

Daniel felt as if he'd been dismissed, so he went out to the wagon and toted all the other items into the house. After everything had been stowed in the right place, he glanced at Mary, who stood beside the windows staring out at her younger brothers romping in the open field behind the house.

"I'll just go check on your father, Mary." He didn't think she had heard him, because she didn't move a muscle. But just before he passed through the open doorway into the hall, her voice caught his attention.

"Thank you," she said.

"You're welcome," he replied.

As he reached her father's bedroom, he heard the back screen door squeak shut and Mary calling her brothers. From what he could understand, she was going to play with them awhile. Just what she needed...and they did too.

He peeked into Mr. Murray's room to see if he was still sleeping. Instead, his eyes were trained on the door as if he was expecting a visitor.

"How are you doing?" Forcing a smile to his face, Daniel dropped into the chair beside the bed. He didn't like the sallow complexion peeking through the stubble on the man's cheeks.

Kenneth gave Daniel a hollow-eyed stare while he rubbed his thigh above his stump, which was clearly outlined under the thin sheet. "Did I just hear Mary go outside?"

An odd question instead of an answer.

He nodded. "I think she's going to play with the boys. Might be good for all three of them."

A weak smile teased at the older man's lips. "At least she'll be gone for a little while. I need to have a serious talk with you, Daniel."

"All right." He leaned forward, his eyes trained on the older man's face.

"Let's talk turkey." His intense gaze blazed toward Daniel.

He nodded. "Go ahead."

"I know things aren't going good with me." A twinge of pain shot across his face.

Daniel didn't know if he should agree or not, so he just waited to see where this would take them.

"The doctor told me that you and Mary had quite a row a few weeks ago, then you high-tailed it out of here for awhile." The older man tried to stare him down.

He hung his head a minute then looked up straight into Mr. Murray's rheumy eyes. "I'm not proud of what I did. I know I was wrong, and I plan to serve Mary and your family until she can understand the tremendous change that took place in my life while I was at my uncle's sheep ranch."

"Good." The older man's fingers fidgeted with the sheet covering him. "That's what I needed to hear. I want a promise from you."

A promise? "What kind?" Daniel clasped his hands together. This was really serious.

"I know I'm not long for this world."

When Daniel started to say something, Mr. Murray held up his hand. "Don't stop me. You can get the doctor out here, and he will tell you the same thing. I haven't treated Mary right since I lost her mother. She needs someone to love her completely. I believe you do."

"With all my heart, sir."

"Don't give up on her.... Take care of her and the others.... Help them keep the farm in the family.... My sons' inheritance." He stopped messing with the sheet, but kept his eyes trained on Daniel.

Daniel took a breath, then measured his words carefully, packing his intent into every phrase. "I don't plan on giving up. I believe Mary is the woman God wants me to marry. And we'll make sure the farm continues in the family."

The tension in the old man relaxed, and he breathed easier.

"And I'm going to make sure a doctor comes to see you tomorrow too." Daniel spoke the words like a vow. And he would never go back on a vow.

Mr. Murray stretched out his hand. "Let me pray a blessing on you. I know I haven't always gone to church, but the good Lord and I are still on speaking terms, even if on my side that's meant mostly grumbling and complaining." The chuckle that erupted from him turned into a hacking cough.

Daniel knelt beside the man's bed and let him put his hand on Daniel's head.

"Dear Lord, give Daniel...Your wisdom and strength. Make him the man my Mary needs. Multiply his knowledge...pour out the blessings you've planned for him...for them. In Jesus' name, amen." Kenneth's hands fell back against the mattress, and he rested against the pillow with his eyes closed.

The blessing that had flowed over Daniel's head felt almost like the oil the Bible talks about that was poured over the priests in the Old Testament. The words encouraged him and lifted him up.

He would never, ever go back on his promise to Mr. Murray...no matter how long it took Mary to accept the change in his life.

CHAPTER 22

*D*aniel didn't want to leave Mary and her siblings alone with their father overnight. If Mary hadn't talked to him about being worried about Mr. Murray, he would have had to come up with another good reason to stay. Now he didn't need to. He would sleep in the barn if he had to, but he was staying.

As he headed back out to the large garden plot, he had a lot on his mind. He picked up the hoe and applied all his strength battling the weeds that had the audacity to spring up between the vegetables.

He prayed that the fire wouldn't spread far from the hotel. Both the house he had purchased and his parent's home were far enough away that they shouldn't be in danger, but other people who attended their church lived closer. He prayed, lifting up each family in turn, asking God to protect them from the burning scourge.

"Daniel!" Frances called to him as she walked across the large, vacant field between the garden and the house.

Her call brought him back to the awareness of his surroundings. "Over here." He lifted a hand above the tall corn stalks so she could see where he was. Leaning his crossed arms on the end of the hoe handle, he watched her step daintily through the jungle of plants. "Did you have a good visit today?"

Charlotte Holden had dropped by this morning. She wanted Frances to come out to their farm and spend time with Milly. Since the Holden farm was farther out from town than the Murray farm, the buggy that brought Frances home hadn't passed by the field where he worked.

The girl stopped in front of him. "Yes, I did." She snapped off a tiny green bean from the row next to the corn, wiped it against her sleeve, popped it in her mouth, and began munching on it.

"I had missed Milly since school let out for the summer. We've had to stay close to home...because of Pa." She glanced up at the sky, her eyes following the clouds gently sailing east. "I was surprised Mary let me go. I usually have a lot of chores."

Daniel's heart softened toward Mary's little sister. When he'd first started coming out every day, she had acted spoiled and scared. He had had to talk to her to help her understand how much Mary could use her help. "Maybe she realized you needed a break."

Frances frowned at him. "Mary needs a break, too, but she hasn't had one."

"I do as much as she will let me to help her." He swatted at a mosquito. "Mary feels the weight of responsibility for all your family."

She glanced down. "I know. I try not to give her any extra trouble. But I know sometimes she wishes I'd do more to help." She put her thumbnail between her teeth and worried with it.

He patted her on the shoulder. "I've noticed you're helping more all the time, and your grouchy moods have disappeared."

She gave a quick snort. "I didn't think anybody noticed I've tried to change."

"You're doing a good job. Just give your sister more understanding, kiddo. Will you?"

She frowned at him before she agreed. Was she mad about the nickname or about having to show her sister mercy? He would never understand the female of the species if he lived to be a hundred years old.

"Where's Mr. Chan? I didn't see him working anywhere, and his horse isn't in the barn." She twisted the end of her braid that rested on her shoulder.

"Today was not a good day in town." Hadn't this girl had enough to worry about without him adding to it? "A hotel caught on fire, and they needed more help. I let him go back after he brought the things Mary needed from the store."

Her bright eyes widened. "Wow! I hope they put it out without anyone getting hurt."

"I wish that was true, but it isn't." He picked up the hoe and sank it into the earth near the roots of a weed. "That's why the doctor wasn't able to come out here to see your father today."

She pulled her bottom lip in between her teeth. "Mr. Daniel, if I ask you something, will you tell me the truth?"

Being a parent must be hard. How did they decide how much information to give to children, no matter what age they were? "I won't lie to you. But I might not be able to give you a complete answer, especially if it's something I know nothing about."

The fingers of both of her hands went back to work on the end of that braid. "Do you think my pa is ever going to be all right?"

Her eyes begged him to say her father would. But he couldn't do that without telling her a lie. Once again, he stopped hoeing. "I don't know for sure what will happen with your pa, but whatever happens, God will take care of him."

"How come God will take care of him when he hasn't even

gone to church much?" Fear shouted through her soft-spoken words.

Even though he was hot and sweaty, he held out one arm. She slipped closer to him and leaned her head on his chest. Her body trembled.

God, give me the words she needs to hear. "I can tell you this. Your father and I had a nice visit this morning, and I know for a fact that he knows God, and God knows him. Sometimes people keep their relationship with the good Lord a private matter. That's what he's been doing. But today he talked about it to me, and he prayed a blessing over me that was powerful. So, Frances, you can trust him to God's care."

His words must have reached her, because her trembling stopped. She turned her tear-stained face up so he could see it. "I needed for you to tell me that, Mr. Daniel. Some things are hard to hear, but just because I'm not an adult doesn't mean that I don't need to know about them."

He gently tugged on her braid. "I'll try to remember that. Okay?"

She pulled away from him and headed back toward the house with a backward wave.

Lord, I'm going to need a lot of wisdom from you in the coming days. Help me be what I need to be for everyone in this family.

He knew he was exactly where God wanted him to be, but he dreaded the things he knew were coming their way.

⁓

*M*ary awakened more refreshed than she had been in several days. With Daniel staying with Pa, and she having played with the boys enough to be completely tired, she slept through the night. Today would have to be a better day.

Sometimes she made breakfast while wearing her robe, but

with Daniel in the house, she dressed before she stepped out of the room she shared with Francie. Because of summer's heat, she bunched her hair on top of her head and pinned it down the best she could.

She put the coffeepot on and went to the smokehouse to get the bacon Tony Chan had brought from town yesterday. *Wonder how much I should slice.* If Tony Chan didn't come back this morning, she could cut down the amount, but she didn't want to take a chance of not having enough. So she sliced plenty.

After gently placing the skillet on the stove so she didn't make any noise, she lined it with the smoked meat. Just as it started sizzling, she heard a buggy come down the lane. She hurried out the front door just as the buggy stopped in the soft light of predawn.

"Dr. Childress, I didn't expect to see you today." She held open the screen door. "Come on back to the kitchen. I need to turn the bacon, and the coffee is on."

When he stepped into the kitchen lighted with oil lamps, exhaustion hung on him like a heavy cloak. "Thank you, Mary. Coffee and breakfast sounds good."

She filled a mug and set in front of him.

"Thank you, Mary." He lifted it and took a quick sip. "Ah, good and hot."

"I can't remember if you want sugar and cream in your coffee." She started removing the cooked meat from the skillet and added another layer.

"Today, black is good. I was up all night with patients." He rubbed his forehead as if he had a headache. "So many people were injured." He looked up at her. "You heard what happened in town, didn't you?"

She gave a quick nod. "That's why I didn't expect to see you out here."

Daniel came through the doorway. "Something smells

really good in here." He stopped short. "Dr. Childress, I didn't know you were here. How were you able to get away?"

"The mayor went to Portland and brought back some doctors. I didn't have to do it all by my lonesome." He covered a yawn with one hand. "I knew I needed to get out here to check on Kenneth. How's he doing?"

Daniel stared at Mary, and she stared right back. Neither said a word.

"Okay. That plus the fact that Daniel is still here answers my question." The doctor heaved himself out of the chair. "I'll go see about him."

Daniel blocked his way. "He's sleeping right now. Why don't you have some breakfast first?"

Mary bustled around and soon biscuits and scrambled eggs joined the bacon on the table. The three of them sat down and Daniel said the blessing over the food. She was glad he did. She wasn't sure she could get the words out around the growing lump in her throat. And her stomach was rebelling against the food she tried to force down.

After the doctor ate his fill, he arose. "I'll go see him."

Both Daniel and Mary started to get up.

"Mary, let Daniel go with me. I might need his help, and I think I hear your brothers and sister stirring."

Relieved, she dropped back into her chair. Then she felt guilty. She should be the one taking care of Pa, but she welcomed both Daniel's help and the doctor's. It meant she didn't have to go in there...just in case Pa wasn't doing as well as yesterday.

"What's going on in here?" Francie was tying some yarn around the end of one of her braids. "I thought I heard voices."

"Dr. Childress is here to see Pa. Daniel went into Pa's room in case he needs help." Mary tried to make her voice sound hopeful. "There's plenty of breakfast on the warming shelf."

George rubbed his eyes when he came through the

doorway with his hair standing up in several directions. "I'm hungry."

Mary smiled at him. "You need to go back and comb your hair."

"Aww, Mary, do I have to?" His voice had a decided whine to it.

She grabbed a tea towel that had covered the biscuits and swatted him with it. "Yes, you do, young man."

He turned around and left, his shoulders slumped. When he returned, his hair was slicked down, and Bobby came with him.

"I'm hungry, Mary." Her youngest brother slid into the chair beside her. "Can I have a glass of milk with breakfast?"

"May I?" She shooed Francie toward the spring house.

So many of the things she said to her siblings were the same things Ma used to say. She even corrected their grammar as Ma had. Today she felt as old as the hills.

While the boys and Francie ate breakfast and talked together, she kept one ear tuned toward Pa's bedroom. She couldn't detect a single sound. Now she wished she had accompanied the men, but they hadn't wanted her to. She'd just have to wait until they came out.

When the others finished eating, Mary gathered up the dirty dishes and put them in the dishpan. She shaved some soap over them then added water from the teakettle. She watched the soap flakes dissolve before she added cooler water so she could plunge her hands in and swirl the liquid until the suds formed.

Usually, she wasn't too fond of washing dishes, but this morning it kept her occupied while she waited. Finally, she heard Daniel and Dr. Childress coming down the hall. She glanced at the clock. Nine o'clock. They had been in there over two hours. Their conversation was muted, and suddenly, her stomach felt as if it dropped to the floor. Something terrible had happened.

With the first glimpse of their faces, she knew she was right. Pa was no longer with them.

"Mary, come sit down at the table." Daniel put his hand on the small of her back and accompanied her across the large kitchen. He dropped in the chair next to the one she took.

Francie, George, and Bobby sat still with wide eyes staring back and forth between both of the men.

Dr Childress looked older and more tired than he had when he went to Pa's room. "This is never easy."

A gasp escaped from Frances, and she pulled her brothers closer to her.

The doctor pinched the bridge of his nose a moment. "A few minutes ago, your father passed on to glory." The words were spoken in a monotone.

Bobby pulled away from Frances and ran to Mary. She drew him into her lap and held him close.

"What does that mean, Mary?" Her brother patted her arm.

Mary wished she could scream and cry... and berate the two men for not letting her see her father one more time. But she had to be strong for Frances and the boys. Her throat was clogged with a lump of tears fighting to escape.

Daniel leaned toward Bobby. He put his face down close to the boy's. "Your pa went to live in heaven with Jesus and with your ma."

He took the boy into his arms. Bobby rested his head on Daniel's shoulder.

"When is he coming back?"

Each word plunged a dagger into Mary's heart.

Daniel patted Bobby's back. "He can't come back... but you'll get to see him when you go to heaven."

Mary cut her eyes toward the doctor, who still stood

between the table and the stove. Now her eyes filled with tears, and she couldn't hold them back.

Wearily, the doctor dropped into one of the empty chairs. "I know you are hurt, Mary." He kept his words gentle... kind. "We were following your father's wishes. He didn't want you there when it happened."

Mary found her voice. "What exactly did happen?" Hurt poured out like an acid with each word. "You told us that amputating his leg would help."

Dr. Childress winced. "I thought we had won the battle against infection, but evidently not. He didn't let on to you, because he knew you couldn't do anything to stop its progression." He started tapping his fingertips on the tabletop. "I know this won't help right now, but he wanted us to tell you that he had made peace with his Maker, and he was ready to join your mother in heaven."

Mary began to sob. Frances joined in. George and Bobby stared wide-eyed with confusion on their faces.

When the crying died down a bit, Dr. Childress looked at them. "He said to remind you that the Bible says that God had numbered each believer's days. And his turn to go to glory is today."

Did Pa and Dr. Childress and Daniel think that made everything all right?

What was she supposed to do now?

CHAPTER 23

$\mathcal{M}$ary stared out the window at nothing in particular, much as she had for the last two weeks. Everything was a blur—the funeral, trying to help the younger children understand what was transpiring. She had been amazed at the amount of help the women at the church had lavished on them. Food the day of the funeral with enough to last several days, help with housework, picking up one or the other of her siblings and taking them home to spend time with children the same ages. For the last fourteen days, one or more of the women from church spent the whole day at the farm with her. Even with the disaster of the hotel fire, they made time to minister to her family's needs. Just thinking about their kindness brought fresh tears to her eyes. She tried to blink them away.

One constant in all of this had been Daniel's presence. His tender care of her and her family slowly broke down more of the wall she'd built around her heart.

Today was the first day no women from the church would be coming to help. Both Daniel and Tony Chan continued their work on the farm, so nothing fell to disuse. Tears leaked from her eyes once again when she thought about their loving care. Even the young Chinese man expressed his affection for her and her siblings with so many small kindnesses. He brought a bouquet one day. On another, almond cookies. Without being asked, he cleaned out her flowerbeds, even adding some plants he'd brought from his home in town.

Mary wondered how long it would be before she stopped crying at the drop of a hat. She would welcome that day. In the meantime, she needed to clean out Pa's room. She had put it off long enough.

She planned to move into that bedroom so she and Frances could have their own bedrooms and more privacy. Mary hoped that staying within these four walls would help the children feel close to their parents.

Of course, Mary planned to make it more feminine. While Pa lived in it those years after Ma died, he wanted it left alone, so six years took a toll on the space. She would air it out and add touches a woman would enjoy. New curtains. Dress the bed with one of the pretty quilts Ma had made and Pa had stored in the cedar chest. Put out some of Ma's figurines and personal possessions. No telling what she'd find that Pa had packed away.

"Mary, where are you?" Daniel called from outside the front door of the house. He had started doing this as soon as Pa was no longer here, waiting on the porch until she let him in.

She went into the parlor to welcome him. She didn't know what she would have done without him these last two weeks. His strength...his support...his prayers. But she had not had the energy or opportunity to properly thank him.

"Come in." She pushed the screen door open and stood back to let him enter.

"So where are the others?" His eyes searched down the hall-way, and he cocked his head. "I don't hear any of them."

"Earlier Reverend Horton came to pick up the boys. He's

taking all the boys their age fishing and on a picnic. He thought they'd enjoy going along." She was so glad she wouldn't have to deal with them while she went through Pa's things. "And Frances is working in the bedroom we share, cleaning out and changing things. I'm going to clean out Pa's bedroom before I move into it."

Daniel studied her for a moment, his left brow quirked in a question. "Are you up to that, Mary? Won't it be hard on you?"

She nodded. "Yes, I need to face that room sometime. I think it's...about time. Get it over with, so I won't have to dread doing it anymore." Her stomach clenched just thinking about what she planned.

"I'd like to help you." He reached toward her, but stopped and dropped his hands. "If you'll let me...maybe my being here will ease some of the difficulties."

She gave him a tremulous smile. "Yes, it will...if you're sure you want to."

"I'm sure." The tenderness in his eyes encased her in comfort.

Daniel had offered his shoulder and arms to her several times during the last two difficult weeks, and she had taken advantage of them. So why did he almost pull away from her a moment ago?

Because you have not told him that you believe he is a changed man. Hasn't he proved it to you yet?

Yes, he had, but she didn't know how to tell him that she knew, she really knew, what he was talking about. So she just led the way down the hall toward Pa's bedroom. *My room now.* Maybe she shouldn't think of it that way until after they finished cleaning out Pa's things. She wouldn't feel comfortable having Daniel in there with her if she called it her bedchamber. That could come after he left.

When she opened the door, she noticed that someone, probably one of the church women, had cleaned up the mess.

Changed the sheets and generally tidied up. She heaved a sigh of relief.

"You haven't been in here since he died, have you?" Daniel's soft words carried a load of comfort with them.

"No." She shook her head.

From behind her, he placed his hands on her shoulders. "Are you sure you are ready for this?" His breath against her hair made curls tickle her cheek.

She straightened her shoulders and swiped the tears from her cheeks. "Yes."

Mary strode across the room and pulled back the faded curtains. With the movement dust and a white powdery substance escaped into the air. She wondered how long those curtains had been on the window. She knew she had never taken them down to clean in the six years since Ma died. She had had bigger things to worry about.

Daniel unlatched the window and pushed up the sash. Fresh air rushed into the stuffy room, diluting some of the lingering stale odor of sickness. Mary stared at the room, going from one side all the way around to the other. Where should they start? All Pa's clothes, hanging on hooks on one wall, looked clean.

"Do you think the women washed his things?" She glanced up at Daniel.

"I'm sure they did." Daniel held her gaze for an extended moment. "Have you decided what you want to do with his belongings?"

Mary didn't know how to answer that question. She hoped that in all the junk Pa had stored she would find some indication of their financial situation. Since Pa's injury, their family had been making it on the money they brought in by selling milk, eggs, and produce, but when the garden was finished for the year, the money would be cut almost in half. In addition, the chickens didn't lay eggs all year long, and the cow went dry sometime each year, only having more milk after she had another calf. Without their own bull, it would cost something to have her bred. There were so many things she'd have to keep up with. Just thinking about them gave her a headache.

She lifted a soft, well-worn cotton flannel shirt and clasped it against her chest. "Pa didn't really have anything very fancy. But didn't some of the people who were caught in the fire lose everything? I understand that a couple of nearby houses also burned down."

"They did." Daniel grabbed a pair of Pa's denim overalls and started folding them.

She almost laughed at him, because they looked like they were sort of rolled, instead of folded as she would have done it. But at least they were neat.

"I'd like to give all his clothing to help some of the men who lost everything."

"Oh, Mary." He laid the garment on the foot of the bed and turned to smile at her. "I'm so proud of you."

At the tenderness in his tone, she returned his smile. "I want to help someone else. So many people have come to our rescue."

Daniel nodded in understanding, then started taking the other clothing off the hooks. "I can take care of these. Why don't you start going through the chest of drawers."

They worked separately for several minutes.

"We need to pack these things for transport into town." Daniel laid the last item on the bed beside where Mary had started putting Pa's socks and handkerchiefs. "There are wooden crates in the barn. I'll bring a few inside."

"Thank you." They shared another smile before Daniel turned away. For the next few minutes, Mary busied herself with Pa's undergarments, stuffing them in a pillowcase, when suddenly she found herself humming. How could this be? She stopped, her hands full of long underwear. When had this happened? Days and weeks of unending toil and pain and despair had left her exhausted and numb. But suddenly, unexpectedly, her heart was alive again, as if a heavy load had been lifted.

And she knew. There could only be one reason for the change. Daniel.

~

*W*hen Daniel went out the back door, he saw Tony Chan trying to round up the cows that apparently had gotten out through a break in the fence. The critters were stubborn, with each one heading a different direction. His friend looked about tuckered out, so he stopped to help. It took nearly half an hour for them to corral the creatures and repair the fence.

With Mr. Murray gone, maybe Mary would let him make some changes to how things worked on the farm. He really hoped so. They seemed to have reached a truce, maybe even returned to friendship. That is, if he read the signs right. But how could a man really be sure he understood a woman?

He quickly gathered up four of the wooden crates and hurried toward the house. He'd spent more time outside than he planned.

Frances almost ran into him at the back door. He dropped the crates and caught her before she fell. "Where you headed?"

"I wanted to go down to the creek and wade in the cool water. Mary said I could." She headed toward the bushes that lined the slow-moving stream.

"Watch out for wild critters." He called after her.

She ignored him...or she didn't hear because she was running.

When he walked into the hall, he expected to hear Mary moving around the room, but dead silence reigned. He pushed through the door and set the stack of crates on the floor beside the bed.

He glanced up. Mary sat on the bed, holding a paper in her hand.

"What's that you have?"

She looked as if she was coming out of a daze as she turned toward him. She held out a yellowed paper to him, tears streaming down her face.

September 19, 1867

I, Angus McKenna, do hereby give my daughter, Mary Lenora, to Kenneth and Melody Murray to adopt and raise as their own child. I promise not to ever try to contact Mary Lenora.

Signed,
Angus McKenna
Kenneth Murray
Melody Murray

Witnessed,
John Overton
Matthias Horton, MD

The words leapt off the page. Her adoption papers. He had known she was adopted, but seeing the information written in a few words like this must have come as a shock to her. No wonder she was crying.

"He didn't want me, so he just gave me away." Her voice hitched on the last word. "What is wrong with me? Why couldn't anyone love me?"

Daniel's heart broke for her. "Mary, you know that Kenneth

and Melody Murray loved you." He wanted to add that he did, too, but a check in his spirit stopped him.

And something about one name on that paper sounded familiar. Angus McKenna. Finally, he remembered meeting with a Mr. McKenna when he'd gone to San Francisco a few months back to meet with the shipper they were considering using. If he was this man, Daniel knew he didn't want to do business with a man who could just give away his own flesh and blood.

"Where was my first mother? Why did she let my first father just give me away like a piece of garbage? I guess she didn't love me either." Mary's shoulders slumped even lower, if that were possible.

He didn't know anything about Mary's adoption, but he knew someone who did.

"Let's go into town. My family came out on the same wagon train. Maybe Mother can shed some light on all this. Explain what happened." He pulled her to her feet. "Go wash your face and do whatever you need to before we leave. I'll tell Tony to watch out for Frances."

Within ten minutes, they were in the wagon headed for Oregon City. Daniel wished he could take all this hurt from her shoulders, but he couldn't. *Please, God, don't let our relationship slip back to the place it was when I ran away.*

Mary stared at her hands. "I found a lot of interesting things in that bottom drawer."

Maybe talking about other things would help her, so he picked up the conversation. "What kind of things?"

"Some nice women's jewelry." She spoke in a monotone. "Probably my moth— probably Melody's."

He felt sure she spoke about her ma that way to distance herself, to keep from getting hurt even more. "I'm sure it was."

"And there were two deeds. One for the farm, and one for the other farm where Ma and my older sisters died and are buried. It belonged to Uncle Leland and Aunt Miriam. They and all their children died at the same time as Ma and my sisters." She stared straight ahead, clutching her hands together in what looked like a death grip to him. "I guess that means Frances, George, Bobby, and I now own two farms."

This was a strange conversation for them to be having. "Sounds like it." His arms and heart ached to pull her close to him and take all her pain away.

"And a wedding picture." She glanced up at him. "It had to be this Angus McKenna and my mother. I look just like her. Maybe they didn't have a good marriage. That's why he wanted to give me away, because I look just like her. What other reason could there be?"

The pain threading through her words pierced his heart.

"Do you want to see it?" Mary opened the drawstrings of her handbag and took out the photograph in an oval frame, then held it out to him.

Holding the reins in one hand, he took a moment to glance at it. The woman did look like Mary, but that man couldn't be the one from San Francisco. The man in this photograph was quite young, but the man in California was old enough to be Mary's grandfather, not her father. He handed it back to her.

After returning the picture to her handbag, she glanced up at him. "And a strongbox." Mary twisted her hands together. "It took me awhile to find the key. It was in the pouch with the jewelry."

He wished he could watch her face, but he needed to make sure the horse followed the curves in the country road. His quick glimpses of her face weren't enough. Every freckle she had stood out against her unnaturally pale face. He hoped she wouldn't faint on the way into town.

"Want to know what was in the strongbox?" Still the monotone.

"Sure." He tried to sound enthusiastic to encourage her.

She turned to stare at him. "Money... Lots. Of. Money."

"How much?" Why had her father lived so frugally if he had lots of money? At least she wouldn't be destitute now.

"After I found the adoption paper, I didn't take time to count it."

She lapsed into silence, and they finished the ride without speaking further. Finally, they pulled up in front of his parent's mansion and Daniel led Mary up the front steps. *Please, God. Let my mother have the answers Mary needs to hear.*

CHAPTER 24

*M*ary caught her breath when they stepped into the foyer of the Winthrop mansion. This was the first time she had been inside. Funny, since Daniel had courted her for a while before their quarrel. All their excursions had been to other places in Oregon City or in Portland. The rest of the time, he came out to the farm where they often sat on the front porch swing, talking, and enjoying the evening breeze.

The beauty of these surroundings stunned her. Marble floor, oil paintings in elaborate golden frames, vases, and delicate knickknacks artfully placed in niches or on tables with tapestry runners. Nothing like the plain decorations in the small house on the farm...her home.

"Mother?" Daniel started down the hall away from the foyer, holding Mary's hand and pulling her behind him. "Where are you?"

Mrs. Winthrop's well-modulated voice answered, "In my sitting room."

Since they had bypassed a parlor Mary caught a glimpse of near the entrance, his mother must have a private place of her very own. Mary hoped she wouldn't mind having them barge in on her. Of course, Mrs. Winthrop had always been kind to her at church.

Daniel stopped outside a doorway and motioned Mary to enter before he did.

His mother laid aside her needlepoint and rose to meet them. She held out both hands to Mary. "Daniel didn't tell me he was going to bring you by to see me. I'm glad he finally did."

When she clasped the proffered hands in her own, Mary felt a special connection to the woman who along with the other church women had been so helpful during her family's recent trying times. "You have a lovely home."

"Thank you, Mary." Daniel's mother leaned toward her and gave her a quick kiss on the cheek. "Now come sit beside me and tell me how you are. And Frances and the boys. I know things have been very difficult."

They both sat on the divan upholstered in cream-colored brocade with a lovely pastel flower design woven in. Mary hoped she didn't have any of the dust or debris from Pa's bedroom on the back of her skirt. She should have made sure before they came inside the house.

"You've been a great help to us all." She folded her hands in her lap, trying to hide the fact that they weren't as smooth as her hostess's hands.

Daniel perched on a chair in matching upholstery, looking very much at home even in this very feminine room. He must come here often to spend time with his mother. "We actually came because we thought you might have some information Mary needs."

His mother looked at Mary, then back at him, with a question in her eyes. "How can I help?"

He nodded toward Mary. "You tell her."

Mrs. Winthrop held up a hand to stop them both. "Mary, would you rather we have a more private discussion? We can send my boy to the kitchen to bother Mrs. Shelton. She is making cookies. She might welcome his attention right now."

Mary glanced at Daniel, wondering if his feelings would be hurt if she agreed.

He gave her an understanding smile. "I think I will check out those cookies." He stood. "Maybe later, we can bring tea and cookies to both of you as well."

The man kept amazing her. He exhibited growing maturity and discernment, which endeared him to her even more. Maybe they could at least become good friends again. Mary hoped so. She watched him give his mother a kiss on the cheek before exiting. A man who showed open affection to his mother. Mary liked that.

"So now that he's gone..." Mrs. Winthrop concentrated all her attention on Mary. "...tell me what's bothering you."

Mary held her reticule close to her heart. "I've known I was adopted as long as I can remember. Ma called me God's blessing because of that fact."

Mrs. Winthrop nodded. "Yes, I heard her say that very thing many times. She loved you so much."

Tears threatened again. Mary blinked them back. "I never knew the circumstances of my adoption."

A gasp escaped from Daniel's mother. "I never realized that. I thought Melody had told you everything. But then you were only ten years old or so when she died, weren't you?"

"Eleven." Mary swallowed the lump in her throat. "Maybe she planned to tell me when I was older."

Mrs. Winthrop agreed. "And I'm sure Kenneth didn't even think to tell you. Men can be so dense about some things."

Mary almost laughed. She didn't realize that other women saw men the same way she did. At least, Pa hadn't paid attention to many things Mary thought he should.

"Adoption is a very personal thing." Mrs. Winthrop patted Mary's arm. "Maybe he thought Melody had told you everything. Now tell me what happened to cause your adoption to upset you today."

Mary opened her bag and pulled out the crinkly paper. She handed it to Daniel's mother.

After the older woman read it, she returned it to her. "I never saw the paper before, so I didn't know what it contained. I can see why it could be upsetting to you."

"Yes." Mary couldn't keep the touch of bitterness from her voice. "Who is Angus McKenna? Why did he give me away?" The words poured from between her lips. "Why did my mother, whoever she was, let him? And why did he promise never to contact me? I...just...don't...understand." To her embarrassment, sobs interrupted the last sentence.

Mrs. Winthrop gathered Mary into her arms and patted her back. "There... there now. It's going to be all right."

When Mary was able to dry her tears, the two women leaned back in the divan to talk.

"I'll tell you what I know." Daniel's mother gazed across the room with unseeing eyes, as if she were revisiting the distant past. "Everyone on the wagon train loved Angus and Lenora McKenna."

"Her name was Lenora?" Mary could hardly believe it. "That's my middle name."

"I didn't realize he gave you her name." The older woman turned to face her.

"He gave me my name. I thought Ma and Pa did." So much new information, Mary had a hard time understanding all of it.

"No. I'm sure he named you. Melody told me that at some time or the other. The McKennas were coming west to open a store at the gold fields in California. They brought a black couple, who had been former slaves. Henry and Odette Marshall. Angus had hired them to work in the store. They had two wagons with each of the families' personal possessions, and a third wagon with things to sell in the store when it first opened."

"So my parents had money?" That was a revelation to Mary. Her family had lived frugally on the farm, but her real parents had money. Of course, so did Pa and Ma, as she had just found out.

"I believe so. He had been some kind of second or third son of nobility before they came to America from Scotland."

"Nobility?" That really didn't fit with the life Mary had led. "How could they give me away?"

"Lenora had a hard time during the last few months on the trail. Her condition deteriorated as we went along. Her difficulties was the reason the wagon train took the easier Barlow Cutoff, instead of crossing the quicker, but more difficult, Dalles. And we ended up in Oregon City instead of Fort Vancouver. The doctor suggested that your mother ride in the back of the wagon on a pallet the last couple of weeks before she went into labor."

"Oh...my." Mary couldn't imagine having to experience anything so arduous. "So what happened to my mother?"

"I'm getting to that, dear child." Daniel's mother got that faraway look in her eyes again, as if she were really reliving every moment. "Some of the women who had already given birth helped the doctor care for her. I was one of them. We stopped the wagons on a cold, rainy night only about three days from Oregon City."

Mary tried to imagine what it was like, but had a hard time. At least, her home on the farm had always been warm and secure.

"Angus was outside the wagon with Reverend Knowles praying for Lenora. She gave birth to a tiny girl with red curly hair. I held her first and cleaned her up before we gave her to her father."

Why did Daniel's mother call the baby *her* instead of *you*?

"Before I got back into the wagon you were born."

"Wait a minute," Mary interrupted her. "I had a sister? What happened to her? Did she die?"

"I don't think so. Let me finish my story. It's a little hard to keep all the details straight."

She didn't think so. Why didn't she know for sure? The thoughts whirling inside Mary's head almost made her dizzy.

"We handed you to Charlotte Holden, and she took you outside to show to your father. He was amazed. No one knew that Lenora was carrying more than one baby.... And then the third one was born. Three identical babies. Tiny little girls, with curly red hair. So beautiful."

Mary's head really was swimming. If she hadn't been sitting down, she would have collapsed. "I'm a triplet?"

"Yes, my dear." Mrs. Winthrop patted her on the hand this time. "I know this is a lot to take in all at once."

"This still doesn't tell me why my mother and father gave me away." Now Mary wasn't sure she really wanted to know. The feeling of rejection she'd fought against most of her life settled on her like an oppressive spirit.

"That's the worst part. I really hate to tell you." Daniel's mother took a deep breath and launched back into her story. "After the last baby was born, Angus came into the wagon to see Lenora. She looked at each of the three babies and gave a wan smile. He leaned over, still clutching the firstborn, and kissed her. When he raised back up, Lenora's eyes closed and never opened again. We took the baby from him and let him have some time alone with her. The doctor had warned them earlier that she was very frail, but I don't think Angus believed she wouldn't pull through. His cries of anguish reverberated through the whole campsite. I can still hear the sound sometimes in my dreams."

Tears poured down Mrs. Winthrop's face, just as they did Mary's.

"Angus loved Lenora so much, he was a broken man. He couldn't face the loss of his only true love. And he didn't know what he'd do with one baby, much less three. So he very carefully chose two families to raise two of his daughters."

Mary wondered how he chose which ones to give away. And why did she have to be one of them? "I found a wedding picture in the box Pa kept. The woman looks just like me. Do you think that is my mother and father?" She once again took the photograph from her handbag.

The older woman stared at it intently. "You do look like Lenora. I'm sure your sisters do as well. The three of you were like three peas in a pod, completely identical."

"There have been times in my life I've felt part of me was missing. I didn't know what part it was, but I missed it very much. I know that doesn't make a lot of sense, but do you think I was missing my sisters?" That was the only explanation Mary could come up with.

"I'm sure you were." Mrs. Winthrop put her arm around Mary's shoulders. "You are a very special blessing, just as Melody told you."

"Why did he choose the Murrays to adopt me?" Mary pulled her hanky out of her reticule and started dabbing at her tear-stained face.

"Melody and Kenneth had two little girls, and she gave birth to another one about halfway across the country."

"Wait. I only had two older sisters, Carrie and Annette." Mary was sure Daniel's mother was mistaken.

"Actually, baby Rebecca died before we got to Oregon. They buried her on the trail."

Mary's heart ached for Ma, who had more than her share of loss. *Thank the good Lord, she agreed to adopt me. She needed me as much as I needed her.*

"Melody had a hard time getting over the loss. She had been serving as a wet nurse for another family, because the mother couldn't feed her own baby. Naturally, they needed wet nurses for the triplets. Angus chose your parents, because he knew they would take good care of you."

Mary stared at the carpet, the colors swirling like her emotions. Did her parents take good care of her? Her mother certainly did as long as she lived. She wondered if Angus McKenna would have given her to them if he knew her adoptive mother would die when Mary was just eleven years old. Or that she would be left to care for three orphaned children after the death of her adoptive father.

"But why did he promise not to ever try to contact me?" This one thing hurt as much or more than any of the other information Mary had just heard.

"No one can really know his thinking on the subject, but I imagine he didn't want the adopting families to love you and your sister but have the fear hanging over their heads that he would come take you back. It was a very noble thing he did, and I know the decision was hard for him to make. He wasn't the same on the last few days of the trip, and he left for California right after we reached Oregon City. Odette Marshall had a baby the day before you triplets were born. She became the wet nurse for Catherine Lenora."

"So no one knows where he is?"

"Not really. He could be anywhere by now." Concern puckered Mrs. Winthrop's brows.

"What about my other sister? What was her name? Who did he give her to?" If Mary couldn't find Angus McKenna and the daughter he kept, maybe she could find her other sister.

"Margaret Lenora went to Joshua and Florence Caine, a couple who had been married a number of years without having any children. They settled in Oregon City and lived here until you girls were about five years old. When they moved away, no one ever heard from them again. And they didn't tell anyone where they were going. It could be anywhere."

Since her mother and father were dead, Mary had a burning desire to find her sisters. Mrs. Winthrop's answers didn't give her much hope of that, but she knew she wouldn't forget the idea. Someday...somehow, she *would* find a way.

Mrs. Shelton came into the sitting room, carrying a silver tray with a teapot, china cups and saucers, and plates of sandwiches and cookies. "Mr. Daniel said you might be ready for this. He didn't want to bring it in until you said he might join you."

His mother gripped Mary's hand. "What do you say, Mary? Should we let that boy come in now?"

She nodded. The way the woman said *that boy* sounded comical when applied to the *man* who had been working on her farm for these last weeks. Mary would not call him a boy at all. But perhaps men were always little boys to their mothers.

Mrs. Shelton set the tray on the table in front of the divan and left the room. Within a minute or two, Daniel sauntered in.

"Is everything all right in here?" His eyes had homed in on Mary, and she felt his nonjudgmental support.

They spent several minutes chatting about inconsequential things and sharing the afternoon tea with Daniel's mother before heading out the door bound for the farm. On the way, Mary kept her eyes trained ahead, pondering all she had learned. After a while, Daniel interrupted her thoughts.

"So, Mary, did you find out what you needed to know about your adoption?"

Had she? She mulled over how she should answer him. "I believe so."

He turned his eyes back toward the road. "I'm glad. I was praying for you while you and Mother were together."

Of course, you were. That was just the kind of man Daniel had become.

"Do you think you can share what you found out with me?"

She hadn't expected that question, but she answered

honestly. "I will want to, but I need to get used to all the information and settle things in my own mind."

"I understand that." He didn't sound upset, and she was glad.

"I'm more at peace than I was before we came to town, but I still have a lot of things to work through."

"I'm here for you any time you want to talk about it."

After driving the wagon for several minutes, he pulled over into a meadow and stopped under the shade of a spreading oak tree. "Mary, I want to ask you something important."

She thought she knew what it was, and she didn't know if she was ready to answer it in the affirmative. Maybe later.

"Do you remember when I came back from my uncle's sheep ranch?"

Staring up into his face, she nodded. "Of course, I do. You told me, 'I came back to serve you. Help you every way you need until you can see into my heart.' I'll never forget that day."

"But you didn't believe I had changed, did you?" He gazed across the rolling landscape with unseeing eyes as if waiting breathlessly for her answer.

She wouldn't lie to him about it, even to make him feel better. "No, I didn't." Her answer was soft and filled with regret.

He looked back at her. "Do you believe me now? Or must I keep on serving and waiting?" There was no censure in his words or his tone.

The time she had hoped for had arrived. She didn't want to mess this up. "Yes, Daniel. I can see into your heart. You truly are a man of God, walking out what you believe in your daily life."

Tension melted out of his back and shoulders, and his smile softened. "So we can be good friends again?"

For a moment, she couldn't keep disappointment out of her expression, but she quickly slipped a smile back in place. "Yes, we are good friends again." Of course, she had expected a deeper relationship.

He picked up the reins and drove back onto the road. "I'm glad."

On the rest of the way to the farm, he talked about doing some repairs to the house, barn, and fences. That's not what she wanted to discuss, but she said *all right* often enough to keep him talking. She buried her disappointment and kept glancing at the trees, the flowers, even the clouds dancing across the sky. Everything around them seemed to display happiness, except her. Her thoughts were in such a muddle.

He stopped the wagon beside the gate to the yard. After vaulting out of the wagon in a single, graceful bound, he reached for her waist and quickly set her on the ground. But he didn't let go. "You agreed with us being good friends awful quickly. But I sensed maybe you weren't happy with that."

Can he read my mind? She hoped not. Some things a woman wanted to keep to herself.

"Well, then, how about this?" He gave her a dazzling smile that melted her heart. "May I return to courting you, Mary?"

"I thought you'd never ask." With those words everything in her world changed. She was in mourning for her father, but now joy burst through in her heart. And for the moment, she simply basked in its warmth.

CHAPTER 25

*D*aniel and Sultan had made the trip from the farm back to town enough times that the stallion knew the way. A good thing, because Daniel couldn't remember any of the trip. His mind was otherwise engaged. Mary had finally forgiven him. They were courting again. His life had taken a wonderful upward turn.

Garrett was still working in the stable when Daniel rode in and jumped from Sultan's back. Any other time Daniel would have taken care of his horse himself, but now he handed the reins off to their driver and headed toward the house.

Mrs. Shelton was serving his parents the soup that would precede the first course of their evening meal. She glanced at him. "So are you having dinner here with your parents tonight?"

"Yes, ma'am. I'll wash up and be down in a few minutes." He dropped a kiss on his mother's cheek, and clapped his father on the shoulder as he quickly passed through on his way to his room. "Good to see you, Father."

When he returned, his favorite potato leek soup was

steaming on his place setting. After he was seated, his father asked for God's blessing on their food.

During the meal, Daniel ate what was set before him without even noticing what it was. His parents carried on an animated conversation, but he didn't enter into the discussion. His mind was reviewing the possibilities of his and Mary's future.

Finally, Mrs. Shelton set a slice of lemon pie in front of him. He took a bite without saying a word.

"Son, what's on your mind?" Mr. Winthrop laid his fork on his dessert plate and leaned back.

Daniel stared at him for a minute. "Why do you think something's on my mind?"

"Well, you haven't said ten words to us since you sat down, and you didn't even acknowledge that Mrs. Shelton made your favorite dessert. Those were easy clues."

When his father laughed, Daniel joined him. "Sorry, I know I'm distracted."

"Does this distraction have red curls and stand about so tall?" Father raised his hand to about the height of Mary.

"OK. You caught me." Daniel took another delicious bite before he set his fork down as well.

"It wasn't a wild guess, Son. Your mother told me about Mary's visit today. Is there any way we need to help her?"

For all intents and purposes, dinner had come to an end. Mother suggested they take their pie and go into her sitting room and relax while they discussed everything.

After they were settled, Daniel told his parents that he wanted to go ahead and propose to Mary. He filled them in on the serious conversation he'd shared with Mr. Murray before he died, including the promise he'd made to the man. And he gave them a brief rundown of the conversation with Mary that afternoon.

"I know she and her siblings are in mourning, but I don't want to wait a year before we marry. I need to be with her and help her in ways I can't as long as we are only courting. We must protect her reputation during the transition time. I'm not sure how to handle this delicately." He took one more bite to polish off the pie. Too bad he hadn't really savored it as he usually did. But Mary was much more important than any dessert, no matter how delicious.

For over half an hour, he and his parents discussed various things that could affect the relationship. They agreed that in Mary's circumstances, maybe a shorter period of mourning would be enough.

Mother set her dessert plate down with half her pie still on it. "It's not unusual in this part of the country for people to have a shortened period of mourning because of the circumstances in their lives. I've known of several respectable widows with small children to marry within scant weeks of their husband's deaths."

"That sounds a lot better than a year." Even though Daniel would rather marry her tomorrow, a few months were reasonable to him.

Father studied Daniel for a moment. "I want to ask you one question. Why do you want to marry her?"

Daniel could hardly believe he had to ask. "Mary has been through so much. I want to help her have a better life."

"Sounds like you want to be her savior, not her husband." His father's gaze turned into a stare.

Daniel shook his head. "I've already worked through that when I was at Uncle Clarence's. He helped me realize that my motivations were all wrong. Then I had a deep experience with the good Lord."

A broad smile split his father's face. "So that's what made such a drastic change in you. I wondered what happened and was hoping you would share it with me."

"You noticed the change?" That was a revelation to Daniel. He didn't figure anyone had, since Mary hadn't at first.

"I did too, Son." His mother patted him on the knee. "We're very proud of the way you have matured."

"Now let's get back to my question." Father was relentless when he wanted information.

"I love Mary, because she is good inside and out. She's strong. She loves the Lord. She has had to deal with some very tough things, and she accepted the responsibility of caring for her siblings, not as a duty, but as a privilege." A vision of her danced through Daniel's head. "And her beauty is breathtaking. All those red curls and her green eyes with flecks of gold that sparkle in the sunlight."

"OK. I'm convinced." His father laughed. "You have my blessing for this marriage."

He could tell that although his mother had been listening, she had more to say.

"Mary's been on my mind a lot since the two of you left this afternoon. Melody was a good mother to her, and she would be grieved about how hard Mary's life has been. Her birthday is coming up in two months. Perhaps we could have a quiet family celebration for her here at the house, make her feel special and loved. And I'd want to help her with the wedding. If she wouldn't think I'm interfering too much." Mother smiled at him. "You could have a church wedding in late October."

Daniel went to his mother and dropped another kiss on her cheek. "You helped her a lot today. I believe she was extremely grateful. I'm going upstairs to change, then I'll be using the buggy tonight. I hope the moon is full."

*M*ary stood by the window and stared out at the deepening twilight, enjoying the muted colors in the sky as they slowly faded. When Daniel left to go home this afternoon, he told Mary he'd come calling on her tonight. That sounded so strange since he had been here every day since he returned from working on his uncle's sheep ranch. Even on Sundays, he came out after services and took care of chores around the farm. But just knowing he was going to be here to court her again brought a whole flock of hummingbirds to her stomach. Those tiny wings that moved so fast they were almost invisible reawakened the embers of love she had buried after he left, fanning them into a bright flame.

She wanted to look especially pretty for him, and the only black dress she had was a serviceable, unattractive one. Mary needed to get enough fabric for at least one really nice black dress to wear when she went to church. Maybe tonight it would be all right to wear her darkest green dress. Daniel had seen her a lot in her everyday clothes. The green had tiny yellow dots in the fabric, and black braid trimmed both the fitted bodice and skirt. Now if she could just manage to get her hair into some kind of pretty style.

A knock sounded on her door. "May I come in, Mary?"

"Yes, Francie." She hoped her sister didn't need something that would keep Mary from getting ready for Daniel's return.

Her sister held her hands behind her back. "I heard Daniel ask Tony Chan to stay later tonight. So I figure he's coming back, and it's not to work in the dark. At least, there's a bright moon tonight."

A blush crept up Mary's face. Francie was growing up. Only a few months ago, Mary had wished her sister would grow up more, but now it was rushing too fast.

"How can I help you?" She continued to brush at her hair, trying to work the tangles from her tight curls.

"I came to help you." Her sister pulled out her hands where Mary could see them. They held ribbon and two combs with pearls on them.

"Where did you get those?" Mary was afraid they were far too valuable for her sister to have.

"When I go to visit Milly, we always fix each other's hair. Her aunt back east had sent her several sets of fancy combs. She wanted to give me two of them, and her mother said I could have them. Now, let's get you ready for your time with Daniel... I really like him."

How could Mary refuse? She would let Francie try her hand at styling her hair. If she didn't like it, she could adjust the results.

Her sister wouldn't let her see what she was doing until she finished. When Francie handed her the mirror, the woman reflecting back at her looked almost beautiful. The combs lifted her hair on the sides, and Francie had tamed the unruly curls into an interesting cluster on top of her head, all except two long curls that draped across the front of her right shoulder. The satin ribbon wove artfully through the creation. She had never looked better.

Mary jumped up and hugged her sister. "Thank you so much. I feel pretty."

While she clung to Mary, Francie whispered, "Mary, you've always been beautiful. I've wished for curls like yours."

"And I've wished for skin like yours with no freckles," Mary teased. The two sisters shared a laugh, all their troubles seeming to fade for a few precious moments.

Their merriment was interrupted by the sound of a horse and buggy. Was Daniel going to take her for a late evening ride?

That question was answered rather quickly, and soon the two of them set off down the country road. They made small talk until Daniel turned into a lane Mary had never noticed before. She pulled her thoughts from admiring the handsome man riding beside her. Some kind of delicious, spicy fragrance joined with the musky, masculine scent that meant Daniel to her.

She laid her hand on his arm. "Where does this go?"

"You'll see." He covered her hand with one of his, holding both reins in the other. "I found this place years ago. I think you'll like it."

Before long, he pulled onto another road, little more than wagon tracks across an open field. After they rode between trees lining a stream, he stopped the wagon in a tiny meadow. At one end, the creek tumbled down a short waterfall into a foaming pool. Mary didn't know there were any waterfalls this far from the town that sprawled across the Willamette falls.

Daniel quickly vaulted from the buggy and hurried to the side where Mary sat. His hands spanned her waist and he quickly deposited her on the lush green grass surrounding them. He seemed reluctant to break the connection of his hands, and she didn't move away. His warmth drew her like a magnet. Being this close to Daniel in the waning twilight whisked Mary away from her mundane life into an extraordinary place filled with fascinating possibilities. Possibilities she and Daniel would face together.

Daniel finally released her and stood in front of her with his stance wide and his hands behind his back. "I wanted to show you this place that is special to me, but even more than that, I have a question to ask you."

His eyes sparkled more than the emerging stars piercing the inky canopy above them. "You are so beautiful.... My heart rejoices just thinking about a future we could spend together."

Mary almost forgot to breathe. She didn't know when she had ever been so happy. But could they agree on what their future should look like?

He led her to a large slab of rock firmly attached to the bank of the pool, but also jutting out over the water. They stepped up on the top surface, which looked much like a stage. Daniel kept hold of one of her hands while he dropped to one knee.

"Daniel, what are you doing?" She didn't want him to let go.

"Mary Lenora Murray, I pledge my love to you from this time forward as long as the Lord allows us to live. Will you marry me?" His soft lips caressed the back of her hand.

She lost herself in the gentle touch that reached all the way to her heart, sending her pulse into a rapid staccato beat. How could she answer? She truly loved Daniel with all her heart, but he had to know that her family would play a significant part in her life until her siblings were grown.

Before she could utter a word, he arose and gazed deep into her eyes, as if he could catch a glimpse of what lay in her heart. The rising moon bathed the clearing in a pearlized light, adding more twinkles to the depths of Daniel's eyes.

"I realize you need to know what this would mean. I will love you and protect you, Frances, George, and Bobby with my very life. I will not make any arbitrary decisions about our lives without discussing things with you. We will seek the Lord's counsel and move the direction *we* feel Him leading us."

Daniel's words touched a hollow place inside her heart. This was what she needed to hear.

"We can work out all the details as we go along." He led her down from the rock, then tucked her hand through the crook of his arm as they ambled along beside the bubbling stream. "Mother made some suggestions, but you can choose to follow them... or not. I won't impose my decisions on you in any of this. Neither will she."

Mary didn't feel rushed. "You do know I'm in mourning."

"Of course, I do. And I share your grief at the loss of your father." His tender voice soothed her. "But Mother thinks three months would be an acceptable length of time for us to wait to get married. That is, if you tell me yes. Circumstances can shorten the time of mourning, even though we'll never forget your father and how important he was to all of us."

These words contrasted to the last ones he had spoken about their future that horrible day at the clinic. She welcomed them into her heart and allowed them to erase all the hurt the others had inflicted.

"We can live at the farm, or we can move into my house in town and bring your siblings with you. The farm will always be your family's inheritance for your brothers." He placed his hand over hers that still rested on his forearm. "There are various ways we can make sure it continues to be productive. We can decide together."

"I'm not even sure how to plan a wedding." Hope expanded inside her like a blossoming flower.

He stopped and turned her to face him. "She doesn't want to interfere with anything you want, but Mother would be glad to help you have the kind of wedding that would make you happy."

Mary felt as if she had cried buckets of tears over the last few weeks, but they had been from grief. The tears filling her eyes right now were from joy...and happiness.

She took hold of Daniel's lapels to keep herself upright. Staring into his dear face, Mary whispered, "Yes."

He studied her intently, a smile spreading across his handsome features. "I think you said something, but I want to make sure I understood what you said. Tell me again, louder this time." Laughter colored the tone of his words.

"Yes." This time anyone within a mile could probably hear her response. "I will marry you, Daniel Winthrop."

He stepped back and reached into the pocket of his jacket, pulling out a small, velvet, reticule-shaped bag. After loosening the drawstrings, he upended the bag over his palm. A gold ring with a large cluster of pearls slid out. "This belonged to my grandmother. I want you to wear it as a symbol of our commitment to each other."

She held out her left hand, and when he slid the circlet onto the third finger, it fit as if it had been created just for her. Holding her hand in the bright moonlight, she admired the beautiful piece of jewelry...and the sentiments it represented.

Daniel slid his arms around Mary and pulled her into an embrace. The whispering of the leaves in the wind and the gurgle of the water faded away as his lips hovered over hers, then dipped into a gentle, tentative touch that made her yearn for more. Finally, they settled over hers with a firmness that sealed their love for each other. Mary's heart floated in a dance with his, entwining their destiny for the rest of their lives.

Daniel leaned his forehead against hers. "Mary, you are God's special blessing to me."

And for the first time in her life, Mary really did feel like a blessing.

The End

Did you enjoy this book? We hope so!
Would you take a quick minute to leave a review where you purchased the book?
It doesn't have to be long. Just a sentence or two telling what you liked about the story!

Receive a FREE ebook and get updates when new Wild Heart books release: https://wildheartbooks.org/newsletter

Don't miss Catherine's Pursuit, book 3 in the McKenna's Daughters series!

September 19, 1885

San Francisco, California

Catherine Lenora McKenna could hardly believe the long-awaited day had arrived. Her eighteenth birthday.

Now she was an adult, and her father would have to stop hovering over her as if she were a fragile china doll in one of his stores. She would be free. Holding her hands above her head like the ballerina in the music box on her bureau, she whirled in a circle that lifted the hem of her blue taffeta skirt to a scandalous height. That didn't matter, because no one was here to catch a glimpse of her ankles, anyway. Not even her personal maid, Julie, who had gone downstairs to grab Catherine a more substantial breakfast from the kitchen before she fainted dead away.

Aunt Kirstin wanted Catherine to eat very light before her party tonight, where a sumptuous banquet would precede the ball. There would be presents to open as well. Catherine hoped her father planned a spectacular gift for her birthday...maybe to send her on a tour of the Continent. Of course, Aunt Kirstin would probably accompany her, but at least she would be able to see more of the world for herself, not just read about it.

Europe should be beautiful in the autumn, or in any season of the year. Since both of her parents were born in Scotland, she wanted to visit there as well as London...Paris...Rome. She had read every book and magazine she could get her hands on, so she knew so much about Europe. A thrill of anticipation shot through her whole body. Visions of crossing London Bridge, strolling along Avenue des Champs Elysees, or touring the Colosseum danced through her head. Pictures she'd enjoyed studying with their Holmes stereopticon. She wondered if Father would accompany her or if he would allow Aunt Kirstin to be her only escort...besides a few servants, of course.

"Where is Julie with my food?" Catherine huffed out an exasperated breath. "Am I going to have to go to the kitchen myself?"

She thrust open the door and hurried down the hallway, the sound of her footsteps lost in the thick cushioning of the carpet. At the top of the front stairs, she stopped to see if she could figure out where her aunt Kirstin was before she sneaked down the backstairs.

Peering over the balcony railing, she caught a glimpse of her aunt's face through the partially opened door to the library. Her brows were knit together into a frown as she stared at someone in the room with her. Catherine had never seen such a fierce expression on her aunt's face.

Father's voice was muffled as he said something to his sister-in-law. *What is he doing home at this time of morning?* Catherine wished she could tell what they were talking about. She had never heard her father use that tone with anyone, especially not Aunt Kirstin. As if he were angry or terribly upset.

Catherine leaned farther over but kept a firm grip on the railing so she wouldn't tumble down. A drop onto a marble floor could be deadly.

Aunt Kirstin gripped each hand into a fist and planted them on her hips. "Just when are you going to tell her?"

Come to think of it, her aunt was using a harsher tone than Catherine had ever heard her use.

Father didn't answer.

Catherine quickly crept down the stairs being careful not to place her foot on the second step from the foyer, which would squeak and reveal her presence. At the bottom, she straightened and checked her reflection in the gilt-framed, oval mirror beside the front door. When she found everything satisfactory, she tiptoed toward the library.

"I don't know." Her father's words stopped her in her tracks.

What did he not know?

"Angus." Aunt Kirstin's voice was firm and insistent. "She deserves to know the truth. And now she's old enough to understand."

Catherine didn't hesitate to enter her favorite room in the house. She pushed the door farther open, and both her aunt and her father turned startled eyes toward her. The two looked as if they had been caught in an act of mischief.

"Tell me what? What will I understand?" Her questions hovered in the air, quivering like hummingbirds without a way to escape the net of tension that bound the three of them together.

Her father glanced at her aunt, then turned his attention back to Catherine. The deep scowl on his face dissolved, and he dropped into the closest chair, dejection dragging his shoulders into a slump. Tears welled up in his eyes and rolled down his cheeks unheeded. He didn't even blink.

"I knew this day would come...eventually." Each word sounded as if it had been wrung from his throat.

Catherine had never before seen her father cry. And he had always been such a strong man. But right now, he was draped in defeat. Her heart hitched in her chest, making her breathless. Something must be terribly wrong. Was he sick with a deadly disease? About to die? How would she live without him? She wanted to grab him in a tight hug and cling with all her might to keep him close.

Aunt Kirstin dragged two chairs closer to where he sat and offered one to Catherine before settling on the other. She smoothed her skirt over her knees and clasped her hands tight enough to blanch her knuckles.

Fear swamped Catherine, trying to drown her in its depths. The strong foundation her life had been built upon shuddered, then she felt as if a crevasse opened deep within her. Tears leaked into her own eyes, blurring her vision as she stared first at her father and then at her aunt, the anchors in her life.

Her father raised red-rimmed eyes toward her, his face a pale, scary caricature of the man she'd always leaned upon. "There's so much you don't know...my precious daughter."

Such a formal way for her father to talk to her, as if they were separated in some unseen way. Trembling started in her knees. She was glad she was sitting, so she didn't sink to the floor in a swoon. The tremors rose over her whole body, and she shook as though a chill wind had swept through the room.

Dare I ask another question? When she tried, her tongue stayed glued to the roof of her mouth, so she waited for him to continue.

Aunt Kirstin didn't utter a single word either.

"I've brought Miss Catherine a bit of a snack." Julie bustled through the open doorway, breaking the unbearable tension for a moment. "There's enough for all of you...and a pot of that new tea you just received from China." She set the tray on the table that stood beside Aunt Kirstin's chair, then exited the room.

Mechanically, Catherine's aunt poured three cups of the steaming liquid and added just the right amount of milk and sugar to match each person's preference. When she handed the saucer and teacup to Father, both of their hands shook, rattling the china.

Catherine received her tea and kept one hand on the cup, warming her icy fingertips.

"Would you like a sandwich or a piece of cake?" Aunt Kirstin's whispered words were only a bit louder than the clink of the dishes.

Catherine didn't think she could get a single bite down her throat that now felt like a sandy desert. She shook her head.

Father didn't glance at her aunt before he handed his cup back without even taking a sip. He turned his gaze toward Catherine and took a breath, releasing it as a soul-deep sigh. "Some things happened when you were born...that I've never shared...with you...with anyone, except your aunt."

She set her cup and saucer back on the tray and waited for him to continue.

"Would you like me to leave?" Aunt Kirstin stared at Father, a look of something akin to pity on her face. "Would that make it easier?"

"Nothing will make it easier." Father roused more than he had since Catherine entered the library, his voice slicing through the room like a sharp dagger. "And no. Since you've opened the subject, you'll sit right there until I'm finished."

Her aunt shrank back against her chair and lowered her gaze to the Aubusson carpet where she traced the intricate pattern as if she had never seen it before. Catherine doubted she noticed any of the colors or flowers right now.

If Father didn't tell her what he was talking about soon, Catherine was afraid she would scream. The atmosphere in the room hung heavy with suspense. She cleared her throat and covered the cough that ensued with one fisted hand.

"There is no easy way...to say this." Father shifted in the chair, the wooden legs creaking under his slight weight. He stared at her. "I'm going to tell you what happened. Please don't interrupt me until I'm finished. Otherwise, I might not get through the whole story. Then you can ask any questions you want."

Her nose itched, but she didn't dare rub it. She didn't want to do anything that might stop this tale from pouring forth from her father. She gritted her teeth ready to face whatever it was, no matter how grim.

"You know that your...mother and I were on a wagon train on the Oregon Trail. Lenora had some...difficulties near the end of our journey." He swallowed, his Adam's apple bobbing convulsively. "She had to ride in the back of the wagon for a couple of weeks."

Catherine knew she was born on the Oregon Trail, and she knew that her mother died in childbirth. Their family friend Odette Marshall had told her that much before Aunt Kirstin finally came to California to help her father. Even though Catherine had been only six years old when she'd heard it, the story was burned into her heart.

"When you were born, one of the women who assisted Dr. Horton brought you to me. I held you in my arms, huddled beside the campfire on that bone-chilling night." A faraway look filled his eyes, and she knew he didn't see her sitting nearby. "I loved you the moment I laid eyes on you....curly red fuzz covering your head....blue eyes."

"Blue?"

He held one palm toward her, stopping her question in midsentence. "They didn't turn green until later."

She hadn't known that. Other questions fought to escape, but she clamped her lips tightly to restrain them. The turmoil inside her made her stomach roil. She swallowed the acid that crept to her throat.

"Before long, a different woman brought another baby girl to me....curly red fuzz....blue eyes. The spittin' image of you. I cuddled both of you close to my heart and kissed each of your cheeks."

Catherine almost gasped. She couldn't remember the last time her father had held her close and kissed her cheek. She knew he loved her, but he wasn't demonstrative anymore. That was why he showered her with gifts so often, wasn't it? To show her he loved her.

"Then a few minutes later, another identical girl was brought to me. I didn't have enough arms to hold all three of you." He rubbed one hand over his chin, the rasp of unshaven stubble loud in the quiet room.

Three of us? How could that be? Did her two sisters die when her mother had? *Sisters!* She had always wished for siblings. Yearned for them.

Grief ripped through her. Tears streamed down her cheeks. To find out she had sisters and lose them all within a few minutes. She didn't feel like celebrating her birthday. Instead, she wanted to mourn the sisters she lost before she even knew she had them.

Catherine started formulating questions in her mind, waiting for the chance to ask them. Before they were half-formed, her father rose to his feet and walked out the door without saying another word. She waited a few minutes in a silence so heavy, it felt oppressive. She realized he wasn't coming back when the front door opened, then closed. Why hadn't he waited until she asked her questions?

"Mr. McKenna wants to talk to you."

Colin Elliott straightened from behind the stack of boxes he had been checking against the bill of lading and stared at the warehouse foreman. "I'm almost finished with these. Does he want to see me right away?"

"The old man's in a strange mood. Has been all day." Howard Lane scratched his head. "Ain't never seen him like this before. Better git on up there to the office."

Colin slashed an X with a piece of chalk on the last crate he'd finished checking and laid the letter-clip board that held the forms on top of the next box. He had been working out here most of the day. Because he often shoved his fingers through his hair, he was sure he looked like a wreck.

That described him to a T. A wreck. Or at least he had been since he lost his ship at sea last spring, along with all the merchandise in the hold. It had taken him several months to recover sufficiently from the severe cuts he'd sustained to his leg, but Mr. McKenna had made sure he was taken care of, even paying him as if he were still a captain. Then the old man gave him this job in the warehouse to keep busy. Still, a dull ache in his gut wouldn't let him forget one minute of the horror he experienced that day, and the limp from his injury kept the memory fresh with each step he took.

Colin headed toward the offices at the other end of the large building. He tried to straighten his mussed hair and stuffed his shirttail farther down inside his trousers. He could try to look neater, even if he did walk like a cripple.

Mr. McKenna's secretary, Roger Amery, glanced up as Colin entered the front office. "He's waiting for you. Just go on back."

He gave the man a distracted nod as he hurried by. The door to his boss's office stood open, so he entered.

"Close that behind you, Elliott. We need privacy." The old man didn't even look up from the paper he was writing on.

After complying, Colin dropped into the chair situated close to the front of the desk. What did the man want? Going back through the events of the last few days, Colin didn't remember anything he might have done wrong, so he slouched into a relaxed pose, hoping to give the impression that being called to the office didn't bother him. Of course, a lot of things had bothered him ever since that ghastly shipwreck, which haunted his dreams at night and his thoughts in the daytime.

Mr. McKenna laid down his newfangled, fancy pen that looked out of place on the scarred desk and clasped his hands together. Colin had never seen the old man look so bad. Haggard. Older somehow. Some calamity must have happened. He hoped it wasn't another shipwreck. Too many of those would put the business in jeopardy.

"You doin' all right, Elliott?" Even his boss's voice didn't sound as strong as it usually did.

He straightened in the chair. "Yes, sir. Better all the time."

"I'm glad. When will you be ready to go back on a ship?" Mr. McKenna peered at him as if he could see right through to his soul.

Colin cleared his throat. *What can I say?* He might not ever be ready to go to sea again. "What did you have in mind, sir?"

"I know you feel responsible for what happened to the *Trinity Bell*, but the storm that hit her came up unexpectedly and was stronger than any we had encountered in a long time." When his employer shifted in his chair, the leather gave a familiar creak. "No one could have prevented that wreck."

Colin lowered his head and stared at his scuffed boots. "Maybe a more seasoned captain could have." He hated voicing the words that wouldn't let go of his mind.

Angus McKenna stood and walked around the desk. "I meant what I said. No one could have. And you did save every member of your crew without considering your own safety." He laid a hand on Colin's shoulder. "I'm really sorry it happened on your watch, but I knew what I was doing when I made you the youngest ship's captain in my fleet."

His words didn't change the way Colin felt one iota. If he lived to be a hundred years old, he would carry the guilt of that wreck to his grave.

Mr. McKenna folded his arms and propped himself on the edge of the massive desk. "I didn't bring you in here to rehash this. Something else is on my mind. It's about time you got back into polite society, my boy."

"I've never been accepted into 'polite society,' sir. I'm just a sailor." He clamped his mouth shut before he spewed words he would later regret. Words about rejection. About never being as good as everyone else.

"Then we'll just have to remedy that. You're a ship's captain. Captains are welcomed everywhere."

Colin stared at an odd-shaped ink stain on the blotter that covered most of the desk top. It reminded him of a half-sunken schooner. "Not anymore."

"Of course you are. And you'll command another ship soon. You have to. It's just like getting back on a horse after you've been thrown. If you don't do it, you'll forever be skittish. We can't have that." His boss went back around the desk, picked up a piece of paper, and handed it to Colin.

He recognized that the address was in a more high-class part of San Francisco than he was acquainted with. "What's this?"

"My address. Today is Catherine's eighteenth birthday. We're having a dinner party and ball for her. I want you there. You might as well start becoming acquainted with more people in the business community. Many of them are also close family friends so they'll be in attendance." He dropped back into his chair.

"I don't have anything suitable to wear to a party, sir." At least he had a good excuse not to attend. A sigh of relief escaped.

"I've thought of that. Roger will accompany you to make

sure you're outfitted the way you should be. I know most of your possessions went down with the *Trinity Bell*." He picked up a piece of paper and started looking at it. "We had insurance on the ship and its contents. So we'll replace what you lost." He lifted a brass bell and gave it a swift shake.

Roger Amery hurried into the office. "How can I help you, sir?"

The way the man stood, Colin almost expected to hear the sound of his heels clicking together.

Mr. McKenna handed the sheet of paper to his secretary. "Take Elliott to town and use some of the insurance money to purchase the things I've listed."

When he gave the two of them a dismissive wave, Colin followed the other man out of the room. He couldn't think of any way to get out of this shopping trip and the subsequent party. He didn't know how he would be able to get through the excruciating evening ahead. Just how many of the people attending the festivities would look down on him? Not only was he a sailor, but he also lost the ship he captained. And his limp announced his failure and weakness to everyone he met.

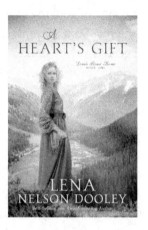

Book 1: A Heart's Gift

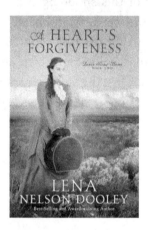

Book 2: A Heart's Forgiveness

Book 3: A Heart's Forever Home

Book 4: A Heart's Rescue

ABOUT THE AUTHOR

Multi-published, award-winning author Lena Nelson Dooley has had more than 1,000,000 copies of her 50+ books sold. Her books have appeared on the CBA and ECPA bestseller lists, as well as Amazon bestseller lists. She is a member of American Christian Fiction Writers and the local chapter, ACFW - DFW. She's a member of Christian Authors' Network, and Gateway Church in Southlake, Texas.

Her 2010 release, *Love Finds You in Golden, New Mexico*, won the 2011 Will Rogers Medallion Award for excellence in publishing Western Fiction. Her next series, *McKenna's Daughters: Maggie's Journey* appeared on a reviewers' Top Ten Books of 2011 list. It also won the 2012 Selah award for Historical Novel. The second, *Mary's Blessing*, was a Selah Award finalist for Romance novel. *Catherine's Pursuit* released in 2013. It was the winner of the NTRWA Carolyn Reader's Choice contest, took second place in the CAN Golden Scroll Novel of the Year award, and won the Will Rogers Medallion bronze medallion. Her blog, A Christian Writer's World, received the Readers' Choice Blog of the Year Award from the Book Club Network. She also has won three Carol Award Silver pins. In 2015 and 2016, these novella collections—*A Texas Christmas, Love Is Patient,* and *Mountain Christmas Brides* have all appeared on the ECPA bestseller list, one of the top two bestseller lists for Christian books.

She has experience in screenwriting, acting, directing, and voice-overs. She is on the Board of Directors for Higher Ground Films and is one of the screenwriters for their upcoming film *Abducted to Kill.* She has been featured in articles in *Christian Retailing, ACFW Journal, Charisma Magazine,* and *Christian Fiction Online Magazine.* Her article in CFOM was the cover story.

In addition to her writing, Lena is a frequent speaker at women's groups, writers groups, and at both regional and national conferences. She has spoken in six states and internationally. The Lena Nelson Dooley Show has been on the Along Came A Writer Blogtalk network.

Lena, now a widow, has an active web presence on Facebook, Twitter, Goodreads, Linkedin and with her internationally connected blog where she interviews other authors and promotes their books. Her blog has a reach of over 65,000.

- Website: https://lenanelsondooley.com
- Blog: http://lenanelsondooley.blogspot.com

facebook.com/Lena-Nelson-Dooley-42960748768

instagram.com/lenanelsondooley

pinterest.com/lenandooley

goodreads.com/lenanelsondooley

x.com/lenandooley

amazon.com/author/lenadooley

linkedin.com/in/lenanelsondooley

WANT MORE?

WANT MORE?

If you love historical romance, check out our other Wild Heart books!

Lone Star Ranger by Renae Brumbaugh Green

Elizabeth Covington will get her man.

And she has just a week to prove her brother isn't the murderer Texas Ranger Rett Smith accuses him of being. She'll show the good-looking lawman he's wrong, even if it means setting out on a risky race across Texas to catch the real killer.

Rett doesn't want to convict an innocent man. But he can't let the Boston beauty sway his senses to set a guilty man free. When Elizabeth follows him on a dangerous trek, the Ranger vows to keep her safe. But who will protect him from the woman whose conviction and courage leave him doubting everything—even his heart?

~

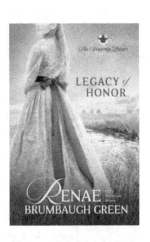

Legacy of Honor by Renae Brumbaugh Green

He's been raised to carry on the legacy.

Riley Stratton has it all, or so it seems. Growing up as the youngest son of the rich and powerful John Stratton, Riley stands to inherit a legacy of greatness in the Stratton Ranch—as long as he does things the Stratton way. On the surface, his family looks like they have it all, but manipulation, deceit, and an ever-present quest for power leave him desperate for change.

After her mother's untimely death, Emma Monroe's dreams to become a teacher are dashed. She takes a job as maid and cook at the local Stratton Ranch, where she endures humiliation and hardship in order to provide for her ailing father and younger brother. Only Riley Stratton, her childhood friend and heir to the Stratton fortune, sees her heart. When she's asked to care for Skye, the young half-Indian girl most family members refuse to claim, Emma finally finds the purpose she craves.

As Riley and Emma choose between honor, dreams, and expectations—not to mention the love they can no longer deny—their first steps prove how quickly the situation can spin into danger. When their best efforts threaten the lives and hopes of those closest to them, it becomes clear the decisions they make will change the course of their lives forever.

~

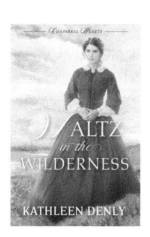

Waltz in the Wilderness by Kathleen Denly

She doesn't need his help. He doesn't need another delay. But God has other plans...

Eliza Brooks's worst nightmare has come true—her father is missing. Now she'll do anything to find him, even if it means taking a chance on who she must trust. But once aboard the steamship bound for San Diego—her father's last known whereabouts—she finds herself in far more danger than she imagined.

Daniel Clarke is a man of his word. Though he never imagined he'd be in California for four years, at least he's finally earned the money he needs to get married. Now he just has to get back to his fiancée in Massachusetts...the sooner the better. Especially since she's stopped replying to his letters.

When he boards a ship bound for San Diego, the first leg of his journey home, the last person Daniel expects to meet is his boss's niece. What could Eliza be thinking, traveling with no escort? With the lecherous captain determined to ruin her, Daniel has no choice but to offer his protection.

From shipwreck to cavalry outpost to the Southern California mountain wilderness, Daniel's entanglement with Eliza forces them—and their hearts—to face a future neither of them ever dreamed.

www.ingramcontent.com/pod-product-compliance
Lightning Source LLC
Jackson TN
JSHW011017130225
79001JS00007B/159